W9-COG-461

The

Lyon Affair

Chapter 1

Lyon, November 1940

The air was full of electricity. Etienne stepped from the train to the platform and narrowed his intelligent, gray eyes which rivaled the color of the mist settling over his hometown in the early hours of the hazy morning. His hand, encased in a tailored black glove, clenched the handle of the patent leather valise he carried, guarding the secret possessions carefully concealed in its double bottom. His young, narrow face with its chiseled features didn't betray any emotion, just like it hadn't when the uniformed, beady-eyed men, who entered the train one station away from the Demarcation Line, spent several minutes in his compartment checking his papers with envious thoroughness. Tall, collected, elegantly dressed – he simply didn't fall under their definition of a criminal. Yet, soon he would become their worst enemy. Etienne's lips barely twitched at the thought, and a permanent mask of aloof detachment settled in place once again.

The mist thickened as Etienne made his way out of the *Gare de Lyon-Perrache*, threatening to burst into a late autumn storm and drench him to the bone. He quickened his pace, determined to get his precious cargo home intact, and excused himself before a man, who he had almost run into while pushing the station door open. Etienne stepped onto the curb of the sidewalk and raised his arm, throwing yet another concerned glance at the clouds gathering above, heavy with water. A taxi cab pulled over at once, sensing a generous tip from an obviously wealthy traveler, and Etienne slipped inside, only now releasing the tension from his shoulders. He leaned back onto the seat, fixed his fedora hat in a practiced gesture, and grinned inwardly, restraining himself from showing any emotion to the unsuspecting driver. Free Zone or no Free Zone, here the policy of the collaboration thrived as strongly as ever, and more than anything he didn't need to raise any suspicion.

Having arrived at the door of his family house, Etienne handed the driver his money and hurried inside, into the safety of the familiar walls within which he had grown up. Only after extracting his punishable-by-prison contraband from its secret compartment, still dressed in his gray cashmere coat, did Etienne allow himself to laugh victoriously, smoothing out the pages of the paper with his hands. The first trip was a success. Now, he only needed to put the whole scheme to work.

Dijon, November 1940

Blanche was putting four more beer mugs in front of the uniform-clad patrons who frequented Monsieur Morin's Bistro, invading the tight, smoke-filled space with their banter, when she felt a hand insolently sliding from the small of her back to her behind. Barely containing herself from slapping the sneering offender, who didn't seem deterred in the slightest by the manner in which she straightened at once, almost spilling the beer on the grease-stained wooden table. Blanche willed herself to keep her anger at bay and forced a lopsided grin on her face instead.

"Would you like anything else?" she asked through gritted teeth, seething at the very nature of being in such a humiliating situation.

Swallowing her anger and repulsion was the only thing that she could afford to do; losing her job at Morin's was not a possibility. After the rationing had been imposed in September, everyone was struggling to keep their belly full. Here she could at least collect scraps after the feasts, in which the Germans indulged almost every evening, and take them home to her mother and two young sisters - not that they showed any gratitude for her efforts. Sometimes Blanche wondered why she exerted herself to please them at all.

The bitter truth was that Blanche had been a stranger in her own home since the day she was born, on a rainy October evening in 1917, much to her mother's displeasure. A small, pale and watery-eyed newborn with a down of ash-blonde hair on the top of her head, she had been scoffed at from the early days of her miserable existence, first by her mother, Anne, then by her father (who grudgingly allowed her to call him *Papa,* even though it was common knowledge that Blanche was a product of her mother's infidelity with some *Boche,* from whom the girl had inherited her pale looks and tall stature), and lastly her sisters, who were born after her father's return from the war.

Anne, a gaunt, weary woman with dull black eyes, and hands that were invariably red and rough from working as a washwoman claimed that the German had forced himself on her. The neighbors appeared to be skeptical of her mother's account of events of years long gone and smirked while debating whether Anne had voluntarily gone with the same *Boche* more than once, hardly minding all the bread and cheese he had brought her during that time. Whatever the truth, Blanche, named after her pallid, almost translucent skin and milky-white hair, was constantly reminded of her dubious parentage both by her family and any willing outsider. And so, she grew, quiet and subdued, yet watchful and resentful, until the past came to haunt both her and her whole country, with the cursed Germans whom she had learned to loathe since her early years.

Blanche held the gaze of the pale-blue eyes, much like her own, of the sneering man sitting in front of her and considered how wonderful, how satisfying, it would be to take that dagger hanging on his belt and plunge it right into his throat so he would choke on his blood together with his beer.

"Anything else?" she demanded again, a tone louder than before after he didn't deign to grace her with a reply.

"Ja." His drunken leer grew wider as he deliberately outstretched his arm to place it firmly on her behind once again. "You."

His comrades broke into boisterous laughter as Blanche stepped away, squeezing her hands into fists. With inhuman willpower, she forced herself not to pick up one of the fresh beer mugs and splash it into his red face, glistening with sweat.

"Pig," she muttered under her breath, then she turned around on her heels, tore the apron from her waist and headed to the kitchen with the sudden resolution to collect her daily pay.

The following morning, in the glow of the rising sun, Blanche gathered her meager possessions, which all fit into a small rucksack. She counted the money that she had been saving for quite some time as if anticipating that something would soon force her out of her childhood home, and headed straight to the railway station. Upon reaching the Demarcation Line, it turned out to be rather simple to find a man who would take her across the border for the right sum. In less than two days she reached her final destination – Lyon.

The morning she stepped off the crowded train in Lyon, it smelled of rain and electricity. Blanche shivered in her worn-out overcoat as she stood just outside the entrance of the *Gare de Lyon-Perrache* and pondered her options. A tall, elegantly dressed man almost stumbled into her in his hurry to hail a taxi cab, anticipating the approaching storm as well, no doubt. Blanche slid her gaze over him with a surge of bitter jealousy, at his polished shoes, warm gloves and the patent leather valise that he carried. Handsome, groomed and rich – everything that she was not. She drank in his features with puzzling greediness while he, oblivious to her scrutiny, disappeared inside the cab and out of sight… But not out of her life, of that Blanche was strangely and inexplicably certain. She raised her gaze to the dreary, leaded clouds gathering above, inhaled a full chest of the wet air which was interlaced with traces of grease and the coal of the train, and started making her way into the heart of the city. She would figure something out. She always did. The cruel world had taught her that skill all too well.

———————————

Father Yves pressed an old, leather-bound Bible to his lips and opened it to the page which contained the subject that he'd been pondering for quite a while now. In his days in the seminary, he was taught to always deliver his sermons to the parish on topics not only relevant to recent events but, more importantly, to always speak of what touched his heart personally. It was drilled into him that every subject matter that concerned the priest must be transferred from him to the parish, for the priest is still a man, though he is a servant of God first, and therefore his conscience is the ultimate litmus test reflecting the conscience of the community entrusted to him. The issue was that Yves had lied to get into the seminary, so his conscience was far from being clean.

His strawberry-blond hair reflected the liquid gold pouring onto his imposing frame from the tens of candles around him, forming a halo above his temple with their radiant light. His palm and graceful fingers gently caressed the lines of the passage that he had prepared for Sunday Mass a day ago. The gaze of his gray eyes, with silver specks in them, was downcast, his brows drawn in concentration. Father Yves cleared his throat and looked over his parish again. The chief of police sat in the front row, as expected, together with his wife and their two children, who always fidgeted despite their mother's constant attempts to hush them. Next to him was the butcher, who never ceased to wipe his round, red face with a handkerchief even in the coldest months of winter, and his spouse and their little clan of five, as rosy-faced and plump as their parents. More civil servants occupied the pews behind them, all solemn, well-fed and thoroughly trying to muster a pious air as if competing with their neighbors. The unfamiliar face of a pale, white-haired girl caught Father Yves's eye just before he returned to the passage in his Bible. He gave himself a mental note to welcome her to his church after the sermon was over. Apart from the mysterious newcomer, Father Yves recognized everyone in his charge, after ten long years.

"Psalm 37:1-6. Do not fret because of those who are evil or be envious of those who do wrong; for like the grass they will soon wither, like green plants they will soon die away. Trust in the Lord and do good; dwell in the land and enjoy safe pasture. Take delight in the Lord, and He will give you the desires of your heart. Commit your way to the Lord; trust in Him, and He will do this: He will make your righteous reward shine like the dawn, your vindication like the noonday sun." Yves's assertive voice reverberated around the marble columns and the statues of the saints, bowing their heads in their everlasting prayer.

The chief of police shifted in his seat, throwing a quick glare at the priest.

Yves noticed his shuffling and opened another page of his Bible. "Deuteronomy 31:6. Be strong and courageous. Do not fear or be in dread of them, for it is the Lord your God who goes with you. He will not leave you or forsake you."

The butcher cleared his throat rather loudly. Yves suppressed a grin, sensing both men's discomfort, and continued nonetheless.

"Psalm 57:6. They set a net for my steps; my soul was bowed down. They dug a pit in my way, but they have fallen into it themselves." Yves raised his gaze to his parishioners, some of them fidgeting uncomfortably; some staring at him with unconcealed apprehension creasing their foreheads. "Today I want to speak to you about our enemies. I have been reflecting for quite some time on this subject, and the conclusion that I have come to is that even the most pious of people have always had enemies. Even the Lord our God Himself. This doesn't reflect on the pious people, though, but more so on those very enemies, who are base and vile to such an extent that they can't recognize the light of the good, upon whom they wish malice. They aren't powerful on their own, and therefore their power is in numbers. They deceive and lure more and more men into their rows to conquer the good. They try to confuse the conquered and spread their venom even among the righteous. They refuse to recognize the light and succumb to the darkness instead. And that, as our Lord said, will be their downfall. I was asked by some of my parishioners a few months ago, before they set out on their perilous journey to defend our land from the enemy, if killing in a time of war is considered a sin and which duty they should choose, of the two most sacred ones: the duty of a Christian or the duty of a soldier? I admit that I didn't have a proper answer for them then, so I advised them to act by their conscience and pray to the Lord so He could give them a better answer than His humble servant. Today, I have an answer for those young men. Jesus Christ, our Lord, was not a pacifist. In fact, He sent Israelis to war Himself, but the war was justified, a war that would prevent bigger evils from happening. We aren't always meant to love our enemies if such enemies are so consumed by darkness that it starts threatening our very existence. And in cases like this, it is our sacred duty to defend the light, even with lifting a sword and taking a life. To the former soldiers, who have been returned to us recently and some of whom are present here today; do not torment yourselves over your deeds, for you are the righteous ones. Do not be afraid, for you carry the light within yourselves. Trust in the Lord our God and remember his wisdom: 'Do not fret because of those who are evil or be envious of those who do wrong; for like the grass they will soon wither, like green plants they will soon die away.' Amen."

A chorus of subdued voices murmured *Amen* together with Father Yves; he turned away to prepare the wine and bread, though he didn't fail to notice the doubtful glares of the parish that once used to be so indifferently compliant. At least there was still something that could stir their apathetic souls, even if it was outrageously against everything that their new leader, Maréchal Pétain, preached. Only, unlike Monsieur Maréchal, Yves didn't believe in collaboration. Or, to put it more precisely, he'd witnessed firsthand what happened when invaders came to one's land, and ardently believed that they had to be stopped before more blood would be shed. Yves was among the righteous who had stopped them once already, during the Great War; only, he had hoped to escape from his past once and for all, hiding within the solemn walls of the church, from the demons who seemed to laugh at such wishful thinking. Far too many lives were on his unclean conscience; too many nightmares that could not be banished with a few Psalms. Eventually, Yves had become used to their presence, and even welcomed it, as a means of some twisted, self-imposed penance. Naturally, neither the ministers in his former seminary, nor his own parishioners were aware of any of those things, and Father Yves preferred to leave it this way.

The chief of police faltered on the steps when Father Yves was seeing his small parish out, blessing their day with a sign of the cross and a parting smile. The priest had expected the man's response.

"A rather... interesting subject you chose for Mass today, Father," the chief remarked. A prominent man of forty with an unnaturally straight back and a narrow, penetrating gaze, he only spoke once his wife and children had been sent on their way down the stairs.

Yves simply cocked his head, waiting for more words to come.

"It is not my place to advise you on such matters *bien sûr*," the man continued, slightly unnerved by the priest's silence, "however, I feel it to be my duty as a civil servant to warn you that such speeches, if overheard by an ear that is not familiar with you and your good nature, a nature that I am personally fortunate to know, might lead to rather... unfortunate consequences."

The chief of police narrowed his dark eyes further as if attempting to better drive his point across. Yves nodded, acknowledging the advice and yet discarding it at once without uttering a word.

"We were fortunate enough to end this war relatively unscathed," the chief went on. "The Germans were kinder to us than we could expect, to be truthful. We happen to live in the Free Zone that they left us, and the only thing they ask of us is to collaborate with them. Why muddy the waters – and young, impressionable people's minds – with such speeches? Leave it to the government, Father; they know better the affairs of the state. Why not preach the good old 'love thy neighbor and forgive your enemies instead? It would be more relevant nowadays."

He tipped his hat and turned on his heel to walk away in a strange hurry, the taste of his own words apparently still sour in his mouth. Yves watched him disappear into his car, wondering whether he rushed to hide from the priest's gaze or his own conscience.

The white-haired girl was still inside, shuffling through the Bible indecisively when Yves stepped back into the dim light of the church. He approached the pew that she occupied, her well-worn rucksack hidden under her feet, and tilted his head curiously.

"You're new here, aren't you?" he inquired in a mild voice.

The girl offered him a somewhat guilty grin and a half-hearted shrug.

"I'm Father Yves," he introduced himself, sensing her reluctance. "Please, feel free to stay as long as you wish. We aren't closing anytime soon. And don't hesitate to ask if you need anything be it a confession or a piece of bread. We've had a lot of displaced people here since the Exodus, and your situation is not new to me."

The girl's pale blue eyes ignited at once, and Yves congratulated himself inwardly on his assumption concerning the girl's situation. She rose to her feet and made an uncertain step forward, offering him her hand but then dropping it as if deeming her action inappropriate to the occasion.

"I'm sorry, Father. You don't shake hands with your parishioners I suppose." A barely noticeable accent could be detected in her voice as she spoke. Not as melodic and free-flowing as the Lyon one. *A Northerner perhaps.*

The girl touched her hair self-consciously. "My name is Blanche. I'm not from these parts. I've been sleeping on the steps of your church for the past two days, but last night the *gendarme* chased me away and almost arrested me... Maybe you know someone, who is hiring help around here? Or I can work in your church if you need a cleaning lady or a cook..."

Her voice faltered slightly, but she collected herself and glanced up at Yves with determination. "I'm a Catholic if that matters. And I can work hard."

"Come with me; I'll feed you first. Then, after you have your fill, we can discuss your employment." Yves gestured for the rail-thin girl to follow him into his living quarters.

Not very priest-like from the Church's point of view but Yves had decided a long time ago to live by God's teachings, and not the ones set by the Vatican. God said to feed the needy, and so he would.

Chapter 2

Lyon, November 11, 1940. Armistice Day

The street was a maddening kaleidoscope of lights, colors, and music. Etienne surveyed the spirited mob, marching with zeal, matching the goose-stepping Germans that he had had the "pleasure" to watch in Paris. Women were draped in prohibited tricolors, their eyes shining with national pride; their hair curled and decorated with red, blue and white ribbons fluttering in the wind; their voices full of resentment and angry patriotism, singing *La Marseillaise* to the faces of the *gendarmes*; the latter only looked away, shamed and laughed at for their uniforms. Collaborators. Traitors of *La République. Boches-lovers.*

Etienne leaned onto the wall, wisely staying away from the marching crowd, seeking to remain undetected by both the communist leaders, using this fine opportunity to hand out their leaflets to all passers-by, and the *gendarmes* who mostly looked at their feet and pretended the parade celebrating the victorious Armistice of 1918 wasn't happening right under their noses. His camel-wool, tailored coat blended perfectly with the wall behind his back, and Etienne stilled, observing the celebration with a bare outline of a smile on his immaculately shaven face, partially concealed under a fedora hat. At least they could still march, he mused with bittersweet melancholy; an outlook a man experiences at the loss of the innocence of his youth perhaps, and the war, which had stripped young hearts of their purity more than anything in the world. Their counterparts in Paris weren't as fortunate as the people of Lyon: repressed, subdued and hungry – not only for food and gas (all strictly rationed, *bien sûr*) but for the loss of freedom most of all.

His gloved hand dove inside his coat, feeling the folded paper inside. Unsuspecting communists – and most of the marching men belonged to the infamous Reds – went on with their leaflets and propaganda, emboldened by the meekness of the police. Etienne scrutinized every single agitator as they turned the corner from the side street leading into the *Rue de la République,* where he had taken up his position; he narrowed his eyes as he spotted the least agitated *comrade,* and observed his movements as the man silently handed his leaflets to the people on the sidewalk.

Unlike his peers, this one didn't shout, didn't seem drunk with emotion or driven by the same mob mentality that pushed the unfathomable parade forward. Etienne pushed himself off the wall and stepped closer to the passing crowd patiently awaiting the quiet communist. When the latter's gaze met Etienne's eyes, his hand stopped mid-air, still holding out a leaflet to him; one who would never fall for its red-lettered calls. The communist's scowl deepened above his attentive eyes, sensing the falseness of the situation in which the well-dressed *bourgeois* took a communist propaganda flyer from him; yet the man stepped nearer as Etienne motioned him closer and discretely slid a paper in his hands, right under the leaflets he was holding.

"You know anyone who can distribute this if I give you more copies?"

The communistbacked away just a step, and Etienne's gloved hand caught his forearm in warning.

"I'm not working for the gendarmes, don't be afraid." Etienne's quiet voice was almost drowned out in the crowd's bellowing. The communist pulled closer, though with visible reluctance, to hear the enigmatic man's words better. "I have a paper from Paris that I'm copying here, in Lyon. But I don't have enough distributors. Do you know anyone who can help me?"

"With all due respect, Monsieur," the communist assessed Etienne with his gaze, "you don't look like a *comrade*."

"I'm not," Etienne replied flatly. The communist relaxed a bit, despite the admission. At least *the bourgeois* was not lying. "If you know anyone who can help me or want to discuss this further, meet me on the *Pont Lafayette,* next Friday at eight in the evening sharp."

With those words, Etienne slid into the crowd of viewers standing on the sidewalk and dissolved without a trace. The communist searched for him with his eyes for a few more moments, then turned back hesitantly and joined the march, walking with more purpose this time.

———————————

Etienne took a silver cigarette case out of his pocket and paused to admire the finely detailed engraving on its top before extracting a cigarette he planned to enjoy before catching a taxi cab home. He had walked a long way, starting from the square itself, where the celebrations continued and in which he had no more interest, after making contact which just the kind of person he had been looking for.

Why celebrate feats of the past? The long-forgotten glory of a triumphant France was years long gone, packed away under layers of naphthalene, and nationalistic slogans only taken out once a year, shaken up and worn for an occasion which seemed like more of a mockery today, when former victors were now struggling under the imposed regime of ones they had presumed defeated some twenty years ago. The past was worthless, just like the new puppet regime, and

Etienne simply saw no point in celebrating the old victory when his country so desperately starved for a new one.

Holding a glove in one hand, Etienne slid his finger across the silver case, smiling fondly at the memories. His father, Etienne Delattre Senior, had awarded him with it when he had graduated from *École Polytechnique* top of his class. Even at seventeen years of age, he was already imitating everything his father did, and smoking had become the latest of such habits. *The key to success in everything – and in life itself – is in moderation,* his father used to explain in his smooth, leveled voice, puffing on a cigarette. And so, Etienne only smoked five cigarettes a day even after his father's death.

It was a rather wasteful death, too; Monsieur Delattre Sr. held the rank of a Major during the Great War but, revolted from everything that the war represented, he returned to his diplomat's duties with immense relief as soon as it was over. Still, when the new war drew near France's borders, he donned his long-forgotten uniform and headed to the front, to die heroically in full regalia only a day before the Armistice was signed. The Germans who had overpowered the position which he'd taken up with his soldiers allowed his men to bury their Major with full military honors – a young Corporal informed Etienne's mother of such in an official letter. Etienne had visited his father's simple, cross-marked grave only once, and had traveled back to Lyon deep with foreboding, wondering what direction his life should take now. He was, in no way, a military man; he was a brilliant strategist, though, a future diplomatic attaché just graduated from the University with honors, with more than a promising career ahead of him... Before the war broke out, that is, and claimed his father's life instead of his.

It was a willing sacrifice, too; Etienne was aware of that from the hushed conversations that his parents held in the kitchen on winter nights in 1939 when the war was merely a topic for hushed discussion and not a brutal reality that would soon smash the nation in the face. Etienne Delattre Sr. was not supposed to travel to the front due to his age and previous honorable service, and yet he made up his mind, weighing his decision carefully as he always did and as he always instructed Etienne to do, greased some hands and took up his son's place thus granting him the gift of life itself.

"Don't try to talk me out of it and don't contradict me," Etienne recalled him saying the only time his father agreed to discuss the fateful decision with him. "You're young, intelligent and earnest; you have a whole life ahead of yourself that can be full of wonderful deeds. I've lived my share; I left an heir; I lived my fill. It's your turn now."

Etienne pondered those words, forever emblazoned into his memory, while the train, headed south, measured kilometers of evergreen meadows, still unmolested, still pure and unravished by the shameless plunder following the invading army that was creeping after his train, or so it appeared in his disturbing dreams. By pure coincidence, only a few stations away from Lyon, having left his compartment to stretch his legs in the corridor, Etienne noticed someone's newspaper, probably forgotten in the haste of getting off the train, laying on the narrow windowsill in plain sight.

Uncertain and bored, Etienne flipped the front-page open and suppressed a shocked gasp just as it was ready to escape his mouth. *La Libération*; an unofficial, criminal, prohibited edition of the underground newspaper stared back at him with its slightly faded, indigo letters, calling for people to join the Resistance and follow de Gaulle's call. At the next station, with the paper burning through his leather valise, he acquired a one-way ticket to Paris and headed back north, a hopeful smile curling his lips upward.

Etienne didn't believe in coincidences, only in some mathematically-predetermined order of things ruling the universe, which humankind was still too unintelligent to comprehend. Therefore, if such an occasion had presented itself and it was him, Etienne, that happened to smoke in that very deserted corridor on that very train on that very day and hour, it was intended for him to proceed with this highly dangerous affair. He possessed all the necessary attributes for it too; otherwise, the newspaper wouldn't have landed into his hands, but into someone else's. The fact that his father's friend, who Etienne Delattre Sr. had advised him to visit in case of his passing, was an owner of a publishing house and might possibly know the people who produced the paper, was also another fateful X fitting into the equation, still unknown to him but in dire need to be solved. Etienne loved solving puzzles and tasks, ever since he was a young boy; this affair was also a task, or at least the way he considered it to be. He had to find the *résistants* publishing the paper, get into contact with them, organize a network of agents to distribute the paper all over France, contact London, offer his services to the Free French under *Général* de Gaulle's command, and drive the Germans off his land – all in his father's good memory. *It was all rather simple if you break it into details,* Etienne smirked to himself. Task by task, equation by equation, one simple affair with him in charge. Feasible, and none would persuade him otherwise.

Etienne flickered his silver lighter and drew a full chest of air, filled with musty whiffs of November leaves, gray transparent smoke, and satisfaction. Only a month had passed, and he had already ticked the first two points off his list; only another four remained.

Suddenly, a thin, blonde girl caught his eye. She was marching purposefully towards a monument that he had been gazing at for the past few minutes, a simple bouquet of flowers in her hand, pressed towards her chest with stubborn determination. Etienne scowled, his gaze shooting towards the *gendarmes* chatting next to the memorial towards which the girl was heading. The *gendarmes* had noticed her too, and straightened their backs, determined to snatch at least one protestor that shied away from the rest of the marching mob; a mob they feared to approach for obvious reasons.

The girl came to a halt in front of the memorial to the fallen heroes of the Great War, gazed at it for a good minute and finally lowered the flowers at its base. The *gendarmes* moved from their position the moment the flowers hit the ground as if that simple gesture was the only sign that they had been waiting for. Etienne weighed all the pros and cons during those few short moments, faltered a mere second, cursed inwardly, stubbed out his unfinished cigarette and moved towards the monument in quick, resolute steps.

She was already struggling in their arms, screaming that she hadn't done anything wrong and demanding to know what was so criminal about honoring the fallen soldiers. Etienne's shadow, emerging in the middle of this commotion, startled and muted all its participants at once, for no one, including the girl, expected such an elegant gentleman to protectively drape his arm around the poorly dressed young woman's shoulder, and offer a most pleasant smile to the *Messieurs les Gendarmes* with his sincerest apologies.

"Pardon my sister, gentlemen." Such fine, dignified notes were released in his baritone voice; such a thoroughly apologetic expression rested on his handsome face; and a twenty Franks bill, concealed in his outstretched hand in such a practiced manner that it remained invisible for any inquisitive eyes besides the *gendarmes* themselves, was so discreetly proffered. "She is not well. Beatrice, what's gotten into you, running out on *Maman* in such a manner? You know perfectly well how it shatters her nerves when you do. Pardon me again, messieurs; she's being looked after by a nurse, but the old woman just can't keep up with our poor Beatrice anymore... Excuse her shouting and rudeness as well; it's common for ones disturbed by the same illness..."

The bill was hastily snatched away, the proffered hand was thoroughly shaken, and the incident was all but forgotten. Etienne, with his arm still gripping the girl's shoulder, led her away before she had a chance to recover from her temporary, and stunned muteness.

Ensuring that they were alone in a narrow side street, Etienne swiftly turned the young woman towards himself and looked at her pointedly.

"Do not ever go near any Great War monuments. Do not speak to communists and never, under any circumstance, keep their leaflets after reading them. Had you tried this stunt in the Occupied Zone, the Germans would be herding you onto a train heading to their fatherland by now. And, in a few more days, you would be breaking your back, hurling stones in one of their working camps. Now go, and keep away from the gendarmes next time."

He had already turned to take his leave when the girl spoke behind his back, "Wait! How do you know about the Occupied Zone?"

Etienne kept walking, ignoring her hurried steps behind him.

"You've been there, haven't you? You've seen it all, right? The *Boches* and what they do."

Etienne looked straight ahead even when she clenched the cuff of his coat, trying to look him in the eye.

"I'm from the Occupied Zone myself. The *Boches* and their cursed occupation are the reasons why I ran."

The girl refused to give up, he noticed, with a sense of mild irritation starting to grow inside his chest. He needed to get rid of her before they stepped from the narrow street into the broad avenue where such a strange pair would most definitely attract unwanted attention. Etienne shook her fingers off his sleeve, coming to a sudden stop to face her once again.

"Yes, I have. Yes, I've seen them. Now, show some gratitude for my rescuing you and head your own way, won't you?"

"You hate them too, don't you? That's why you helped me; I understood everything at once." A passionate gleam shone in her pale blue eyes as she caught his sleeve once again. "Do you know anyone from the Resistance by chance? Anyone who wants to fight... I'm new to this city and don't know anyone yet—"

"Have you completely gone off your head, asking a man who you just met something of this sort?!" Etienne hissed at the girl. "I could be an undercover Vichy police agent, looking to arrest people like you!"

"You aren't; otherwise why would you have helped me?" She gave him a tentative smile. "I saw you in the train terminal a week ago. I wasn't sure that it was you at first, but now I know. You just came back from the Occupied Zone, correct?"

Etienne didn't betray himself by even a single bat of an eye, even though the possibility of this strange girl recognizing him and poking at his private matters was the least desirable turn of events in his mind. His mind began processing information at the speed of light.

"I travel for business. And that business of mine is none of yours." He interrupted her before she even had a chance to open her mouth for yet another question. "Now, off you go."

"You don't travel for business. Businessmen are all collaborators. I know it; I'm not stupid. So, you're into something different then. I won't ask another thing of you, not even your name; just put me in touch with the right people, and I'll be out of your hair once and for all."

Etienne eyed her for one very long moment and then asked, articulating every word, "What did the Germans do to you that you have such a grudge against them?"

"One of them gave me life; a life that everyone around me turned into a kind of hell, just for that very reason," she responded with unconcealed resentment in her voice. "Maybe if I kill enough of them, I'll finally get rid of the stigma of being a half-German bastard."

Too impulsive, too unreliable and too angry for her own good. Uneducated, from a struggling, unloving family, and her only motivation is pure revenge; motives for which she has got it all wrong. Confused and troubled; not a good recruit by any means. Nevertheless, a simple fact outweighed the rest: Etienne needed her out of his hair, and the sooner, the better.

"If I promise to put you in touch with the right people, you must promise never to seek me out again, to never inquire about me and completely erase this meeting from your memory. Understood?"

"Yes." She nodded readily.

"One of my men will find you on *Pont Lafayette* in two weeks. You'll meet him Monday, eleven in the morning. He'll be wearing a green scarf and posing as a seller of postcards. The code words he'll say will be 'You have such a pretty face, Mademoiselle. Will you allow me to take a picture of you?' To which you'll respond, 'Only if you give me a copy to send to my husband. He's a prisoner of war.' Then you'll follow him to wherever he leads you; he'll take your picture and that will be placed on your new papers. Bring your old ones and give them to him; he'll fix you up with a completely new identity. From there follow his instructions. Is that clear?"

"Yes." She nodded once again.

"Good. Goodbye then."

"Thank you, Monsieur!"

Etienne winced at her joyful farewell, fighting off a feeling of unease, and hurried back onto the avenue to quickly blend into the crowd.

Chapter 3

Blanche danced around her new lodgings. Her room was small and modestly furnished with a narrow bed, a closet and a square table with a single chair, but it was hers; for the first time in her life, she didn't have to share anything with her sisters. When Father Yves offered her the opportunity to temporarily stay on the church's grounds on the condition that she would help the elderly widow, Madame Freneau – also a refugee and the only woman who also lived on the premises – with cleaning and cooking, Blanche was delighted beyond measure.

Despite the hard work polishing the wax off the candle holders and scrubbing hard marble floors, Blanche threw herself into every task with inexhaustible energy, eager to not disappoint her new generous hosts. Madame Freneau helped her find a much-needed job in the town center, and even though it meant once again putting on an apron that she loathed, Blanche at least was spared the unwanted attention of the *Boches* and got to keep all the money she earned instead of giving most of it to her mother.

Now, within the space of only two weeks, her life would take an even more drastic change, and she would have her revenge... Only, the problem was that Blanche sometimes questioned herself on who had wronged her more: the *Boches,* or her countrymen. She sat on the edge of her bed, deep in her brooding once again.

It would all get clear in time, or so Father Yves said. And since he was the first person who had treated her with true kindness, something she had hardly ever encountered in her life, Blanche willed herself to believe him.

Father Yves was a man like no other. He was kind, quiet, intelligent and serious – quite the opposite of the type that Blanche used to encounter throughout her whole life, and during the last few months in particular. How wonderful it was, just to share meaningful silence with him whenever the occasion presented itself and Blanche caught him alone and contemplating something from one of the front pews, his steel-gray eyes staring, without blinking, into space while his fingers counted the beads of the rosary. Blanche experienced some inexplicable guilty pleasure from watching him like that, without him noticing at first. But when he would shake off his everlasting brooding, feel a pair of eyes watching his every move intently, he always offered Blanche the gentlest of smiles and shifted slightly, offering her to share a pew and a prayer with him. Yes, Father Yves was a man like no other. Only he understood her. Maybe, eventually she'd be able to share her new life with him, and who knew, if he would even want to share it with her as well...

She counted the days till the eagerly awaited Monday, and flew through her daily routines, as driven as ever, her pale eyes shining with a new ferocious energy. The night before the momentous morning, Blanche lay wide awake unable to fall asleep due to the overwhelming anxiety washing over her with a hot, fiery wave despite the chilliness of her room. *Tomorrow. Tomorrow her life would change at last. Tomorrow she would become a new Blanche, no, not even a Blanche but someone entirely different, shedding the old name which sounded like constant taunting to her, always reminding her of her mother's sin; a sin for which she had been made to pay for, whatever the reason.*

The dawn stalled to break that morning. The sun didn't deign to make its daily appearance at all, slumbering with a lazy indifference somewhere behind the fog-bearing clouds, heavy and unmoving, ready to drench the whole of Lyon in their icy November downpours. Blanche shivered in her thin overcoat, pulling the ends of a black shawl under her chin – another generous gift from Madame Freneau. Widowed and childless, with the uncertain heart of a lonely woman, she took to Blanche with the shifting senses of mistrust and affection, fearing yet another eventual loss yet clinging to the overpowering need to care for someone besides the statues of the saints. In the few weeks that Blanche had spent in Lyon, Madame Freneau had become more of a mother to her than her birth mother ever was.

Blanche hastened her pace on the way to the bridge, not only due to the bone-chilling cold but also by the need to arrive on time. She had asked directions on how to get to the bridge the day after she'd met the mysterious gentleman who had saved her from the *gendarmes*. She had even timed her way from the church to it, rehearsing her walk several more times over the next two weeks. Blanche smiled conceitedly as she noticed the time on the big clock near the *Metro*, opposite the bridge: she was fifteen minutes early.

Counting her steps in a vain effort to curb her anxiety, Blanche stopped in the middle of the bridge and turned away from the river so that she could look in both directions. Leaning against the railing, she kept turning her head left to right, peering into the faces of every passing gentleman in search of one with a green scarf. Just as she thought she had noticed someone fitting that very vague description, a voice spoke softly above her ear, startling her.

"You have such a pretty face, Mademoiselle. Will you allow me to take a picture of you?"

Blanche turned swiftly and let out a nervous giggle. The connection that the mysterious gentleman had sent appeared to be much younger than she had expected, yet there was something hidden in the depth of his hazel eyes that aged him just by the sheer force of his gaze; the gaze of a very old man on the face of a very young one. Blanche suddenly realized that she had forgotten the code phrase. He waited patiently until she quickly collected herself and muttered, "Only if you give me a copy to send to my husband. He's a prisoner of war."

The young man grinned, nodded and extracted his camera, motioning Blanche to pose in front of the river. She leaned against the railing and tried to look relaxed and at ease even though she was positive that her smile was constricted and anything but sincere.

"Maybe a few more in my *photo atelier?*" he inquired, tilting his head to one side. "You would do me an honor if you allow me to make some professional portraits of you."

Blanche nodded and followed him off the bridge, falling into step with his purposeful strides. However, his whole demeanor changed as soon as they slipped into a side street with broken cobbles under their feet and sheets stretched in between the windows concealing them from curious eyes.

"Why on earth did you turn your head without stopping on that bridge?" He growled at her, clearly irritated. "Weren't you instructed to walk there inconspicuously and wait for me, gazing at the water?"

"I didn't want to miss you by accident." Blanche blinked a couple of times. "I thought you might not recognize me and in that case—"

"In that case what? You would have called out any man wearing a green scarf and asked him if he would like to take a picture of you?"

Even though his voice was low and barely audible, to Blanche it equaled him actually yelling at her.

"N-no…"

"Listen to me carefully before I take you anywhere." He stood right in front of her, and though they were almost of the same height, Blanche cowered involuntarily under his penetrating, heavy stare. "If you want to work for us, you need to understand one simple thing: always follow instructions. That's rule number one of survival, simple as that. You don't follow the instructions, you fail the operation, you reveal yourself, you die, and, what's worse, you take others from your cell with you. Do you understand or not?"

"Yes, I understand." Blanche nodded earnestly.

"Next time someone tells you to stroll towards the bridge and stand with your back to everyone gazing at the water, you stroll, you turn around and you gaze. Is that clear? You're lucky you weren't in the Occupied Zone where the Gestapo pigs are at every turn, just waiting for an opportunity to grab someone like you. And you broke almost every single instruction today, running towards the bridge like a lunatic, looking at your watch every five minutes and staring at every passer-by making it more than clear that you were waiting for someone when our meeting was supposed to be accidental."

Blanche lowered her eyes, her cheeks taking on a crimson shade.

"How do you know I ran towards the bridge?" she mumbled, not finding anything else to say.

"I followed you of course. Had to make sure that you didn't bring anyone else on your tail," the young man grumbled, with barely concealed annoyance.

"I didn't notice..."

"And that's another mistake of yours. Let's go, enough of wasting time here."

The walk was fast and silent. The *photo atelier*, to which he'd brought her, was warm and cozy, albeit small and clouded with cigarette smoke. A brass bell chimed, announcing their arrival to the dim anteroom which had a burgundy rug in front of a small counter, and a cash register standing on its top. Samples of portraits and postcards with local views were displayed both in a small window and the wall above the cash register.

Her new acquaintance went past the counter and slipped behind heavy, burgundy red curtains with a fringe adorning them. Blanche followed him into an even dimmer room with a single sheet of white paper stretched on the opposite wall and a camera facing it. On the other side stood a beautifully executed Viennese chair in front of a small table decorated with flowers and a painted scenery behind it.

"For weddings," a woman's voice clarified in response to Blanche's inquiring gaze. Blanche jumped, not expecting anyone to speak from behind her and chastised herself once again for not paying attention to her surroundings. These people just seemed to live in the shadows, just like this smirking woman, who separated from the dark corner and stepped into the light, looking Blanche over. "But you're here for something different, right?"

She arched her dark brows and exchanged handshakes with the young man. *Communists,* Blanche decided at once. Only their women shook hands with their comrades – that much she knew.

"This is Lucienne." The young man motioned his head in Blanche's direction.

"I'm Blanche," she corrected, feeling guilty for no apparent reason.

"Not anymore, you're not." The woman chuckled, shamelessly scrutinizing Blanche. "I hope you haven't forgotten to bring your old papers?"

"No, they're all here." Blanche dug in her rucksack and handed the woman everything she had. "My birth certificate, my passport, and my ration card. But I was told by the priest who shelters me that it's of no use here and I will have to apply for a new ration card…"

"You haven't yet, I hope?" The woman frowned.

"No."

"Good." She took all the documents and disappeared with them into the back room. Returning barely a minute later, she beckoned Blanche to sit in front of the white sheet. "Hold your head straight."

Blanche froze in her seat, but the woman was still studying her, in no hurry to take the photo.

"You said it's our new Lucienne?" she asked the young man once again.

"So I was told."

"Lucienne's legend is that she's a girl who distributes cosmetics catalogs. Does this one look like she sells cosmetics? Look at her. Would you buy anything from her for your lady friend?"

"I don't have a lady friend."

"It's a hypothetical question. Look how pale she is. Invisible almost. No, that won't work, I tell you."

"So what do you suggest? We need to send her on her first trip this Thursday."

"I think I can make her look like Lucienne, the cosmetics catalog girl. Give me a couple of hours with her, and you won't recognize her, I promise."

Blanche kept shifting her guarded glance from the man to the woman while they were exchanging their remarks, feeling more and more uneasy. They hadn't even introduced themselves, then they took her papers away and now this woman wanted to alter her appearance to send her on some trip for who knew what purpose... Blanche swallowed a nervous lump in her dry throat and told herself to keep still. She knew what she was getting into, didn't she?

Before she could answer herself, the woman lifted her face by the chin, scrutinizing every feature with a skeptical look, feeling her hair and nodding to some thoughts she was obviously having.

"Yes. We'll definitely cut your hair, curl it and color it. It's too limp and lifeless now; no one will believe you're a cosmetics girl. And your face, that too. We need rouge. A lot of it. Mascara and eyeliner – you can't go without them. And lipstick is a must in your case, Lucienne."

Lucienne. Blanche kept tasting the new name on her tongue, still unsure if she liked it or not, while the woman, who had finally introduced herself as Margot (even though Blanche was more than certain that it wasn't her real name), clipped off Blanche's long blonde tresses. Blanche entrusted her new self to Margot's strong, skillful hands and slowly allowed her old, invisible, persecuted self to dissolve in the small clouds of smoke that the woman puffed out with such natural ease as if the cigarette was glued to her mouth. Blanche suspiciously eyed the reddish paste in the bowl that Jules – another alias most likely, but now at least Blanche knew how to address him – brought in, together with a sturdy man with his hair and mustache colored in such an unnatural shade of black that it shined into blue every time he turned his head. More chemical smell, more hair pulling and wrapping it around small iron cylinders that the blue-black-haired man – the hairdresser – had brought with himself; more tweezers above her eyes, already burning from the acidic smell; more *"don't blink now, look up, look down, press your lips together…"* Just when Blanche thought that it would never end, all three of them stepped away and took turns exchanging glances and tilting heads left to right, grinning like conspirators.

"Now, that's more like it," Margot declared with satisfaction. "This is a Lucienne; this one I'll believe."

"Well… she draws attention, that is a fact I can't possibly dispute." Jules pursed his lips.

"So?" Margot snorted, crossing her arms over her chest.

"So, every *Boche* will be staring at her. Are you sure that's what we want in our situation?"

Margot arched her brow, offering him a knowing grin. "That's precisely what we want. If you were a *Boche,* would it come to your mind that this girl, with so much paint on her face and red hair, could possibly be a Resistance member smuggling something illegal?"

Jules smiled, at last, acknowledging the validity of the argument.

"I suppose not."

"May I take a look?" Blanche chimed in tentatively.

Margot grinned with one side of her mouth and motioned her head towards the small mirror hanging behind Blanche's back. Blanche slid off the uncomfortable chair and slowly turned around. She leaned forward as if not recognizing her own reflection, and stepped closer, her hand hovering near her rouged cheek, her scarlet lips slightly parted in amazement as her brain tried to process the sheer possibility that this woman in the old, clouded glass with brownish stains on it, could be her, Blanche.

No, it was a mask most certainly, like the ones *femmes fatales* wore on movie posters. This was no Blanche from Dijon; impossible. Women with fiery red locks like she was now sporting were either some big shots' mistress - scandalous, pouting and invariably carrying some small dog under their arm - or women of an even more disreputable profession, like those cat-calling German officers from under darkened corners in her native Dijon.

"I think our little Lucienne is in shock." Margot snorted with amusement and without further ceremony pulled Blanche by the elbow back into the photo room. "Let's get on with it and take your picture for your new papers if we want them to be done in time. You can stare all you like at yourself later. Oh, and I'll make a big headshot for you, too, so you can use it as a sample and learn how to apply makeup by yourself every day."

"Every day? But I can't go back to work with all this on my face…"

"Work? What work?" Margot's brows shot up, and her nicotine breath hit Blanche's senses. "You don't work there anymore, girl. That blondie girl who did, she stepped through our doors to never return. This is the ultimate rabbit's hole, *ma chérie,* and you can only come out of it as an Alice. Or Lucienne in your case. And Lucienne sells cosmetics."

"But…"

"Don't concern yourself with money," Jules replied to her unspoken question. "We'll provide you with everything needed. All we need in return is your loyalty and compliance. The rest, you just leave to us."

The rain was drenching the streets of Lyon when Lucienne stepped outside the doors of the photoshop, her red locks and scarlet mouth the only bright spots against the bleak canvas of the city. She opened her borrowed umbrella and hid her face from the rest of the world.

Chapter 4

Etienne pushed the massive iron gates open and gestured for Jules to follow him inside. Of course, the name "Jules" was just as fake as the young man's metal-rimmed round spectacles and newly grown beard, but Etienne had never known his real name, and he didn't want to know. Jules was introduced to him as Jules by his late father's friend from Paris – the owner of the publishing house – and was already provided with new papers, which suited Etienne just fine.

After the temperature plunged two nights ago, an intricate ornament of frosty designs had spread its shimmering spider-webs over sleet and mud as the winter professed its rights, arriving fashionably late like a typical southern aristocrat at a sophisticated soiree. The glassy film of ice, covering the puddles where the winter had caught the remaining water unawares, crunched and cracked under their feet as they made their way towards the imposing mansion.

A feeling of abandonment and solitude was becoming more and more evident as they followed the paved road, now barely recognizable under the layers of leaves and mud. They stopped near the fountain, no longer white but covered with greenish moss, cracked and muddied just like everything around, neglected and forgotten, with years of inadvertence deliberately but mercilessly eating away at its formerly grand stance.

"What do you think?" Etienne's voice sounded loud despite the softness of his tone. It was strange to think that they were on property bordering the city limits and yet the scenery had changed so drastically. "Impressive, isn't it?"

Jules nodded, slowly scanning the mansion with his thoughtful gaze.

"It is. Difficult to believe that no one lives here anymore. It's a rather vast property."

"Yes. But the problems with the law that the banker, who owned it, had, were even greater. He faced up to twenty years in prison for embezzlement and some shady deals with the Americans – in the mid-twenties I believe – so, he decided to make a run for it with the help of the said Americans and now resides somewhere on the Golden Coast from what I heard last. The city seized the mansion as it was the only property that was left after his escape, and after all the legal issues were sorted out, they set it up for an auction about a couple of years ago. And by then everything was already in the condition that you see it now and no one wanted to invest money into fixing it. So, it still stands, cheap as dirt, and yet there is still no buyer." Etienne shuddered from yet another gust of wind and tightly fastened the collar of his coat while Jules waited unassumingly for him to continue. "I'm thinking to buy it. Put some keeper's family there, a legit one of course, and use it for our purposes. Maybe set up an orphanage in it and leave the cellar for us… I haven't decided yet. What do you think? Is it a distant enough location? Do you think the *gendarmes* will get wind of what we will do in here?"

"If you indeed decide to set up an orphanage here, I don't think they will. It's a perfect ruse if you ask me. And the place is far enough from the city for no one to care what we do here. Excellent location."

"Good." Etienne nodded to himself affirming his own thoughts. "I'll buy it then."

His father had taught him from an early age that the decision-making process must be approached with utmost seriousness, and that hastiness and hot-headed rushing never did anyone any good. And so, Etienne always carefully evaluated everything, looked at the issue from every possible angle and only when he was about ninety-nine percent sure of its correctness would he ask someone their opinion, mostly to confirm his own already-correct one. People that he used for this purpose were also selected with utmost thoroughness, and Jules had already proved himself to be a reliable, level-headed man despite the short period of their knowing each other.

"Is our Lucienne on her way?" Etienne turned to his friend, switching to a new pressing matter. That was another trait that he had inherited from his father: efficiency.

"Yes. I watched her board the train on Friday. She seemed to be doing all right considering it is her first time. Not too nervous. I sent her to Marseille and from there to Nîmes. She's supposed to return in four days with the report."

"Did you tell her what exactly she's carrying?"

"No. I just told her which catalog to give to our men in each city. I hope she follows the instructions this time."

Etienne looked around, brushed the leaves off the edge of the fountain and sat on it gingerly, careful enough not to muddy his coat. "Do you think it's a good idea? The whole Lucienne persona. Be honest, please."

Jules also cleared a small spot for himself and lowered himself next to Etienne, hiding his hands in his pockets to keep them warm.

"I don't know. She seemed too antsy to me at first, then fearful, then eager... As if her emotions were all over the place. Not good liaison agent material, to be truthful. But then I remembered myself in my first days in the Resistance and realized that she was doing fine by all measures." He chuckled. "How I survived to have this conversation with you now is beyond me."

Etienne waved him off.

"You're too modest, my friend."

Jules only nodded, averting his gaze.

"I brought you here to ask one more thing of you." Etienne waited for Jules to look him in the eyes once again. "Will you go to England with me? For a few days only, and then we'll return to work here."

"What's in England?"

"Général de Gaulle."

"You aren't used to tip-toeing around matters, are you?" A hint of amusement reflected on Jules' face.

"I'm just tired of walking and feeling my way around like a blind man. What good is there having one-way communication when the directions that we're receiving from him cannot be verified, discussed, shared between different cells… I've managed to create quite a net of Resistance members on both sides of the Demarcation Line. It would be a shame not to offer him my services. Also, I have a proposition for him, or MI6 or whoever else will agree to listen, but we will discuss that on British soil. So, what do you say? Will you accompany me?"

"How are we going to get to England?"

"Through Switzerland and with the help of fake passports, *bien sûr*." Etienne grinned.

Jules started shaking his head at once. "You can't be serious. With my face plastered on every wall in every *préfecture* all over the country, showing up at the border will be pure suicide, for both of us."

"No, no, no; we won't cross to Switzerland through an official border," Etienne rushed to reassure him, laughing. "We'll cross at night. And from there we'll travel like the two honest gentlemen that we are. Well? What do you say?"

Jules's response came in tow with a one-shoulder shrug and a smile.

"You saved my life getting me through the Demarcation Line once. I owe it to you now. Of course, I'll go with you, only…" He faltered.

"What?" Etienne tried to catch his elusive gaze. "Jules, what is it?"

"Don't tell Général de Gaulle that the Gestapo are looking for me. He won't want to have anything to do with us if you do."

"I understand. I won't say a word, I promise."

The monotone cadence of the train slowly lulled Blanche into sleep with its gentle, hypnotic rocking. Using the collar of her new coat (generously supplied by Margot on the day when Blanche went by to receive her new papers and the heavy stack of the catalogs, which had beautiful women smiling cheerfully from their covers) as a kind of pillow behind her head, Blanche allowed herself to relax, at last, to melt into her seat and to close her eyes just for a few moments. The sack of catalogs was snuggled tightly between her calves, and her attention remained focused on her precious cargo despite her reposeful state. Her first meeting in Marseille had gone enviously smoothly, however, Blanche was determined to keep herself on guard until she met with the second man in Nîmes. It was the first task that the Resistance had delegated to her, and she couldn't afford to fail. Margot hadn't failed to warn her in her usual nonchalant tone that failure also meant arrest and quite possibly imprisonment and torture.

"So, staying diligent is in your interests, first and foremost," Margot concluded while offering Blanche a firm parting handshake. "And in case you do blow your cover and decide to sell us to get a lighter sentence, we'll deny even knowing you. No one keeps any compromising materials in this *atelier*, so the gendarmes will come and leave empty-handed. And you'll end up in jail. Understood?"

Blanche nodded and hugged the cumbersome sack of catalogs to her chest.

Only one more catalog needed to be passed to one of their connections' hands, and then she would officially become a part of their cell. Blanche sighed blissfully and drifted off to sleep, not forgetting to wrap the canvas of the sack's handles around her wrist. This way if someone touched it, she'd wake up at once.

The central train station in Nîmes welcomed her with an uncommonly warm breeze and turquoise sky, smeared with whipped butter clouds. Blanche took it as a good sign and headed towards the taxi cabs waiting for their newly arrived clients just near the entrance. Blanche noted to herself, with a healthy dose of cynicism befitting the situation, that it was a blatant mockery to call a bicycle with a small carriage attached to it a proper "taxicab"; only, in the new France, people had stopped laughing at such matters a long time ago.

Upon arriving at her destination point – *Boulevard Victor Hugo* – Blanche paid the cabby and moved along the sidewalk with deliberate slowness, taking in the unfamiliar surroundings and searching for the name of the place that Margo had indicated she should go to: Salon *Chez Louis*. A man strolling on the sidewalk looked her over appreciatively and tipped his hat when passing her by. Blanche willed herself to erase yet another silly grin from plastering her rouged face; she still hadn't gotten used to all the attention that she, as Lucienne, was getting.

Salon *Chez Louis* hid under a bright yellow striped awning, advertising the best *perm* and highest quality peroxide in the whole of Southern France. Apparently, even though the Germans were kept behind the Demarcation Line (by some miracle, no doubt), the fashion for bleached blonde hair had somehow slipped through the Line, as if local women expected that the miracle wouldn't last long and that the appearance of new uniformed masters of the Free Zone was merely a question of time. So, everyone readied themselves the best they could: women by dyeing their hair and men by handling highly criminal affairs for the Resistance – all under the same roof.

Blanche stepped through the door, displaying the brightest smile she had learned to muster as she practiced in front of the small mirror in her room in the church.

"Bonjour!" she chirped, directing her charms at the first man she saw – a short, pudgy hairdresser with a permanent look of disdain imprinted on his pasty face and scissors which seemed to never leave his unexpectedly delicate hands. "My name is Lucienne Bertin, and I'm looking for the owner, Monsieur Louis Colas."

"What do you need him for, Mademoiselle?" He scrunched his nose slightly at her northern accent.

"I sell cosmetics and have the newest catalogs just delivered from Paris. I'm sure he would like to see them."

"Paris?" The hairdresser arched his brow, expressing in this simple manner his scorn towards the French capital. "What are they offering this season, I wonder? Camouflage face paint?"

The young patron in his chair with thin cylinders of *bigoudis* in her hair giggled readily.

Blanche responded with a tight-lipped smile and shifted from one foot to another. "Is Monsieur Colas in or shall I come back later?"

"Why, you're a persistent one, aren't you?" The hairdresser smirked but at least motioned his head toward the row of chairs lined up alongside the window. "Wait there. I'll get him for you in a few minutes."

He took his time finishing the thorough arrangement of narrow rows of bigoudis on his patron's head and only then headed to the back of the salon, with an audible sigh and visible reluctance. Blanche decided that judging by his attitude, he wasn't involved in his boss' affairs and took her for what she tried to pass for; a pestering sales girl and not a secret liaison agent delivering something of great importance.

What was it that she was delivering though? This thought had crossed Blanche's mind many times since she had begun her journey, but then a tall and elegantly dressed man appeared from the back, and Blanche's attention switched to him.

"*Bonjour,* Monsieur Colas. My name is Lucienne Bertin. Madame Toussaint from Lyon sends her regards." Blanche stopped after saying the exact words that Margot had taught her.

"How is her business doing nowadays?" The man offered his reply.

"Thriving."

"Always good to hear. What does she recommend this time?"

"A new mascara is a true wonder. She swears by it. I will supply it exclusively to your salon, of course."

"I wouldn't have it any other way." The elegant man grinned and held his hand out, expecting a catalog.

Blanche lowered her hand into her canvas bag, counted the fifth one without looking and handed it to the handsome salon owner. He put it under his arm without looking through the pages and asked the last question.

"What is it called, this miracle-working mascara of yours?"

"Midnight in Paris. Page forty-seven," Blanche supplied, and, with that, the two parted ways, until their next meeting.

Blanche walked briskly towards a sunlit square, elated at her recent success. Only one thought wouldn't leave her mind: what exactly was encased into those catalogs in between the pages that she wasn't allowed to see?

"If you don't know what you're carrying, you won't speak during the interrogation in case you get caught," Margot's voice sounded in her head.

"Always follow the rules. We need obedience and compliance from you," Jules's voice joined Margot's.

Blanche took a deep breath and decided to listen to them. For now.

Chapter 5

Father Yves's unblinking gaze, impenetrable and morose, was transfixed on the worn-out floorboards, completely devoid of any movement, unlike his long, skillful fingers which were doing their work with effortless gracefulness. Practiced movements, well-learned and performed too many times in the years, long forgotten, needed no supervision. Disassembling the gun and cleaning and polishing every part of it equaled the same form of meditation to him as counting his rosary beads. God forgive his sinful soul, it probably even pacified him more.

Having finished polishing the gun – his loyal friend which had given him protection and taken others' lives with even more zeal – Father Yves sat motionless for some time, contemplating his life. It seemed that no matter how hard he tried to bury the faceless ghosts of his past they still found their way back to him, to taunt him with the painful memories from which he thought he had escaped, no matter how well he disguised his true self in his black cassock. Who was he trying to fool with this masquerade? He had too much blood on his hands that no years of service to the Lord, nor humility, nor repentance, nor any amount of good deeds would ever wash off.

Father Yves had breathed out in relief when the short war was over in mere weeks, and the Germans "graciously" granted the Southern half of France their so-called independence. It still bothered him, of course, their invisible yet looming presence. However, he was satisfied that even with such concessions from the occupying forces, he at least didn't have to see them daily… Because God only knew if such proximity would awaken the old demons that were still slumbering inside him, controlled by an almost inhuman willpower, but vigilant as ever and ready to be unleashed.

He thought he had found his comfort and relative peace, and yet with the appearance of this girl his whole life threatened to be turned upside down once again. Father Yves didn't mind her living in the church quarters while she sorted herself out and her helping Madame Freneau while attempting to engage him in superficial chatter whenever he happened to be around. But when she almost crashed into him while trying to sneak into her room unnoticed, and turned a shade of beet red that rivaled the rouge covering her pale cheeks, Father Yves almost regretted his hospitality. He suspected what was going on even before she opened her mouth, and regrettably proved himself right after her hasty explanation had followed.

"Father…" Blanche muttered, stepping away and clenching the collar of her new coat on her chest. "This is not what it looks like, I swear!"

He stood silent and motionless, observing the new fiery red locks and the shocking amount of cosmetics that had turned her face into a mask.

"I'm sorry, Father," she mumbled again, lowering her eyes. "I'm not supposed to say 'swear', right? The Bible says something against it, doesn't it? I'm sorry, I don't remember the verse."

Father Yves only shook his head slightly and stepped aside, allowing her to walk away; she didn't.

"I know what I look like, but I promise you that it has nothing to do with anything immoral."

"It depends on what you consider immoral, Blanche," Father Yves responded calmly and started walking away.

Blanche hurried after him, much to his annoyance.

"I'm not one of those women, Father!" She caught up with his long strides and tried peering into his eyes. He stubbornly kept his gaze forward. "It's a disguise..."

He stopped and looked at the girl, silently imploring her not to say anything else. The priest in him softly asked him to stay and to not abandon her, but the Yves from ten years ago wanted nothing to do with her confessions, which would only drag him into all this business again; he knew it right away, he sensed it in his gut.

"I can trust you, right?" She tilted her red head to one side with a pleading expression on her face.

"Of course, you can, Blanche. I'm a priest after all," he spoke somewhat tiredly.

"I joined the Resistance, Father!" Blanche whispered, her eyes shining with excitement.

Father Yves caught himself thinking with detached curiosity that he had probably looked the same when he was exactly her age: inspired and with high hopes, setting off on the road to a metaphorical hell which would change his whole life with no chance of redemption.

"I want to help France, Father," Blanche went on, seemingly surprised by the lack of reaction from his side, as if he had known already what exactly she was going to say. "But for them to accept me I needed a new identity, and so... Here I am. Lucienne Bertin, a cosmetics catalog girl. I'll be their liaison agent they told me. I'll travel from city to city and pass their messages to others. I just wanted you to know that I had to change my looks to help France, and not to do anything... immoral."

Immoral. Again, that damned word. Father Yves cursed inwardly, and at once made a mental note to himself to recite certain passages later to make up for it. He almost laughed at his hypocrisy.

"It's a noble goal, Blanche. Lucienne, I beg your pardon." He corrected himself. "We need to be careful with your new name, don't we? I'll tell Madame Freneau to pay attention to what she calls you from now on. But you'll be traveling a lot now if I'm correct? So, it shouldn't be a problem, I believe. We'll hardly see you."

Blanche nodded, even more confused with his unexpectedly calm demeanor and impenetrable gaze.

"If that's all, I will have to ask you to excuse me," he said with a polite but distant smile. "I have duties to attend to."

He had already started to leave when Blanche spoke softly behind his back, her voice betraying her unsatisfied interest.

"How long have you been a priest, Father?"

Father Yves stopped and pondered something for a moment before turning around to look at her. Something menacing flashed in his eyes, the color of cold steel, some long forgotten wound freshly disturbed.

"Ten years as an ordained minister, not counting the seminary," he replied with curtness.

"You're nothing like other priests," Blanche pressed carefully, an uncertain smile playing on her face. "The ones that I knew couldn't even talk like ordinary people. They would only reply with a certain scripture to every question as if reciting a prayer twenty-five times would solve all problems."

Father Yves snorted softly, agreeing with her. She was right about that, truth be told. He hardly ever told his parishioners to recite scriptures as punishment for their sins or as a means of enforcement against a wavering spirit. He preferred speaking with them at length instead and to help them come up with the right decision. *The Lord likes the ones who help themselves*, he liked to say. *After you sort yourself out, you can always thank Him with a prayer later.*

"What did you do before you became a priest?" Blanche stepped a little closer.

At once, the light was gone from Father Yves's gentle smile.

"Nothing to be proud of," he muttered softly, and he walked away in haste before she had a chance to ask him anything else.

Now, sitting in his room and still holding the gun that felt frightfully natural in his hand, Father Yves closed his eyes and prayed; he prayed that he would never have to use it again.

———————

The immaculately tailored civilian clothes that the man wore were supposed to deceive his visitors into believing that he was a mere middleman. However, it was his perfectly maintained composure, like that of a trained hound combined with the penetrating look of his blue, watered-down eyes that betrayed his belonging to a much higher echelon of power than he wished to pass for. Etienne grinned slightly and returned the man's firm handshake, taking in all these details.

The man had introduced himself as Mr. Brooks, just seconds ago. No rank, no official position, no explanation as to why Etienne and Jules were escorted to see him instead of Général de Gaulle as they initially had asked. *Très bien, let it be Mr. Brooks*, Etienne conceded, if it was even his real name. MI6 was known for using aliases just like they, the Resistance, now did.

Jules remained noticeably on edge throughout the whole journey, even though it had proved to be an uneventful one, just as Etienne had predicted. Two masterfully executed fake passports and a generous sum of money paid to the smugglers got them across the border without any questions asked. Due to his late father's connections, securing a meeting with an official who had access to the General in exile was also an enviously easy task. However, when an MI6 agent appeared at the door of the hotel where they were staying and kindly asked them to follow him – with typical British politeness which left no choice – that's when their luck seemed to run out. Jules ceaselessly threw glances at Etienne along the way to MI6 headquarters as if asking a silent question: *what if it's me who they're after?*

Etienne shook his head in a barely noticeable manner and patted the young man's clenched fist with his gloved hand. *Stay put, Jules. I'll handle everything.*

He was a diplomat's son after all; a gift for negotiation ran in his blood. Jules nodded, but his scowl remained in place.

Mr. Brooks assessed both men with a fleeting glance and at once assumed Etienne to be the leader. One more detail that gave away his ability to read people – an attribute of a typical intelligence officer. With an almost sincere smile, he insisted that he was here only for paperwork.

"We get a lot of volunteers these days and many of them wish to offer their services to the General. Someone has to sort all of them out."

"Most certainly." Etienne nodded his understanding and declined Mr. Brooks' courteous offer of whiskey.

"So, gentlemen. Let's not waste any more of your precious time then." Another polite smile followed as Mr. Brooks interlaced his fingers together. "As I understood from your friend's words you two wish to get involved with the General's Free French movement?"

Etienne hesitated a moment, wondering if he should put all his cards on the table with this mysterious Mr. Brooks without even knowing his official standing and rank. Clearly, Mr. Brooks would withhold that information until he knew what exactly Etienne and Jules had to offer, and so Etienne decided to reply honestly.

"Yes, we do. We know that the General is in dire need of a good network that will allow him to manage loyal people on French soil more efficiently, and I believe that with the help of the network which I have personally organized and which I'm currently supervising, it'll make his work much easier."

Mr. Brooks leaned forward slightly, a flash of interest just barely detectable in his hawk's eyes.

"Could you describe your network a little bit more specifically, Mr. Delattre?"

"I have about fifty people, in several different cities, working under my charge. Some of them are communists, some – just ordinary patriots willing to take a risk for the sake of their country. That last fact is particularly favorable if you think about it, for, unlike the communists, they aren't on any government radar and therefore have much fewer chances to cause suspicion. Particularly those who work in the Occupied Zone."

"You have people working for you in the Occupied Zone?"

Mr. Brooks' interest was apparently piqued.

Jules fidgeted in his seat while Etienne simply nodded his affirmation.

"Yes. In Paris and Dijon namely. We're trying to spread our network to more locations, but as you probably understand we must tread very carefully. The Gestapo is not an organization which should be discounted as inefficient by any means. They infiltrate the cells far too often for us to run the risk of employing people who aren't recommended and vouched for by one or more of our members personally."

"I certainly appreciate you being so cautious. It's a much-needed quality that too many people in our business are lacking, much to our disappointment." Mr. Brooks offered Etienne another smile. "What exactly do they do, these people? If you don't mind me asking, of course."

"Why would I? We're allies, aren't we?"

Etienne grinned, adopting a distantly polite attitude which mirrored that of Mr. Brooks. The technique, becoming a vis-à-vis's metaphorical twin during negotiations, was something that the late Monsieur Delattre had taught Etienne a long time ago. Etienne employed this technique quite often, becoming completely unreadable to his opponent and therefore impossible to manipulate. He needed to find out why MI6 was so interested in him and his network because he knew all too well that the British didn't take Général de Gaulle seriously, and therefore didn't bother too much with his business, assuming he did not have any real power over the Free French or anyone else on French soil. Why such interest in his organization then?

"They print and distribute an underground newspaper, *La Libération*," Etienne explained, noticing Jules's growing uneasiness. Any mention of anything connected to the paper or Paris unnerved him, but Etienne had decided, as soon as he met Jules, not to ask why exactly. *The less you know, the less you'll be able to give away during an interrogation.* It was the first rule that Etienne taught his people, and which he himself always observed. "Also, they're storing weapons after having bought them from the barracks and army storages just before the Germans raided them and took everything under their control. So far, following Général de Gaulle's instructions, we have abstained from any hostile action towards the occupants; however, our people have proved themselves to be trustworthy and reliable, and they are ready to act as soon as he gives direct orders to do so."

Mr. Brooks remained silent for some time, contemplating something. Etienne leaned back in his comfortable leather chair and started observing the interior of Mr. Brooks' office. Dark wood, immaculately clean surfaces, a neat stack of papers and the complete absence of any personal items reflected the owner's personality with painstaking precision. The office was as faceless and undetectable as Mr. Brooks himself.

"What if I told you that while you have a lot to offer Général de Gaulle, the Général himself has nothing to offer to your Resistance yet?" The MI6 agent suddenly tilted his head to one side with an enigmatic smile.

Etienne restrained himself from frowning instinctually and replied with the same grin, "I would say that I find that rather surprising. From his speeches, I gathered that the General was more than capable of managing people if only those people were given to him."

"Unfortunately, I regret to inform you that those speeches are the only thing the General has to offer the Resistance, Mr. Delattre. French people need a French leader to inspire and lead them. So far, due to certain circumstances, the General can only inspire, and we let him do so. As for the organization of the cells and resources – I assure you, he has none. No skilled people, no structure, no chain of command and no technical supplies."

During the long pause that followed Etienne finally congratulated himself on his guess of what Mr. Brooks wanted from them, and now waited patiently for the agent to voice it.

Mr. Brooks didn't disappoint.

"We, on the other hand, can supply you with the above-mentioned. We'll send you liaison agents that will gather intelligence and report directly to us, supply you with radios to communicate with us, and instruct your people through our agents with direct orders that we'll communicate to you through those radios."

"And in exchange, you're only asking us to pledge our allegiance to you and not Général de Gaulle?" Jules spoke for the first time since the meeting had started.

"You don't have to pledge anything to anyone, Mr. Gallais. The only difference between MI6 and your highly regarded General is that we possess the resources that he doesn't. After all, as your compatriot wisely noticed, we are allies."

"Stalin and Hitler used to be allies, too," Jules muttered when he and Etienne stepped outside the headquarters and each lit a cigarette.

"He left us no choice. We had to agree to accept the deal on his conditions. Besides, the British won't collaborate or even sign for peace with the Germans after all the havoc that the *Luftwaffe* created here, right in their capital." Etienne exhaled a grayish cloud of smoke and pulled his hat over his eyes, shielding himself from the raw December windstorm. The street itself was barely visible, hidden behind a wall of icy mist. Humid London air made the horrid weather even more unbearable, throwing gusts of wind in the men's faces.

"Do you think he was telling the truth?" Jules stepped in front of him and searched Etienne's thoughtful face. "About the General?"

"I don't see how lying would benefit him in this situation. So, yes."

"But this means that we'll be working under the charge of MI6 then?"

"It was either that or nothing at all."

They walked in silence for some time, each immersed in his thoughts.

"Don't fret, Jules." Etienne slapped his shoulder amicably. "We got what we came for after all."

"Why, then, do I feel like he played us somehow?" Jules countered, taking a drag on his cigarette before throwing it into a snowdrift.

"Because he did," Etienne replied with a nonchalant shrug. "But it's only the first round, Jules. The game has just begun, and without him, we wouldn't have the means to continue it. So, let him have this round for now. We have much more ahead of us, my friend. That's why I said, don't fret."

Chapter 6

Blanche hastened her steps both due to the snowstorm attacking the people of Lyon with a viciousness rivaling that of the German army, and the ever-growing impatience that seemed to penetrate every cell of her body together with the cold. Even the canvas bag entrusted into Blanche's eager hands by Margot mere minutes ago didn't appear to be as heavy as usual. Margot hadn't forgotten to nearly suffocate Blanche with the clouds of tobacco smoke billowing from her mouth, while she reminded the girl, once again, that the catalogs were not to be touched under any circumstance. However, Blanche's curiosity was getting the better of her, heating up her blood and shining her eyes, as she squinted against the raging weather with excitement.

The church stood gray and graceful, stretching its gothic towers towards the low-hanging clouds that ceaselessly poured their diamond powder on top of the crosses and gargoyles. Blanche circled round its walls, shook the snow off her red curls, inappropriately bright against the churchyard's austere elegance of dark stone and ivory snow, and pushed the heavy wooden door, letting herself inside its modest living quarters. Animated and breathless, she ran up the stone steps and hid inside her room, like a thief impatient to discover what amazing goods he had managed to snatch from an unsuspecting victim.

Blanche dropped to the floor and, with her perspiring back pressed against the door, she carefully released the stack of catalogs from the bag and counted to the fourth one in the stack. It was the copy she was supposed to take to Dijon next week. For some inexplicable reason, she refused to go back to her hometown without knowing what exactly she was carrying, even if it might be the biggest mistake she could possibly make, according to that know-it-all, Margot.

Having carefully separated the two stacks so as not to misplace the catalog that was lying on her lap – the greatest mystery waiting to be revealed – Blanche flipped the first page, then the second one, the third, her searching eyes looking for underlined words or hidden messages that she expected to be dotted in between the pictures of women displaying insincere but bright smiles. But there were no cryptic messages hidden inside; only a two-page newspaper which seemed to be printed by some amateurs, neatly enclosed between pages thirty-two and thirty-three, its ink as blue as the blonde's eyes on the advertisement next to it.

Confused and glowering, Blanche scanned the contents, and the more she read, the deeper her scowl grew. She tried to guess if the paper was telling the truth or if it was a piece of anti-German propaganda, deliberately depicting the new occupants of France as merciless beasts. After all, who could verify if the names of the men that were rumored to have disappeared into the Gestapo jail in Paris were real? Who could confirm that the firing squad indeed executed teenagers who were supposedly aiding the rebels? Could it be true that a new law had just been passed, bestowing unrestrained power into the Gestapo's hands, allowing them to take hostages and execute them in the case of hostile action against the Germans? And all because some Resistance fighter shot some naval officer in Paris, and disappeared into the night?

Blanche closed the catalog, burying the underground newspaper and its contents into the magazine's glossy embrace; only, it proved to be much more difficult to bury her doubts concerning the words that she had read. They swarmed around in her restless mind, mixing with her memories and assumptions of the recent past. She knew them well enough, those Germans; she'd lived near them for quite some time, and even though she'd grown to despise them for their drunken bouts and pig-like behavior, she never saw them actually hurt anyone. It was against the rules of the armistice, wasn't it? The citizens were to be left alone, and criminals were to be dealt with accordingly – but by the French gendarmes. What was this paper then? A tiny piece of truth that the Resistance fighters were trying to reveal to the people while the official government blasted their propaganda through the official newspapers and state radios? Or just a conniving means of attracting more people into the Resistance ranks? Blanche bit her nail, deep in thought. She could hardly find out until she traveled back to the Occupied Zone and saw everything for herself.

"They were hiding a simple newspaper from me, can you imagine?" She snorted softly while announcing her discovery to Father Yves later that evening.

The two shared a modest supper like they always did, with one difference only: that night Madame Freneau was absent from the table, falling sick a day ago and muttering that she had no appetite to all of Blanche's offers to bring her some food to her room. Warm candlelight glowed softly in the small dining room: the hardships of the occupation had slowly started to slither through the Demarcation Line into the Free Zone. Electricity was not to be wasted, according to the new regulations passed through the *préfecture* into the hands of the citizens of Lyon, who, while grumbling their discontent, were so utterly powerless against them.

"Must be one important newspaper then," Father Yves noted with a soft smile and served Blanche the rest of the cauliflower.

Blanche mumbled a somewhat embarrassed thank you, still not used to such a kind attitude being directed at her. Maybe it wasn't doting, but Father Yves was being nice, and that's how people were supposed to treat each other, weren't they? Blanche didn't know. All she knew was that she had been yelled at far too often by far too many people, including her own mother and siblings, and therefore couldn't possibly differentiate between politeness and interest. She stole a quick glance at the man who was sitting across from her and noticed that his gray eyes looked almost black now, due to the dark ambiance. There was a mysterious air about him, which she tried so desperately to penetrate, yet she failed miserably every time. However, she kept feeling drawn to the enigmatic hollowness marring his handsome features, as if all life had been sucked out of him a long time ago. It reminded Blanche too much of her own emptiness inside, the same dejected gaze aging both of them beyond their years. She'd never felt the warmth of love. She was an unwanted bastard of some German soldier, hated solely for that; what had happened to Father Yves though? Perhaps it was something even worse because it wasn't resentment and sadness that looked back at her every time she wasn't quick enough to lower her gaze after her shameless scrutinizing. No, there was something much more despondent and forlorn. He looked simply dead inside. And yet, Blanche held her breath each time his fingers grazed her lips on Sundays.

"Body of Christ." She took a thin white piece of bread from his hand. His warm breath caressed her forehead, and all she could see was the blackness of his cassock in front of her because she's too afraid to lift her gaze to his. She wants to drown in this darkness together with him...

"You shouldn't have looked."

"Pardon?" Blanche's cheeks blushed bright red at his words as if she feared that he might have guessed her sinful thoughts.

"The newspaper. You shouldn't have looked at it." Father Yves was as calm and reserved as always as he spread a film of butter, glistening in the dim light, on top of a fresh baguette. "And you shouldn't have told me about it either. Didn't they teach you that, in that cell of yours?"

Blanche observed his confident movements without replying.

"The gendarmes might catch you and take you for questioning," he continued, in a mildly scolding voice, after handing Blanche her piece of bread with strawberry jam generously applied to it. "What will you do then? And if they come to me and start asking me about you? Have you thought of that? What if I tell them all I know at once? Lying is one of the mortal sins. What if I'd rather not sin than keep you safe? Have you considered that?"

Blanche almost buried her head in her plate, squeezing her toes inside her shoes as tight as she could, abashed from his shaming. Then she suddenly lifted her chin defiantly and proclaimed, "Well, I trust you I guess. And I know that you won't give me away to the gendarmes, sin or no sin. I don't believe that you're so pious anyway. I don't even believe that you're a priest."

Father Yves only chuckled softly in response. "It would be rather difficult, to keep such a façade and to deceive the whole congregation for such a long time, don't you think?"

"You somehow managed."

"Such blasphemy against the Lord's servant in God's house."

"See? Even now you sound ironic. What kind of priest would joke about something of that sort in his church?"

Father Yves barely suppressed a grin, rose from his chair and bid her good night, ignoring her question. In the doorway, he paused, though, and spoke before leaving. "You are meddling with some dangerous business, Blanche. I don't want anything to happen to you, that's all."

"What do you know about dangerous business, Father?"

"More than I wish I did."

The indigo velvet of the night transformed the route into a maze of shadows, illuminated only by the shimmering waves of the blizzard cutting through it each time the wind picked the snowflakes up off the ground. As the two figures navigated their way knee-deep in snow, the steel-gray crescent of the moon followed them silently from behind its hideout of threadbare clouds, thinly painted across the sky. Breathing heavily while mounting yet another hill, braving the cold with admirable stoicism, the two figures hardly spoke to each other, choosing to cover their faces so that only their eyes, shining with determination, were visible above their scarves.

Finally, the couple came to a halt at the top of the hill to observe their surroundings and to catch their breath. The taller figure pulled his sleeve up, revealing a beautifully executed hand watch and squinted his eyes in an attempt to see the time in the dim light of the uncooperative moon.

"Surprisingly, we're on time. We have exactly half an hour left before the British drop their cargo."

"Is your man waiting for us?" the other man asked, his voice sounding muffled behind the multiple layers of a heavy scarf.

"Yes, down the hill, right there, where the forest starts. See?" He pointed his gloved hand towards the woods looming up ahead, indicating the direction.

"Are you sure we're in the right spot?"

"Quite sure. If the compass doesn't lie, of course."

They started making their way downhill, panting and sliding in the snow which was covered in a thin film of ice, rendering the easy descent almost impossible to navigate.

"Have you been here before?" the shorter figure demanded, hoping not to lose sight of his comrade in the dark.

"Only in summer. My father and I came here to ride horses quite often."

"How are we going to find your friend then?"

"Don't fret. He'll find us." The taller figure seemed to be much more confident than his companion, even after admitting to himself that he was just as helpless at navigating through snow-covered mountains in winter, and particularly at night, as the other fellow was. "He's a hunter; he knows the forest and his way around it like the back of his hand."

The couple, with their backs now completely covered in snow, caught each other's hand to steady themselves from sliding on a particularly steep part.

"Etienne."

"Yes, Jules?"

"I think you should leave it to me."

"Leave what to you?"

"This whole affair, with the parachutists. It's not just a simple newspaper anymore. This is... They'll shoot you for this."

Their breath was still coming in short gasps as the two stopped to peer into each other's eyes, Etienne's matching the silver shade of the moon.

"So, you would rather get shot instead of me?" His voice sounded mildly amused but with notes of sadness at the same time.

Jules lowered his scarf, revealing his mouth which was pressed into a hard line.

"It is only sensible and fair, Etienne. Those parachutists, if captured, must under no circumstance reveal who is in charge of the whole enterprise. You are too important, far too important for the Resistance. And, therefore, you should stay in the shadows and supervise everything without revealing yourself. I think that you know it perfectly well yourself... You're just too noble of a man to admit it."

"Understanding it and agreeing with it are two rather different ends of the spectrum, Jules." Etienne turned his face away and resumed his walking.

Jules trailed after him, unwillingly admiring the grand scenery unraveling in front of his eyes. The Lyon mountains, within several kilometers of the city itself, were even more imposing now, with the impenetrable wall of the forest rising right in front of their eyes.

"War is a strange thing," Etienne continued, in what seemed to be musings which he had decided to pronounce out loud, into the stillness of the night. "It changes a man and even his way of thinking. And while the sensible man in me agrees with you wholeheartedly, the honorable man in me won't listen to any of those very sensible arguments. I can't sacrifice your life to keep mine safe, Jules. It simply wouldn't be right."

"You're right about the war, Etienne. And yet, you're wrong about one thing: sometimes a man must sacrifice the honorable man in him and all his moral qualms for the sake of a bigger cause. Even a few months ago I wouldn't have said any of this to you because I didn't understand this myself. Then something happened—"

"Don't tell me."

"No, I want to. I killed an innocent man, Etienne. An innocent man, whose only fault was the uniform that he was wearing. I knew before I set out to kill him that I would never look at myself in the mirror the same way again. I knew that I would be a changed man after I went through with the gruesome deed. But as you said so yourself: it's the war, comrade. And it's us against them. And if we don't kill them all, they will kill us, simple as that. And after I realized that, all of my moral qualms and the honorable man in me didn't matter anymore."

They stood in silence a moment, sharing the most intimate truth between them. Two conspirators, with souls bared, in a rare moment of precious sincerity, as if it might decide the whole world's fate; or so it seemed under the cover of that velvet night, under the light of the crescent moon, still peeking curiously from behind the curtains of the clouds.

"So, you're the legendary Ghost then? The one who shot that naval officer in Paris?" Etienne's words came out in a mere whisper. "I can't say that I didn't suspect as much after my father's friend, Monsieur Demarche, asked me with utmost urgency to smuggle you out of the Occupied Zone. I wondered what you did to cause such havoc all over the North. How do you know Michel though?"

"My sister has a contract with his publishing house. She asked him to shelter me and then help me get out of Paris before the Gestapo got a hold of me."

"What's her name?"

"Giselle Legrand."

"Really? I must say, I very much enjoyed that novel of hers, with Jean-Marc as a protagonist, what was its name...?"

"A Good Man's Bayonet."

"That's right. My father loved that book, too. He fought in the Great War, so he understood it better than me. She stayed in Paris then, your sister?"

"She did. She's one of the writers for *La Libération,* you know."

"You're joking, most certainly? Our *Libération,* the one that we're reprinting and distributing?"

"That's right."

"I thought all of the writers were men."

"Giselle is a man, only in a woman's body." Jules smirked. "She always had more guts than I did. And the sharpest mind to match. Helps her get all that information for the paper, obviously, from that Nazi lover of hers."

"Nazi lover?"

"Yes. She lives with a *Boche*. And a formidable one on top of it."

"What?"

"Ah, long story. She's getting married to him, too. I have no idea what's going on in that mind of hers and why she's acting like a dog in the manger – being with the Resistance on the one hand, and refusing to let go of her high-ranking Nazi on the other. I can only hope she will choose the right side sooner rather than later. By the way, since tonight is the night of revelations, my real name is Marcel. I thought I owed you at least that after you saved my life. Or maybe because I don't want to die nameless." He snorted mirthlessly.

"It's an honor to meet you, Marcel." Etienne outstretched his hand, and the two exchanged firm handshakes. "No matter what you think of yourself, you're still a hero in my eyes. And in the eyes of many people, too."

"I told you my story for two reasons," Marcel spoke mildly after a pause, seemingly glad that Etienne walked in front of him again and couldn't see the tears that shone in his eyes against his will. "The first one is to persuade you to leave this to me. And second, for you to know that I am capable of whatever needs to be done in the name of the Resistance."

"Even though it would mean that you would most likely put a gun to your head after the war is over because you won't be able to live with yourself?"

"Yes."

The howling of an owl interrupted their conversation, and the two men stopped at once, gingerly listening for the second one to follow. After it did, Etienne cupped his hands, brought them to his mouth and replied in the same manner. Barely a minute later, another figure appeared from behind the dense growth of the trees and started approaching them in a resolute step.

"Comrades," the harsh voice grumbled from under a scarf, also shielding the man's face from the weather as he stopped to shake hands with the two men.

"This is Jules. Jules, this is Patrice; he'll help you collect our parachutist and take you both to safety."

Etienne's voice sounded slightly strained as he proceeded with the introductions in his usual collected and efficient manner; only this time there was another reason behind his hastiness. The sensible man in Etienne had listened to Jules' – *Marcel's,* Etienne mentally corrected himself – story, and realized that the only reasonable decision was the one that Marcel suggested. The honorable man in Etienne recognized that he should become a faceless puppet master, governing the whole affair from behind a curtain of anonymity, unknown and devoid of the honor of a true fighter, and yet so very indispensable and necessary for the greater cause. He had to turn around and leave, now.

"You're going then?" Patrice's voice gave way to surprise as he watched this strange bourgeois, whom he had met during the Armistice parade when he gave him his first copy of that paper, *La Libération,* to then simply stride off rapidly in the opposite direction.

"Yes." Etienne threw the words over his shoulder. "Jules will explain everything to you. And forget that you ever saw me."

Chapter 7

The visitor shifted uneasily from one foot to another, his agitation obvious to Father Yves, who'd been observing him for a few silent moments. He rarely ever crept up on his parishioners in this manner, watching their backs without making a sound when he happened to catch them unawares between the services; only, this man was not one of his parishioners, that much Father Yves knew from the very moment he had spotted him. Instead of removing his cap and making a sign of the cross, the man stood indecisively as if taking in the new and unfamiliar surroundings of the church.

Father Yves wrapped a rosary around his fingers and cleared his throat with intentional loudness. The visitor visibly jumped and turned around swiftly.

"You startled me, Father."

"I beg your forgiveness. I didn't mean to." Father Yves's voice was as serene as the atmosphere in the empty church – one of the rare islands of peace and silence from the world outside, raging with the madness of the war. "How can I be of service?"

The man approached him gingerly, outstretched his hand in a somewhat nervous gesture but then, as if on second thought, quickly retracted it, hiding both calloused palms in the pockets of his worn-out leather jacket.

"Sorry, Father. Priests don't shake hands, do they?"

Father Yves lowered his head, concealing a coy smile, and asked instead, "And communists don't usually seek priests without a seemingly good reason, do they? Isn't your ideology supposed to be atheistic?"

"How do you...?" the man stuttered, then shuffled anxiously once again and lowered his gaunt face that had a shade of visible stubble on his square chin. "Well, it doesn't matter I suppose. It's even better that you know who I am; saves me time as I don't have to go into long explanations."

"How can I be of service?" Father Yves repeated, gesturing his unexpected guest towards the nearest pew, polished to perfection by his own hands during one of those nights when the demons of the past wouldn't let him sleep, and he would serve his self-appointed penance by rubbing the dark wood with ferocious obsession in order to clean it, together with the blood on his hands that he swore was still visible.

"I heard from my comrades that you... well..." The communist threw a quick glance over his shoulder and, despite the church being empty, lowered his voice to a mere whisper. "They say that you're not too fond of the Vichy government, and Maréchal Pétain in particular. They say, during your speeches—"

"Sermons," Father Yves corrected him.

"Sermons, right. That during your sermons, you call for denunciation of the Vichy and for standing up to the oppressors."

A shadow set across Father Yves's face, settling deep into the lines creasing his brow and annihilating the kindness in his gray eyes, leaving them cold and dead.

"I don't call for anything. I merely quote verses from the Holy Book. I'm not responsible for how my parish chooses to interpret them."

"No need to put on such a defense, Father." The communist grinned, still not offering his name. "I don't work for the *gendarmes*."

"I would be rather surprised if they started hiring communists." Father Yves sighed and looked his guest square in the eye. "I know who you work for, and before you say anything else, let me state this clearly: I don't want to get involved. I've seen my share of fighting already, and have no desire to get entangled within another war. Take care of your fighters, and I'll take care of my parish. Let's leave it at that."

Father Yves made a motion to get up when the persistent communist caught his sleeve, imploring him only by the sheer force of his deep brown eyes to sit down. Father Yves lowered himself on the pew, obliging him with visible reluctance.

"Just one more question, Father, and I'll let you go, I promise. Do you care only for parishioners of the Christian faith?"

Father Yves knitted his brows in confusion. "It's a Catholic church. I think it implies that all of my parishioners are of Christian faith."

"Of course, Father, I understand that. But what if I told you that there are people of a different faith who might be in more desperate need of your help than their Christian counterparts?"

"Are you talking about Jews?"

"*Bien sûr.* Who else could I possibly mean?" The communist chuckled mirthlessly.

"Why would they be in 'desperate need' as you called it? And besides, I always thought they gravitated more towards your communist lot than our Church."

"I'm not talking about Jews from the Free Zone, no. They're fine and well, joining our legion in Africa in the hundreds, and especially the foreign ones, which the Nazis kicked out of their homes in their own countries. They're hell-bent on taking their revenge on the *Boches*, that much you're right about. And who would blame them, right?"

Father Yves didn't laugh with him, instead patiently awaiting further explanation. Regardless of how little he wanted to deal with the communist, he had to admit that he intrigued him.

"I am talking about the Jews from the Occupied Zone, Father." The man regained his serious look. "The *Boches* are plotting something against the poor devils, I'm afraid."

He pressed the tips of his fingers to his lips, smiling at Father Yves apologetically. "I beg your pardon, Father. I shouldn't say 'devil' in the church, right?"

Father Yves dismissed his apologies with a simple wave of his hand.

"Don't worry yourself over it. I listen to confessions from sinners far worse than you, and if they haven't been stricken by a bolt of lightning by now, I'm quite sure that you're safe. Get to the point, please. I have to prepare for the Mass."

"My comrades were right. You are not a typical priest. I think you would be perfect for our plans, if you agree to them, of course."

"You still haven't revealed these mysterious plans of yours."

"Would you agree to shelter several families here from time to time? We'll be smuggling them across the border, and they need to stay someplace safe before we get them new papers and sort out their new living arrangements. It won't take long; a week or two at the most for each family. We'll pay you for the food, *bien sûr*."

Father Yves sat, letting the beads of the rosary run through his fingers while pondering on the request. He had had no dealings with Jews before, only prayed together with everyone for the poor souls whenever news poured across the border that the Nazis were acting more and more savagely and ruthlessly towards them. Wasn't it his Christian duty to care for them? Only, he wasn't that much of a Christian. Father Yves smirked slightly at his unhappy thoughts. An imposter in a black robe, who thought that he would find solace and forgiveness in the holy, marble-clad house of God. God hadn't spoken to him once; not that Father Yves blamed Him.

"What do you say, Father?"

What should he say? Maybe this was it, his chance for redemption?

He turned to the communist, put the rosary away and offered him his hand.

"I'll do it."

The communist looked at the priest's palm in surprise but grasped it after a moment of hesitation and gave it a firm parting press.

———————

Marcel balanced on the edge of the sturdy wooden windowsill, his gaze glued to the Brit's nimble fingers that seemed to fly over the *Paraset* radio transceiver, now almost completely taken apart. Last night, after recovering the parachutist from the tree, in which the straps of his parachute had the misfortune to entangle, the three of them braved the storm that had regained power while Marcel and Patrice searched for their radio man.

The British plane had dropped him a little off the designated location, and it took them longer than expected to finally locate him and take him to the safety of a small hut, in which the forest overseer used to live, but since his death, had stood abandoned, mostly used by hunters – according to Patrice. Shaking from the cold and having lost almost all sensitivity in their frozen limbs, the three of them dropped down onto the floor as soon as they stepped through the doors of the hut. They fell asleep right on the floor, huddled tightly together for not one of them could muster enough strength to light the fire; their fingers simply refused to listen to them.

In the morning, after a royal breakfast of smoked sausage, a loaf of bread (all produced from the depths of the resourceful Patrice's backpack) and even coffee, which Patrice brewed on top of a small stove, the men felt almost completely recovered from their ordeal and even felt alive enough to start exchanging jests and chuckles, ridiculing the "preciseness" of the British pilot. The young British fellow, who had suffered the most from his parachute mishap, acquiring several scratches gained after falling through the branches, rubbed his sprained ankle and even grumbled under his breath that he would report the pilot to his superiors in the first radio message that he sent. Only, as soon as he sat down to see to this task, the radio stubbornly refused to cooperate.

He introduced himself as Tommy, immediately sending both Frenchmen into a fit of chuckles.

"What could be a more suitable name for a Brit?" Patrice noted with obvious irony. "It fits you as perfectly as Fritz would fit a *Boche*."

"That's the point of it," the svelte young man with golden hair, who had an air of being a rascal about him, countered nonchalantly, not taking any offense at the joke. "Now, if asked about me, you will only be able to say that you had a *tommy* with you. Which interrogator would accuse you of lying?"

His amber eyes twinkled with mischief as he offered the two comrades a wink.

Now, Tommy hissed and cursed in expressions that would put any sailor to shame while trying to get the radio to work. Marcel and Patrice had nothing better to do but trade accounts of their progress with *La Libération* within their different cells, and agree on a new set of rules that were to go into effect now that they had a direct line with their allies in England.

"Think of it as a measure towards being overcautious, but I believe it wouldn't hurt us if, when recruiting a new member, we could sort them out in three-member cells," Marcel suggested to Patrice, who kept nodding solemnly. "The initial two members should be the 'old fighters', though. This way we will be able to kill two birds with one stone; the recruit will learn from them – number one; number two –

if the recruit turns out to be an agent infiltrated by the Gestapo or the *gendarmes* he will only be able to sell out two people from his cell and not the whole chain."

"I like the idea." Patrice patted his pockets in search of cigarettes, produced a crumpled pack and offered Marcel one. Tommy managed to snatch one for himself without even taking his eyes off the radio in front of him. Patrice snorted softly and stood up to help the British radio operator with the matches. "Also, it would be smart if each cell had a certain structure. Let's say, a ringleader, a liaison agent, and an engineer. There should be an engineer if you ask me. Or a sharpshooter. Or an expert in bomb-making, I don't know. But if they're all ringleaders or are all only good at talk and no action there's really no point in the cell itself. Someone has to do the job, physically that is."

"Soon both liaison agents and bomb-makers will be dropping on you from the sky in such quantities that you won't know what to do with them," Tommy remarked nonchalantly, once again indicating that he, in fact, attentively listened to every word the Frenchmen exchanged, despite the utter concentration in which he seemed to be immersed.

"That would be grand. Only, first, you will have to fix that radio of yours." Patrice's sneer, which was intended to look mocking, came out kind-hearted for some reason.

The young Brit's charming boastfulness and typical arrogance reminiscent of youth couldn't possibly be met with contempt solely because of the sheer innocent naïveté of it. The boy was talented; there was no doubt about it. MI6 wouldn't send him here if they weren't sure of his qualifications. He was too handsome, with the whiskey-colored eager eyes of an eighteen-year-old who had only seen war, in textbooks and probably loved romanticizing it with the all-knowing air of a university professor, while puffing on a thin cigar and discussing what Napoleon did wrong with his own similarly eager-eyed young men. He most likely believed that

71

now, having analyzed and discussed all of Napoleon's mistakes, he would most certainly avoid them, and maybe even beat the Germans single-handedly. It was all understandable, too. When one was eighteen, one didn't believe death was on the horizon. It was too far away, too contrived and fictitious when one was too full of life and the conceit of youth.

"Don't worry yourself about my radio. It'll work perfectly fine in just... Ah, sod it!" Tommy suddenly slumped to the back of his chair, sending a small screwdriver flying across the room.

Marcel caught himself smiling. Tommy even managed to make temper tantrums look charming.

"You can put a fork in this radio, for now, mates. It's done." Tommy declared calmly, his demeanor changing within seconds from one of a pouting child who had just discovered that his favorite toy was broken to a self-assured professional. "Need to get new bulbs for it. Without them – say bye-bye to the communication line and therefore to the bomb-makers raining on you from the sky thanks to the generous MI6."

"What kind of bulbs?" Marcel frowned.

"Well, obviously not ones that you would put in your chandelier." Tommy snorted with laughter and scrunched his nose comically at the overpowering tobacco stench of his cigarette, something he was apparently not used to. "I need very small ones that are used in portable devices like this one. The problem is, if you go to an electrics store and ask for them, the chances are that they'll know that you're getting it for a radio. I know that it's a Free Zone but... Will it not put you on the radar of the gendarmes?"

"We don't know," Patrice replied after exchanging glances with Marcel. "We don't know how diligent our gendarmes are in their work, that is. Never had to deal with them before."

"That's a problem." Tommy nodded several times, carefully taking the thin broken glass out of his now useless radio.

"Wait a minute. What about professional cameras which they use in *photo ateliers*?" Marcel snapped his fingers at the idea. "Do they use the same bulbs?"

Golden specks shimmered in Tommy's eyes as he squinted them slightly, regarding Marcel with an attentive gaze.

"Quite possibly. I don't specialize in cameras, but... Could be."

"We'll never know until we try it, right?" Marcel shrugged as he spoke, grinning in reply as the contagious smile of the young Brit brightened up his face once again. He turned to Patrice. "What do you say, comrade?"

"I say if we want to make it before sunset, let's get moving."

Ten minutes later the old cabin looked just as it had before the three men had appeared – old, abandoned, and devoid of any trace of the recent presence of the men. Just as when the sun had occupied its highest position in the sky at midday, the gusts of wind completely concealed any footsteps, imprinted in the luminous crystals of the snow. The three figures disappeared without a trace.

Chapter 8

Blanche caught a fleeting glance of her reflection in the glass of the revolving door of *Gare de Lyon-Perrache,* before letting herself inside the familiar foyer with its marble-clad floors and tall ceilings. A subtle smile played on her painted lips as she walked resolutely towards the teller's window to buy her ticket to Dijon, feeling nowhere near as nervous as she had been during her first few trips. She still remembered how her hand had been shaking when she gave the stern-looking man the money, and how perspiration dampened her back under her coat as anxiety covered her in one nauseating wave after another.

That fearful girl had disappeared somewhere along the way, lost between the railway stations, and forgotten like an old dress that Blanche had decided to shed once and for all. She was *Lucienne* now, and Lucienne had nothing to fear. She wasn't some *Boche's* bastard daughter; neither was she a neglected child to whom even her mother paid no heed. Lucienne was confident and attractive, even though it was all a mere mask made of thoroughly applied makeup and hair dye, imprinted in her new papers. But, slowly, Blanche was growing into the new person her papers said she was.

She'd adopted new mannerisms that she learned from observing good-looking women, wrapped in silk and bright jewelry as they accepted the adoration of the men around them. She had spent hours in front of the mirror trying to smile as mysteriously and seductively as the actresses in those black and white movies that she could finally afford to see; she taught herself how to walk looking straight ahead, holding her head proudly under the lingering glances of men, whose wives usually pulled them by the crook of their arm the moment they spotted Lucienne. Even Yves (for Blanche stubbornly refused to call him Father while giving in to her not such holy thoughts) had complimented her appearance a couple of days ago, noticing how becoming her new hat was.

Around her, he still acted the same as he did when she had first stepped through the doors of his church. It seemed like ages since they had first met, but he retained the same air of indifferent melancholy and ignored all of Blanche's attempts to penetrate the wall that he had seemingly erected and which he flat-out refused to discuss. Yet, each smile and each word of encouragement, each blessing he softly whispered while making the sign of a cross in front of her face before she set out on yet another trip, fueled the feelings that she, at first, had refused to acknowledge, soon creating a veritable fire that seemed to consume her soul at the mere thought of the holy man, who Blanche suspected was a much bigger sinner than she was. It was a fire that made her assign meanings to the most ordinary words he uttered, look for something deep in his glances, and create pictures of the future in her mind that painted a natural rosy radiance on her face, that made her smile seem so dreamy and that made the grip of her gloved hand much more relaxed on the canvas bag with the catalogs that she carried. Yes, she was an attractive young woman now, and soon he would give in to her charms and let her inside his world, at last, Blanche thought, just as yet another man lifted his hat and moved out of her way, looking her up and down appreciatively.

Blanche bathed in the new attention and in her confidence that day and even felt bold enough to ride the train in one of the first cars, which the Germans usually

75

occupied as soon as the train crossed the Demarcation Line. Such reckless action proved to be a mistake.

An officer strode in at one of the transit stations, followed by two younger uniformed men, with the arrogance of a man who held the whole world in his gloved fist. Blanche felt the air leave her lungs as he set his icy blue eyes on her, a look of mild curiosity settling on his clean-shaven face. Blanche took in the deep, cruel lines around his mouth, the leather coat with a rich fur collar, the markings of the SS on his uniform cap, the shoulder-boards on his coat that held too many knobs to signify anything good, and realized that she was as good as dead. *The Gestapo.* She had never encountered any of them before but had heard enough about them to induce a lump in her throat. It only expanded under the Boche's scrutinizing glare, threatening to suffocate her if the menacing silence lasted any longer.

"How far are you traveling, Mademoiselle?"

His voice had a barely detectable accent, which took her aback with its mildness. Like honey, in which an unfortunate bee can get caught in and die; the fleeting thought flashed in Blanche's mind for some reason.

"Not far." She forced the words out, her confidence melting away as he stripped her bare with penetrating eyes, looking into her very soul, it seemed, and guessing all of her most guarded secrets. "Dijon."

"That's still at least a two-hour trip," the German noted with the same enigmatic grin. "Certainly, you don't want to spend it in the company of these scoundrels."

He motioned his head towards the soldiers occupying the train car. Blanche waited for what he would say next, holding her breath.

Exit the train car, please. We know who you are and what you're here for.

You're under arrest, Mademoiselle. Our men in Dijon have been following you for some time now.

You will have to come with us now. It would be better for everyone if you start talking right away. Maybe then we'll make your execution swift and painless.

The two black-clad men behind his back stood like two silent shadows, guarding their master. He shifted slightly, and Blanche heard his glove brush the leather of his coat, breaking the perfect silence.

"You can ride in my compartment if you'd like." He casually dropped the words. "I suppose you'll be much more comfortable there."

Without waiting for her reply, the German turned on his heel and headed to the front of the car, where a couple of private compartments were situated. Blanche threw a helpless look at his two henchmen, who patiently stood in the same spot, clearly waiting for her to follow their boss. Fighting a sudden wave of nausea, Blanche picked up her bag, trying to contain her reluctance, and headed in the same direction as the German.

He stood in the doorway of his compartment, holding it for her in the most gallant manner. Blanche went inside, willing herself not to begin openly shaking.

"Friedrich, bring us some coffee, *bitte*."

The two somber looking men were dismissed, the door was closed, and Blanche found herself face to face with every Resistance member's worst nightmare.

"Well, Mademoiselle -" His soft voice sent shivers down her spine as he took the canvas bag out of her hands and placed it on the seat next to him. "It's time to, how do you French call it? *Faire votre connaissance, ja?*"

All of a sudden, she felt trapped and claustrophobic in the narrow space of the private compartment, standing mere centimeters away from the German. Still observing her with curiosity, he removed his uniform cap and smoothed out his platinum hair with a practiced gesture. In such proximity, Blanche realized that she had mistakenly assumed that he was a young man. Now, seeing deep lines in between his brows, the net of smaller ones around his eyes and, more than anything, that air of superiority that he emanated, she concluded that he must be well into his forties.

"Allow me to take your coat? The compartment is heated, and you'll find yourself most uncomfortable if you keep it on."

Judging by his outstretched hand, it wasn't a polite request; an order was more like it. Blanche started silently unbuttoning her coat, unable to look away from him. It was almost as if he held her in a hypnotic daze with his stare. After taking the coat from her hands, he hung it near the door and went to remove his leather one. The full view of all his ribbons and military awards terrified her even more, and Blanche lowered to the seat only because she was certain she would most definitely faint if she didn't.

"Don't be afraid of me, Mademoiselle." He sat across from her, his legs crossed and a coy grin in place. "I don't bite."

Blanche willed herself to smile back, even though she was sure her smile resembled a pale, frightened grimace more than anything.

"Standartenführer Jürgen Sievers, at your service, Mademoiselle. Shall I continue calling you 'Mademoiselle' or do you have a name, perhaps?"

His soft-spoken manner and the teasing tone completely confused Blanche. She hardly remembered what her alias was in that moment.

"Lucienne. Lucienne Bertin."

"Lucienne Bertin," he repeated with intentional slowness as if tasting her name on his tongue. "It is my pleasure to make your acquaintance, Mademoiselle Bertin."

"As it is mine to meet you, Monsieur Sievers."

His grin widened.

"Are you visiting someone in Dijon?"

Against her better judgment, her gaze fell on the bag that the German had placed next to him. He followed it with his eyes, arched a brow inquisitively and before Blanche had a chance to utter a word, he lowered his hand into it and extracted one of the catalogs.

"I sell cosmetics." She finally found her voice as he flipped through the pages nonchalantly.

"Cosmetics?" Sievers looked up at her, the corners of his eyes creasing as he grinned. "Fascinating. Do you have a lot of customers in Dijon?"

"No, just one. What I sell is rather expensive, and most of my clients demand exclusiveness. So, I travel between cities, thus making up my numbers."

"*Ach,* I see."

Much to her relief, he put the catalog back into the bag and concentrated his attention on Blanche instead. "Does your husband, or some lucky young man, mind that you travel all the time?"

"I'm not married, and nor do I have a 'young man', Monsieur Sievers." Blanche caught herself blushing for some reason. "So, my long absences don't bother anyone."

"*Schande.*" He tsked several times, shaking his head. "Had you been living in the Reich, some young, dashing officer would have long snatched you up, the lovely little thing that you are."

Blanche caught herself smiling, unexpectedly pleased with the compliment even though it came from such a feared man.

"What about your family?"

"I don't have anyone. My father died in the war, and my mother died giving birth to me. I'm an orphan and was raised in a church orphanage." Blanche gave him the full story which she had carefully rehearsed with Margot until it became emblazoned in her mind to the point that she could repeat it without a single stutter even if awakened in the middle of the night.

"I'm sorry to hear that." He sounded almost sincere. "Where do you live now?"

"Lyon, Monsieur."

"Lyon." He went silent for a few moments, pondering something. "And how is the mood nowadays in Lyon?"

"It's good. Maréchal Pétain visited it recently, in November, and there was a grand parade all over the city. People welcomed him with such emotion; you should have seen it! We couldn't be more grateful to him for everything he has done for France and its people." She repeated this additional, carefully studied lie with the brightest expression she could possibly muster.

The German snorted softly, suddenly becoming very interested in his nails.

"Interesting. That's not what I heard."

"Anti-Vichy propaganda," Blanche suggested with a slight shrug, offering him another timid smile.

"*Nein.* I don't think so. There were too many communists and criminals that ran across the Demarcation Line before we closed it last month. And they all settled in Lyon because it was already infested with liberals, Jews, and even more communists."

"I don't see that side of the city, Monsieur. All my friends and neighbors are ardent supporters of the Maréchal and Vichy. And so am I, naturally."

"Naturally. However, I don't think you would have told me, had you been a liberal, or a Jew, or a communist." He chuckled.

"I'm none of those things, Monsieur. I'm just an ordinary girl who makes her living selling cosmetics."

"I'm sure you are. *Ach,* here's our coffee. And I thought that Friedrich had forgotten about us." He spoke teasingly as his adjutant advanced into the compartment carrying a small tray. "Put it on the table near the window, Friedrich. *Danke.*"

After the young man disappeared behind the doors, Sievers inquired about how Blanche preferred her coffee, poured some cream into both cups and then added sugar to hers only.

"Have you been to Dijon, Monsieur?" Blanche broke the silence after sipping the hot, steaming Arabica, savoring its taste. She had forgotten when she last tasted real, good quality coffee.

"My office is in Dijon. Some coincidence, eh?" He winked at her playfully, much to her dismay.

"Do you... work for the government?" Blanche asked carefully, trying to figure out who exactly she was dealing with.

The German burst out laughing. "The government? Your government works for us, Mademoiselle Bertin."

"Pardon." She felt her skin reddening once again and cursed her fair complexion for instantly giving away the slightest of her emotions. "I didn't mean to offend you. It's just that I'm not well-versed in politics and not quite sure what all your offices do. Or ours, for that matter."

He returned her smile before answering.

"No offense taken. I work for the *Sicherheitsdienst.*"

Blanche's brow furrowed as she tried to repeat the new word in her mind. She was certain she had never heard it before.

"SD. The Secret Service," Sievers clarified, obviously amused by the girl's confusion.

"Is it similar to the Gestapo?" Blanche inquired quietly.

"The Gestapo is subordinate to our organization."

What could have possibly been worse than the dreadful Gestapo? The mysterious and sinister SD, apparently. Blanche shifted in her seat warily.

"No need to be alarmed." He caught onto her apprehension at once. "You said it yourself; you're just an ordinary girl who sells cosmetics. Therefore, you have nothing to hide and nothing to be afraid of. Right?"

That last word of his, or actually the intonation with which he pronounced it, made Blanche spend the rest of the way on pins and needles, wondering if it was indeed a simple coincidence, or if he had toyed with her intentionally, playing some sick game with his defenseless victim before announcing to her at last that he knew everything about their cell, that she'd better give him names before he made her, that... But he only helped her off the train, tipped his cap and handed her a small card after scratching something on it.

"Give me a call next time you're in Dijon. A pretty girl like you shouldn't work yourself to death without any breaks. I'll take you to the opera. Do you like opera?"

Blanche only nodded absentmindedly and muttered something in response to his goodbye, barely stopping herself from running away as far from the man as she could.

Chapter 9

Etienne exited his car, checked his watch, and took out his cigarette case while squinting slightly into the light pouring out through the French windows of the Bouillon mansion. Raimond Bouillon, the owner of the estate, had already left the mark of the typical *nouveau-riche* while redecorating his recently acquired property, Etienne noticed with a sad smirk, observing the gaudy marble lion that appeared right in the middle of the stairs, and an oversized gilded lamp above the front door. With a shake of his head Etienne expressed his disappointment at how the once elegant mansion had now been adorned, pondered taking out a cigarette and having a quick smoke, but changed his mind at the last second, hid the case in the pocket of his cashmere coat and ascended the stairs, throwing yet another disapproving glance at the offending lion.

A butler with a most impassionate face ushered him inside, and Etienne tried not to grimace when he observed how even more gilding had appeared on the panels (*and even the ceiling!* Etienne grunted inwardly) than had been there the last time he visited the mansion with his father. Yes, he was alive back then, and the host, his father's dear friend, was still alive even though a little frail, but still carrying himself with the grace and poise of a true aristocrat. Etienne remembered his kind smile that seemed to light up his tan, weather-worn face, due to his love for the outdoors, gardening and hunting; his brown cardigan and almost snow-white hair; his mild voice and the wrinkles in the corners of his eyes; and how his foot shuffled slightly on the mosaic floor after his first stroke…

At least Bouillon didn't touch the mosaic, Etienne noticed with relief when walking through the familiar hallway towards the dining room, in which Monsieur Bouillon awaited him, according to the butler.

Was there really a need for a butler, in times such as these? Etienne's family had never had one, even in times of peace, his father always welcoming the guests himself.

Etienne took a deep breath and stepped into the brightly-lit room, putting on the mask that seemed to have become his second face. It was certainly no time to show his emotions to those whose help he needed, so no matter how much he despised the man, he would smile, shake his hand and be his most respectful and polite self. After all, Bouillon was the newly appointed Prefect of Lyon, and therefore the man who could help Etienne with his recent project. If he wanted this to work, he would just have to swallow his pride.

The room was the embodiment of opulence, with a new crystal and bronze chandelier, hanging above the dining table that could seat at least twenty persons. An enormous bouquet overflowed onto the silk tablecloth in the middle of the table, and new silver cutlery, no doubt someone else's heirloom bought from some auction, seemed to glare at him just like the oversized portraits of people the new owner probably didn't even know, that now proudly hung on both walls.

Raimond Bouillon, an imposing man in his late thirties, put away his brandy and opened his welcoming embrace to his guest, smiling a gleeful smile. Etienne shook his wet palm with the same enthusiasm and complimented the host on his excellent taste, surprising himself with how sincere his words sounded. It seemed that day after day he was mastering the art of deception so necessary for all diplomats... or Résistance leaders.

"This German invasion is the best thing that could have possibly happened to France, I tell you!" Bouillon was already fawning over his guest, gesturing him towards the immense table set only for two, and motioning the butler to get on with the aperitifs. "All of my factories in Paris and Bretagne have tripled their profit in just a few months! I wish they had invaded us earlier, ha-ha! To think about it, the ridiculous money they're paying, eh? My government never paid me this much!"

Etienne chuckled politely and smoothed out a napkin over his lap. A maid in a black uniform and a starched apron appeared, pushing a tray with appetizers in front of her.

"I didn't have a chance to congratulate you on your recent appointment." Etienne lifted his flute of champagne that the butler had just filled.

"What can I say? Having German friends comes in handy nowadays, doesn't it?" Bouillon toasted his glass with his guest, his small brown eyes glimmering under heavy eyelids. "They removed all of the liberals from the administrative posts, and rightfully so if you ask me. The old Prefect was an idealistic fool, who allowed all this riff-raff into the city. And for what? They don't bring anything except for their rabid communist propaganda and trouble following it. And the Jews? Do we really need more Jewish refugees here? Why he allowed them into the city in the first place is beyond me."

"Anyway. Congratulations, *Monsieur le Préfet.*"

Bouillon, visibly pleased with how his new title sounded coming from an acquaintance who belonged to a circle of members who wouldn't give him the time of day several years ago, straightened a little more in his chair and smoothed out his prematurely receding hairline.

"I have to admit, and this is just between the two of us," he muttered, lowering his voice and leaning closer to Etienne, "I know nothing about politics or governing a city. Business, yes, that I know very well. But when it comes to anything concerning administration, I'm afraid I slightly lack in qualification."

Etienne didn't acknowledge Raimond's words, looking more interested in his seafood soup that the maid placed in front of him. Bouillon needed something from him, and it made his task asking for a favor in return even easier. Now he just had to wait patiently for the new Prefect to show his cards.

"You're a diplomat's son, Etienne. And a highly-esteemed one at that."

Straight to the business then. Etienne concealed a grin and stirred his soup some more.

"Would you do me a favor and help me out?"

The man definitely didn't shy away from the real reason Etienne was here.

"Don't get me wrong, it will be an official, paid position on the payroll of the *Sous-Préfet*, with a very generous salary – not that you need it, but why not take the Germans' money, right? – And you will have all the freedom you like on top of it. I won't even meddle in your affairs; I don't have the slightest interest in them, to be honest. But the *Kommandant* of the Gross-Paris recommended me for the post, and I didn't have the heart to refuse him. We became rather good friends, you see, haha! I even tried to decline his offer, told him that I'm a businessman, not a politician, but he wouldn't listen to my arguments. He thinks that if they, military men, can be good administrators, so can businessmen. Who am I to argue?"

Bouillon finished his thought with his signature, artificial laugh, which Etienne guessed to be a nervous habit.

"I am flattered by your proposition, Raimond, and by your trust in my abilities. However, I'm afraid I must decline," Etienne stated with his usual politeness. "I am actually planning to start a rather big philanthropic project that will take up all of my time and attention, and I simply won't be able to supervise matters of politics."

"What kind of a project?"

"I want to buy out that old, abandoned mansion near the city, the one that the bank seized after its owner ran away with his money to America."

"I know exactly which one you're talking about. I was looking at that place myself, but it's falling apart! What are you planning to do with it?"

"I want to house all of those orphans from the Alsace area over there. The Germans expelled all the French population from there and are putting their people there now. Those children live with nuns now, but even the nuns will soon have nowhere to go. So, I wanted to ask if you could sign the release papers for the mansion so I could buy it out."

"It's a brilliant idea!" Bouillon exclaimed, much to Etienne's amazement. "But you can easily combine both things. Be a sub-prefect and watch over your little orphans. Why, it will be a perfect reflection of Lyon's new image under the new administration! A new Prefect and sub-prefect who do more for French children under the German administration than their liberal predecessors did! And you don't have to buy anything out. Think of it as the city's gift to you, ha-ha! Only accept my proposal, please. I could really use your help, Etienne."

Etienne sipped more of his champagne and pondered Bouillon's proposal. He would have to deal not only with the businessman, but most likely with his new German partners as well, a matter that he tried to escape by all means possible, and especially after his recent activities. Being on their radar was the last thing he needed.

On the other hand, the position would allow him access to information that in any other case would be far beyond his reach. That would help their cause tremendously. But what if they get wind of his involvement not only with the

Resistance but with the British MI6 as well? That would become his ticket straight to the gallows, with no questions asked. Not that he was afraid to die, no. His father gave his life for France, and so would he; that wasn't what bothered Etienne. What was truly the issue was that without him holding all the ends of the little strings between all the cells, that he managed and organized, they would simply fall apart like a house of cards.

Etienne carefully wiped his mouth with his napkin and smiled at Bouillon.

"Absolute freedom, you say?"

"Absolute freedom!" Raimond's eyes glistened as a wide grin spread across his face. "I travel a lot to supervise the production of my factories. You won't even see me most of the time."

"And the mansion is mine?"

"I'll send my secretary with the notarized papers tomorrow morning."

Etienne outstretched his hand and allowed Bouillon to enclose it in his sweaty grip. For some reason, his father's words surfaced in his mind, deepening a sense of foreboding that had nestled somewhere in the pit of his gut: *diplomats and lawyers shake hands with the devil so often that they become the most intimate friends on first name terms.*

"I really can't thank you enough, Etienne."

"It's nothing, Raimond."

Blanche paused at the entrance of the *photo atelier,* trying to collect herself. All the way from Dijon to Marseille, and then to Nîmes and back to Lyon she couldn't shake off the feeling that she was being watched. She turned around on every corner and had almost got lost a few times simply because she had purposefully taken unfamiliar streets to shake off her invisible pursuers. Or was it just nerves and paranoia, and there were no pursuers at all? No matter how many times she glimpsed in her mirror or tried to catch her "shadow's" reflection in a glass window of yet another store, she saw no one suspicious. Yet, she decided that it would still be wise to warn her superiors of her suspicions, and so, straight from the train, Blanche headed to their cell's "headquarters".

A little brass bell chimed its usual tune announcing her arrival. Margot, with her usual cigarette billowing its fumes from the corner of her mouth, hardly looked up from the paper she was reading.

"Why the personal appearance? What happened to the flower arrangement?"

Right from her early days in the Resistance, Jules had warned Blanche not to loiter around the photoshop without any apparent reason, as it might attract unwanted attention. And so, it was decided that as soon as Blanche returned from her trip, she would place a potted geranium in her bedroom window that overlooked the street. This would be the signal for someone from the cell to stop by the church in the morning to see that everything was fine. Hoping not to raise Margot's suspicion, Blanche shifted from one foot to another.

"Nothing. Just need to talk to Jules in person. Is he in?"

"Is everything all right?" Margot looked at her with suspicion.

"Yes," Blanche lied with a bright smile.

Margot grunted under her breath and disappeared behind the velvet drapes, leaving a grayish cloud of smoke to hang in the air. Blanche waved her hand in front of her face, somewhat clearing the air.

Jules was also seemingly surprised to see her judging by his look.

"What's wrong?" he demanded instead of greeting her properly.

"Nothing. Can I speak to you alone? *Oh, bonjour.*" Blanche switched her attention to a young man, who appeared from behind the curtains as well.

"Bonjour." The handsome young man replied cheerfully, quickly shook Jules's hand and excused himself, passing Blanche on his way to the door.

"Who was that?" Blanche asked as soon as the man was gone.

"No one you should know about."

Blanche's cheeks flared at Jules's dismissive attitude and how he always managed to find new ways to put her in her place. The young man who had just left was obviously a recruit, and she had been working with Jules and his cell for over three months now, and yet she still hadn't seemed to have earned their trust. Nevertheless, Blanche wisely decided not to show that she took offense as she followed Jules outside; it was not a good time and place, especially with the news she was about to announce to him.

The two walked in moody silence along the street, careful not to step into puddles of sleet along the way. The sun had recently graced Lyon with several days of weather that were unusually warm for the end of February, prompting the early snowdrops to peek their heads from under the ground, and chestnut trees to turn their bare branches towards the azure sky, bathing them in the generous sunshine. Blanche unraveled her scarf and unbuttoned her coat, also giving in to the early spring day. Jules remained as somber as always, his hazel eyes behind his metal-rimmed glasses fixed steadily on the ground and his face still partially hidden in his scarf as if imitating one of the underground posters that had started to appear on the walls of the back streets just recently: *Comrade! Say nothing. You never know who's listening.*

Blanche was surprised when he eventually uncovered his face as they occupied a corner table in a café that advertised real coffee, and not the chicory version. The only other patron was finishing his late breakfast at the bar, but Blanche still eyed the establishment suspiciously.

"Is it safe to talk in here?"

"Yes. The owner is our man." Jules had shed his jacket and sat in front of her with his hands clasped. "Well? What happened?"

"I don't know. I'm not sure myself," Blanche admitted, picking at a splinter of wood at the edge of the table, with her eyes lowered. "Maybe, it's nothing, a coincidence only..."

Jules pulled forward.

"What happened?" he repeated in an even quieter tone but with an intonation that made Blanche swallow a nervous lump in her throat.

She took a deep breath, collecting herself, bit her lip and finally lifted her eyes.

"There was a Gestapo officer on the train to Dijon. Not the Gestapo even... What was the name that he said? The SD. Yes, that's what it was, but I don't remember the full-on title. He told me in German, and it's some kind of unpronounceable word. Well, long story short, as soon as he entered the train car he noticed me and offered for me to share his private compartment with him. I was so terrified that I couldn't say no and I went with him... I thought he was going to apprehend me and arrest me but all he did was just talk to me, that's all. We parted ways as soon as we got off the train in Dijon. And I watched my back closely not only in Dijon but in Nîmes and Marseilles, too. I didn't see anyone following me. I think it was just a coincidence, yes. But I thought I would tell you anyway, just in case."

Jules rubbed his neatly trimmed beard while scrutinizing Blanche.

"Whether it was a coincidence or not, is not for you to decide. Was he alone?"

"No. He had two other soldiers with him."

"Was it an ordinary paper check-up?"

"No, no, they weren't checking papers at all. He was traveling to Dijon from... Oh, he never told me where he was traveling from. He came in during one of the transit stops, so he could have been coming from any place."

"Why would he enter a common train car then? They all usually travel in the front."

Blanche nodded and smiled gratefully at the bartender who had appeared with their coffees. At least it delayed the dressing down that she would most certainly receive after she told Jules the truth.

Jules waited patiently for the bartender to go back to the bar and then bore his eyes into Blanche, silently demanding her reply. Even stirring her coffee, she felt his glare.

"He did enter the front car," she admitted, at last, her downcast gaze still glued to the steaming liquid in front of her. "It's just... I rode in the front as well."

"Merde!" Jules hissed under his breath and ran his fingers through his hair, trying to get a hold of his emotions so as not to start yelling at her openly. "What the— What in the bloody hell were you doing in the front train car?!"

"It's less crowded in there than in the back. Everyone knows that the Germans like the front cars. Everyone is afraid to ride with them, so there are always free seats, and no annoying children crying," Blanche muttered in her defense. "And if I ride at night, it's impossible to sleep sometimes, with all those babies wailing. Have you ever tried riding a common train car at night?"

"Yes. Yes, I have. I was the courier before we entrusted you with the responsibility. Mistakenly so, as I see now!"

"Jules, please, don't assume the worst about me! It was just one little slip, and only because I wanted to see if it was safe to ride in the front. It was merely a coincidence that he happened to get on the train that day, I tell you! If he suspected me of something, don't you think he would have checked my papers?"

Jules sat with his arms crossed, virtually seething with fury.

"It was nothing, Jules, really. Just a stupid mistake of mine, and it won't happen again, I swear!"

He was silent for a moment, and then spoke quietly, "Do you know what happened to a friend of mine who made the mistake of underestimating the Gestapo and the *Boches* in general? And his mistake was a far less stupid one than yours, mind you."

"What?" Blanche asked warily, already guessing the answer.

"He got shot. Together with his brother and his father."

The clock on the wall chimed a quarter to eleven. Blanche dug into her pigskin purse and took out a wrinkled handkerchief to dab her eyes with her shaking fingers. Jules remained unconcerned with her distressed state.

"I'm sorry," she whispered, finally getting a hold of herself.

Jules shook his head and picked up his cup.

"Did he introduce himself?"

Blanche nodded with a timid smile, sensing his tone softening a little.

"Yes. He said his name was Jürgen Sievers."

"Never heard of him. What about his rank?"

"I'm not good with their ranks," Blanche admitted.

"What kind of insignia did he have? The high collar with the SS letters on one side and knobs on the other?"

"Mm, no." Blanche shook her head, recalling the officer's attire. "He had a black uniform on. It was more of a regular jacket with a white shirt underneath and a black tie. I think he had a single oak leaf on each lapel."

"*Bordel.*"

Blanche had never heard Jules utter such crude curses before.

"Is that bad?" she asked in a tremulous whisper.

"Yes and no. I'm not sure yet." He went silent for a moment. "I don't think that high-ranking officers like him would personally hunt minor couriers like you. Maybe, you're right, and it was just a coincidence."

For some reason, Blanche wasn't so certain that Jules believed his own words.

Chapter 10

Father Yves ran his fingers over the text, let out an exasperated sigh at the words that seemed to escape his attention and blend into nonsense that evening, and slammed the Holy Book shut. Perhaps he had never learned to read the Bible when in need of spiritual guidance after all. He possessed a phenomenal memory and could effortlessly, and with envious ease, pull out a verse that was required for an occasion from the depth of his mind; and yet, when he needed it for himself, the words lost their power and sounded so miserably pathetic that he felt he had insulted the Holy Book by his inability to relate to its wisdom. And so, he would put it away, and returned to polishing his gun with graceful, practiced movements. He found it rather disappointing that such form of a meditation felt much more natural to him than one that his vocation demanded from him.

Ten years a priest, and he apparently still had little clue what to do with the Bible just as on the very first day when that kid Simone had thrust it into his hands against his will. Father Yves smiled and shook his head at the memory, the young and eager face of the boy still alive in his mind. Simone was most unfitting for the gruesome setting that circumstances had put him in, with his golden locks, too long for a young man of his age, and eyes too honest and unbearably blue in the midst of all that dirt and blood in the trenches. It surrounded them one endless wall after another, but that worn-out, well-read Bible felt as soft and golden as the skin of a peach once it was pushed into his grasp.

Simone had been an utmost mystery to Yves, a walking miracle, the only one of their regiment who didn't seem affected in the slightest by the endless nightmare of dreadful shelling, which would cease only to be replaced by deadly fumes creeping up towards them in vicious clouds, and then off they went to yet another offensive, bayonets secured on their rifles, like grim reapers who would take the lives of those who failed to take theirs. Then, as soon as they dragged their depleted bodies back to the dirt of the trenches, to fill their bellies while they could and to drink themselves into oblivion until the rum had run out, Simone would sit away from everyone, as serene and unaffected as ever, whispering verses under his breath from the utterly useless book that Yves despised.

"Useless?" Simone beamed at him with such a radiant, natural smile when Yves confronted him once about his spiritual inclinations that Yves scowled, finding it difficult to resist his sincere charm. "It got me through three years of this war. Without it, I would have long been dead."

Yves sneered with all the contempt he could muster and patted the wooden handle of his rifle affectionately. "This got me through three years all the same."

With those words, he took another hearty swig from his canteen, filled with rum instead of water that evening, wiped his mouth with the back of his hand and pointed at the new medal, shining proudly on his chest.

"One eighty-four confirmed ones. How about that, eh?"

Simone only glanced at Yves, his rifle and his medal with pity, and said in a quiet voice, "Don't brag about the lives you're taking. War is a dirty business as it is and one must kill to protect his land, but that's one thing. It is something else entirely to feel proud of killing."

"What is that supposed to mean?" Yves glowered and squeezed the butt of his rifle tighter.

Simone only shrugged in response. "They're not targets in the Platz. They're people. Someone's husband, son, father, brother, and comrade. Men who will be missed dearly. Men, like us."

"Bullshit! They're fucking *Boches*! They deserve to be shot, each and every one of them!" Yves shouted, his nostrils flaring with an anger that even he couldn't explain.

Simone simply shook his head and lowered his eyes to his Bible, paying no more attention to Yves. That maddened Yves even more. He grabbed the young man's Bible and threw it in the mud under his feet.

"If you're such a *Boche*-loving *nancy boy,* why don't you go and fight on their side then?! Well, go ahead, trot along! I'll even warn the sentries not to shoot you while you cross the front line. Well?! Go ahead, I said! *Boche*-lover!"

Simone sighed with infuriating calmness, reached for his Bible, brushed it off carefully and, as soon as his gaze picked up the line where he had left off from, he was back to his angelic self, too clean and innocent for this world and too good for arguments with the likes of Yves. Yves snorted his despise, and couldn't resist kicking Simone on his leg before he walked away, muttering more curses under his breath. By the next evening, the boy was dead.

Yves had lain in his foxhole, his trained eye searching for an unwitting target to claim as soon as the shelling started and the *Boches* had nowhere to run from the shell-holes they had jumped into – their only salvation from the enemy shrapnel hissing, screeching and blowing up dirt into their pale, terrified faces. Yves spotted his target, a young German about his age, not more than twenty years old, with tears and mud smeared across his face, crawling on his stomach towards one of the shell-holes, his foot, barely attached to his leg by a thin string of flesh and mangled bone, dragging after him. *Killing him will be doing him a favor, really. Put him out of his misery.* Yves's finger hugged the trigger like the gentle embrace of a lover, and he had just started pulling it when another figure jumped into the periphery of his vision.

"What are you doing?" Yves whispered incredulously, observing Simone fall onto his stomach after his run, crawling towards the German with fearless determination. "*Merde…* Leave him, you fool!"

Simone didn't hear him of course. And even if he did, he wouldn't have abandoned the injured man, Yves realized with painful clarity. He was dragging him towards the hole as if his own life depended on it, yelling some words of reassurance that the *Boche* couldn't have possibly understood, pulling the German's clothes and covering him with his body as the artillery redirected its aim and started pouring its lead-filled torrents onto the small figures scattered all over the battlefield.

Yves's finger dropped off the trigger as his target stopped moving. Just as the golden-haired boy next to the German went still also.

He stumbled out of the trench after the ceasefire and walked unsteadily among the bodies, with their glassed-over eyes staring at the sky and their mouths open in silent plea; an image that would remain in Yves's memory for the rest of his days. He finally approached the two figures, so frighteningly similar despite the different uniforms. But even the colors of their uniforms started blending into a picture of desolation and death, blood-soaked and no longer distinguishable.

No one uttered a word about Simone's heroic deed. They put him together with the rest of the dead men their regiment lost that day, leaving the German where he was for his kin to take care of. For an endless hour, Yves sat at the foot of the mass grave that evening, pressing the crimson-colored Bible to his chest. The captain wanted to bury it with the boy, but someone told him Bibles weren't meant to be put in graves; so, Yves took it. For an endless hour he sat, sober for the first time after such a brutal offensive, and then opened the book and started reading out loud some passages that he knew nothing about, but doing something that he felt deep inside would please the dead boy, and that would let his soul find its way to his Creator that he loved so much. That night, while all his comrades slept soundly, huddled together, Yves crept out of the trench, found the German's body, dragged it towards the nearest shell-hole and buried it with his bare hands, digging into the ground with force, trying to fix something irreversible that he still couldn't quite comprehend...

A knock on the door from the first floor made his senses snap to attention. *Once a soldier, always a soldier,* his captain used to say, and, unfortunately, he was right. Father Yves hid the gun in the pocket of his black robe, opened the door of his room, descended the stone stairs soundlessly and moved the heavy bolt to let the night visitor in.

"I'm Patrice," a man who he didn't recognize said. Half hidden in the darkness of the night, with the meager light coming from the hallway illuminating his stern and noble features, he nodded to Father Yves. "My comrade told me you agreed to help him accommodate a couple of our friends?"

Father Yves motioned him inside, but the man stayed in the shadows. A woman stepped from behind his back, holding a young girl firmly by the hand.

"I better be going. No need for me to be seen loitering by your quarters, Father. No offense. And thank you."

With that, the mysterious Patrice was gone. Father Yves held the door wider for his guests as each party looked at the other apprehensively.

"Shall I do something before we go inside?" The woman spoke, at last, pulling the ends of her shawl closer to her face. "Shall I cross myself? We're Jewish. I wouldn't want to insult your church in any way."

"You don't have to do anything." Father Yves's lips gave way to a gentle smile. "Please, do come in. You must be cold and starving. My name is Father Yves. I'll be taking care of you for now."

"I don't know how to thank you enough, Father Yves."

In the dim twilight of the only lamp hanging above their heads she looked like one of the saints from the ancient frescos: gaunt, desolate and with onyx eyes full of unshed tears. A masterpiece of suffering embodied in one woman, with a gaze that was as full of pain as his own heart was. Father Yves found himself mesmerized with the riveting, yet heartbreaking, look in the woman's face.

"I'm Augustine. And this is my daughter, Lili."

"Welcome to Lyon, Madame Augustine. Lili." Father Yves found himself smiling at the little girl who couldn't have been older than eight and yet carried herself with an air of an adult who had seen her share of life already. "Will your husband be joining us too? I'm only asking because I need to know if I will have to move another bed into your room for your daughter."

"Papa is in the German *stalag*. He's a prisoner of war," the girl answered instead of her mother, and as soon as Father Yves glanced up at the woman, he understood why.

Her lips trembled as she made an inhuman effort to pull herself together and not to break down in front of her daughter. Those eyes of hers told him everything and no words were needed. Her husband was dead, and she couldn't bring herself to announce the news to her brave little girl.

"Please, don't worry about anything," he whispered. "You're safe now. I will see to it."

Augustine nodded, looking as if she were restraining herself from throwing her body into Yves' arms, to weep the thousands of tears that she had contained for far too long. Father Yves nodded his reassurance once again and turned to the staircase. For the first time in many years, he felt his heart beating with purpose.

Etienne smiled contentedly as he watched Marcel wolf down his lunch. Marcel hardly ever came to his house, preferring to meet in neutral locations, but apparently, he had something important to report to him.

Etienne dismissed the maid as soon as she set the table for his guest, asking only for a cup of coffee for himself, to keep Marcel company. For some reason, he recalled his father's war stories and how Monsieur Delattre Sr. had admitted to him once that the brightest moments of his service were to watch his soldiers eat their rations.

"Why?" A young Etienne snorted with laughter in response.

A shrug followed. "They'd survived another day and hadn't lost their appetite and their will to live and fight. Whenever I saw a soldier leave his meal untouched, it was always a bad sign. At war, you feel your end nearing, I suppose. If you eat – you're alive."

Etienne hardly had a couple of years on Marcel, and yet the same paternal feeling overcame him at that moment. His own father gave his life to protect his, and so would Etienne for this man; yes, he would give his life for the men in his charge.

"I'm sorry. I missed my breakfast," Marcel mumbled with his mouth full and offered Etienne a guilty grin. "Patrice and I were scouting the mountains all night and all morning, trying to find the best drop-off spot."

"Were you successful?"

"Oh, yes! Tommy has already sent the coordinates to London. We're all set for this Thursday."

Marcel attacked his pancakes and jam with renewed vigor.

"How many people are they sending?"

"Tommy says just one. If everything goes smoothly and the *gendarmes* don't get wind of anything, they'll send more."

"What are they? Spies for MI6?" Etienne carefully placed a small silver spoon next to his porcelain cup and took a sip of bitter, black coffee.

"They're all from some sort of a diversion unit, as Tommy explained it to me. Half of them will go straight across the Demarcation Line, but they will be reporting to us, of course. They'll be blowing up German commute routes, train tracks, cut their communication lines... Cause them all sort of trouble, in short. Our task, for now, is to take them in, check their papers to make sure that they're all up to date and have all the necessary stamps and send them on their way."

"Papers won't be a problem. I'll be the first one to know about all the new changes, now that I'm a sub-prefect." Etienne followed his words by a mirthless chuckle.

Marcel put down his fork, wiped his mouth with a napkin and said carefully, "Maybe it's not my place to say, but I don't think it was a good idea."

"What? To accept Bouillon's proposal?"

Marcel didn't reply, but only searched Etienne's face with his eyes.

"Let me worry about that." Etienne's tone sounded sharper than he intended.

"Bouillon is a well-known collaborator. You're muddying your good name agreeing to work with him. What if, when the war is over—"

"When the war is over, then we'll worry about all *what ifs*," Etienne interrupted him coldly, and regretted his rudeness at once at the sight of Marcel's pained look. He resembled a pup, whose owner had just kicked him for the first time, and rather painfully as that. "You worry too much about others, Marcel. Just worry about yourself, won't you?"

Marcel nodded and picked up his fork again, but only used it to push his food around the plate, seemingly losing all interest in it.

"How's your new roommate?" Etienne decided to change the subject, softening his tone as much as he could. "Are you getting along?"

Marcel's face brightened at the mere mention of the British radio operator. "Yes. He's a great fellow. We're getting along just fine. He's incredibly good with radios and all sorts of mechanics, and, well, everything really; he's sharp like a blade! And he knows so many amusing stories; you won't believe it! I wish I had half his wit!"

Etienne smiled at such a gushing description, but then his dreamy expression changed, as a desolate feeling of loneliness crept up on him without any warning. He was apart from them now, from these men and their cells; cells that he had personally created and interweaved into an intricate lace of men, working in the shadows, underground, and through half-whispered messages. He would never shake this rascal Tommy's hand, just like he would never personally welcome any recruits into their secret club of men who were ready to die for their land. Instead, he would have to shake Raimond Bouillon's hand, well-greased with the *Boches'* money, and try to persuade himself, just like he had tried to persuade Marcel, that he'd manage to come out of this swamp somewhat clean. Who was he trying to fool? If he came out of it alive, that would be a miracle... *But let's worry about it when the time comes,* he thought to himself and he forced another pained smile on his face in response to Marcel's beaming.

"How's our Lucienne doing?"

The light disappeared right away from Marcel's gaze. "She's the reason why I'm here, actually. Apparently, our little Lucienne got herself in some big trouble with the Gestapo. Not the Gestapo even, the SD."

"Why didn't you tell me earlier?" Etienne paled at the news. "Has she been arrested?"

"No, no, nothing like that," Marcel rushed to reassure him. "That silly girl decided that the back of the train was too overcrowded and noisy for her liking, and took a seat in the very front, with the *Boches*. And what do you know? One of the leather coats got in the same train car, noticed her and asked her to ride with him in his private compartment. She had no choice but to agree. She reassured me that he only spoke to her about trivial things, and she doesn't think that the Gestapo is onto us. Just a coincidence, probably. But I still didn't want to send her on any new trips before I heard your opinion."

Etienne sat quietly for some time, digesting the information with his dark brows drawn tightly together. In cases like this, rushed decisions always led to grave mistakes that could cost people their freedom, or even their lives. Gut feeling was also not such a reliable companion when it came to an opponent such as the Gestapo, let alone the feared SD.

"How about you send her on her trips, just as they're scheduled; only, don't put anything in her catalogs," he suggested to Marcel after a few moments of pensive silence, squinting his eyes slightly. "This way even if someone is indeed following her, they won't be able to accuse her of anything illegal. That is if we discount the possibility that she can actually meet with this SD big shot voluntarily."

"Why would she voluntarily meet with him?"

"Money." Etienne shrugged calmly. "He could have offered her money in exchange for information."

"You think she would have sold us out as easily as that?"

"I prefer not to think and speculate; I would prefer to know the facts. And we'll only know the facts if we confirm them ourselves. Now, finish your lunch and have some more coffee with me. You have another big task coming."

"What task?"

"You'll have to find me a man who will be in charge of our little 'orphanage' as soon as I finish the reconstruction. Preferably a priest. This way we'll raise less suspicion. Who's going to poke their nose into a children's orphanage run by a Catholic priest, under the direct control of the sub-prefect?" Etienne grinned. "And then put all the British agents there you want; you won't find a safer place for them, that much I can guarantee you."

Marcel beamed right back at him. "I think I already know the priest who fits the criteria."

Chapter 11

Blanche was wandering aimlessly through the streets of Dijon, her hometown, and yet it had felt hostile to her since the day she was born. She had mistakenly assumed that Lyon might have been kinder to her but had faced bitter disappointment, just as it always seemed to happen with her and her terribly unjust life.

Jules had hardly spoken to her after the dressing down he had given her in the café with tables full of splinters and the bitter coffee that matched her mood. The next time she saw him he was with the good-looking young man whom she had seen in the *photo atelier*, who hid behind his back and whispered something into his ear. Jules handed her a canvas bag with its usual contents, glared at her with disdain accompanied by his mysterious friend's mischievous giggling, and left her to her own devices, without even wishing her a safe trip as he had always done before. Not that she didn't deserve the cold shoulder treatment after her silly mistake, but the more distance she put between Lyon and Dijon, the more isolated Blanche felt, like a tiny twig thrown into the ocean without anyone caring as to what was going to happen to it.

She deserved at least some respect, didn't she? She risked her life for them, after all! And now some new woman with charcoal black hair and with eyes the color of molten onyx had appeared out of nowhere with her daughter and seemed to take up all of Yves's time and attention. Just like Jules refused to reveal his new friend's name to her, Father Yves's lips turned out to be sealed as soon as Blanche started prodding him about the church's new tenants. Whenever Blanche saw them together, their heads were almost touching above the Bible, Yves invariably in the process of teaching the woman some new prayer, which she diligently repeated after him, word for word, like a lesson that had to be learned to pass some important examination. Blanche was excluded from their company, left to feel alone and unwanted, like so many times before.

Having satisfied her hunger with a croissant smeared with butter bought from a street vendor, Blanche sat on a bench facing the busy street, a used napkin crushed between her lifeless fingers, deep in her brooding.

"What happened to your smile, Mademoiselle?" a young man on his bicycle called out to her, grinning widely. "Cheer up! You're too pretty to be sad!"

He had already sped away, but Blanche sat on her bench, a silly grin plastered all over her face.

Why, he's right, she thought to herself, digging in her purse for her lipstick. *I am pretty and young, and life can't be all bad. It's just one of those days... Tomorrow will be a new one and I will feel back to myself.*

A small card fell to her feet. Blanche scowled as she picked it up, and then hesitated when she recognized the handwriting.

Standartenführer Jürgen Sievers. *Call me next time you're in town, Mademoiselle. I'll take you to the opera. Do you like opera?*

She had never been to the opera...

Blanche contemplated the card in her hand, painted her lips absent-mindedly, pondered her choices some more, and then rose from the bench and headed towards the phone booth across the street. Her fingers trembled slightly as she dialed the number, and the words she had planned to say caught in her throat when a voice with a distinctive German accent replied on the other end.

"Standartenführer Sievers' office."

Blanche's immediate reaction was to hang up the phone and flee from the phone booth, to never come back. Yet, something stopped her from following her first instinct, and, drawing a breath, she spoke as confidently as she could into the phone.

"Can I speak with Monsieur Sievers, please? He gave me this number. My name is Lucienne Bertin."

Beads of perspiration appeared on Marcel's forehead from the concentration needed to complete his task… Or from the intent gaze of Tommy's amber eyes, fixed steadily upon him. The young British radio operator sat across the table from him, his long fingers playing lazily with a pencil, as his signature enigmatic grin shone on Marcel completely distracting him from the radiogram in front of him.

"I give up." Marcel finally threw his own pencil down and slumped to the back of his chair, angry at himself for looking so pathetic and incompetent in his handsome counterpart's eyes. "Numbers and all these ciphers are not my thing! I'm a history student; I don't understand any of this!"

Tommy rose from his chair with the poised grace of a feral cat, circled the table and lowered above Marcel, almost resting his chin on the young man's shoulder as he placed his hand over Marcel's. Marcel froze, trying to breathe steadily as if it didn't bother him. Only, it did. Everything about Tommy bothered him, stirred the strangest range of emotions; causing his cheeks to flush whenever the exasperating British boy started pestering him with his ciphers; to nearly choke with romantic joy at having him so near; to melt into a puddle of pure delight just because the golden-haired boy's hand was close to his. It was like the Brit purposely did everything to unnerve Marcel and laugh with his eyes at his uncomfortable squirming; eyes that were so unbearably golden and handsome, as if made of pure sunlight, soft Mediterranean sand and everything sinful that existed in the world.

"You're not a history student anymore. You're a Resistance fighter," Tommy explained with infuriating calmness and started crossing out numbers with Marcel's hand in his still, forcing him to move the pencil across the paper, taking away any possibility for Marcel to think straight. "And Resistance fighters must know the basics of decoding."

"No, they don't," Marcel grumbled, forcing himself to concentrate on the paper. If only Tommy's pine aftershave didn't invade his senses, completely replacing the air in his lungs. Marcel didn't want to breathe anything else.

"You must, at least."

"What makes me so special?"

"We live together." The young man started counting, only bending Marcel's fingers instead of his own. "You know what I do. I trust you. If I get killed, you can continue my job."

"You won't get killed," Marcel blurted out, far more fervently than he wished to, and bit his lip, lowering his head away from the golden prying eyes.

"It's the war, Jules. We can both get killed."

"My name is Marcel. I've told you a million times before."

"And I told you that I want to forget that I even heard it the first time. You're Jules." The intent eyes were peering into his again, so hypnotizing and ruthless in their unbearable depth. "If I get captured, and they start interrogating me, Jules will be the name I want to say, understand? *Jules*."

Tommy's face was too close to his own.

Marcel turned away quickly. "Whatever."

"I'm glad we're on the same page." A familiar grin played on the Brit's angular face as he went back to his seat. "Now, be a good lad and finish decoding the radiogram just as I taught you."

An unexpected guest rapping on the front door saved Marcel from yet another failed test. He smiled triumphantly and headed to the small hallway to discover Etienne on his doorstep, much to his surprise.

Even though the new sub-prefect managed to successfully conceal his face under a wide-brimmed fedora pulled down low enough to shield his eyes, he had never appeared at Marcel's apartment before for fear of being recognized by Marcel's neighbors.

"I had to come myself," Etienne explained after Marcel ushered him in, closing the door right away. "You will have to go to Dijon with Lucienne next time she goes. Pretend to be a couple. And when you two are in Dijon, head straight to this address and ask for Monsieur and Madame Vignon. Lucienne will be in their charge from now on."

"Who are these Monsieur and Madame Vignon?" Marcel glowered, feeling positively confused.

"Our new liaison agents in Dijon. They will be in charge of everything."

"But who on earth are they? I've never heard you mention them!"

"Friends of an old friend. You'll understand everything once you see them." Etienne gave him the parting wink of a conspirator together with a firm handshake and disappeared before Marcel had a chance to ask him anything else.

Blanche accepted a plate that Mariette – or Marie as Yves called her, with a fondness that he couldn't conceal from his voice no matter how much effort he thought he put into it – offered her and even smiled at the woman, even though the look in Blanche's eyes remained harsh. Mariette and her daughter Claire tried to be as agreeable as possible and had even taken up all of Blanche's former tasks concerning her duties around the church. Mariette certainly knew her way around the kitchen and managed to make a feast out of the simplest products, Blanche would give her that. With Blanche, they acted with the utmost amicability and respect, and yet Blanche couldn't help experiencing the most hostile feelings towards the unsuspecting woman, whose only fault was that she had arrived without invitation and had become Blanche's rival for Father Yves's attention.

"Claire!" Mariette's voice distracted Blanche from scrutinizing Father Yves's face and the subtly affectionate smile playing on his lips. The girl had already stuck her fork into the chicken breast on her plate but she immediately froze in her place, startled by her mother's voice. "Aren't you forgetting something?"

Claire checked the napkin on her lap, her hands – ensuring that they were washed most likely – and glanced at her mother again, positively confused.

"The Grace, Claire. We have to say Grace before the meal, don't we?"

The girl's face lit up with recognition at once, and she compliantly lowered her head over her hands to recite the prayer in her melodic, high-pitched voice.

They aren't Christians; it finally hit Blanche with indisputable clarity. Jews, most likely, and ones who had run from the Occupied Zone. They couldn't cross the border anymore; the Germans had closed it to them. Of course, that explained everything. Why else put so much effort into learning prayers and studying scripture all the time? To pass for good Catholics, no doubt.

Only, why was Yves hiding them in the first place? Lyon was full of their lot; there was no need for them to hide in churches after they made it safely through the border... Unless they were some sort of criminals from the Occupied Zone.

Criminals. That's probably what Jürgen Sievers called just about anyone who didn't belong to the good Aryan race or who disagreed with the Reich's policies. Their meeting that took place just a couple of days ago was still fresh in Blanche's memory; how he sat across the table from her in a pose that was full of relaxed confidence, bordering on arrogance even; how he lazily waved the waiter off with a simple flick of his wrist while musing aloud on matters that Blanche had no clue about; how he sent away the most exquisite dishes, barely touched; and how she was afraid to eat her dinner, in that brightly lit restaurant full of German military elite and their French mistresses, simply because she didn't know which fork to use for certain dishes.

What was also still fresh in her memory, emblazoned somewhere deep under her skin once she experienced it, was the feeling of power that emanated from all those men in their perfectly starched uniforms, so different from the soldiers that she had had to deal with before she ran away to Lyon. How she basked in this power, absorbing it, breathing it in, taking it into her very pores with every low bow of a waiter, with every envious glance from her fellow female counterparts, with every new glimpse of luxury thrown at her feet by this man who she feared... but couldn't help but admire.

"They're all nothing but a bunch of petty criminals, ja," he mused aloud, *swirling the burgundy wine in his glass, his tone sardonic and mocking. "All those so-called Resistance fighters. Noble defenders of their land? No. Just a bunch of lowlife thugs who are mad at us simply because their women like us better."*

He burst out laughing, making a circle with his hand around the restaurant. "Am I wrong? Of course not. All those Resistance fighters are a bunch of Jews and communists, without any good leadership or any kind of power whatsoever. They sit holed up in their underground hideaways and talk about booting us out of the country. Gut. I say, let them sit. My people will eventually get them all. I can't even quite take it in, what they're hoping for? They will never succeed in their plans. Simply because we're superior. A superior race with superior intellect. It's the law of nature, for the superior species to be on top of the food chain. The rest is only – food."

Blanche smiled meekly, feeling her cheeks flare up under his scrutinizing gaze. "I guess that makes me food then."

"Ach, but no, my dear Lucienne." Another Cheshire cat smile flashed onto his face as he played with his golden lighter. "You're here with me, and that makes you part of the clan, and definitely not food. Playing around with the Resistance, that would make you food."

A long, pregnant pause settled between them as Blanche felt all the color leave her face. The cruel lines around his mouth seemed to have become more prominent.

"But you're a good girl, aren't you, my sweet little Lucienne?" Sievers smiled again, almost kindly, even though his cold gaze dissected her with its sharpness. "You don't want to be living in hiding with Jews and communists, do you? You want to be on the right side of the power balance, ja?"

Blanche lifted her eyes towards Mariette who was eating her chicken silently, then to Yves and finally to little Claire, sitting to her right. After trying lobster served on the finest porcelain, chicken, no matter how deliciously it was prepared, just didn't taste the same to Blanche anymore.

Blanche put her fork down, pushed her plate away under Yves's concerned gaze, and excused herself from the table.

She spent the next few days in her room barely moving from her bed, her resentment towards Mariette, Claire, and even Yves, growing stronger with each hour, as she replayed Sievers' words in her mind, giving in to their hypnotic, poisonous power. A wounded, rejected pride swelled up in her chest as she heard yet another exchange of soft voices somewhere in the hallway, outside her closed door, Yves's voice sounding with notes that he had never used with her. *Well, if he chooses Mariette over me, then he's an idiot, and a worthless one on top of it,* Blanche thought, letting anger overtake her completely and fill her from inside. *One had to be an idiot to choose a Jew over her. So be it. Let them all rot here, in their underground hideout.*

Yes, she did want to be on the right side of the power balance. The thought snaked and slithered its way into the back of her mind. *Let them all rot... And Jules, and Margot, too...*

Jules had recently confirmed that they would be traveling together to Dijon on a new assignment. Apparently, she wasn't trusted anymore and needed a nanny to watch her every move. Still, Blanche decided to act like a dutiful orderly for now, and not show her temper to her immediate superior, and, so, the two spent almost the entire journey to Dijon in the most uncomfortable silence.

"Where are we going?" Blanche inquired when Jules headed towards the metro as soon as they got off the stuffy train car.

"To meet your new superiors."

Blanche stopped in her tracks for a moment but, seeing that Jules didn't even turn around to see if she was following him, hastened her steps to catch up with him.

"What is that supposed to mean? I won't be working with you anymore?"

"You will. They will be your superiors here, in Dijon. Whatever they tell you, you do. Got it?"

Too many superiors for one subordinate, Blanche caught herself thinking grudgingly, but only nodded instead.

After they ascended the stairs from the metro, Blanche scrunched her nose involuntarily at the sight that lay ahead of them. It was most certainly an industrial part of the city in which she had never been before, an area that was even more run-down than her own side of the town, which wasn't a comfortable place to live in by any means. They made their way along the concrete fences shielding the factories that lay behind them and changed narrow streets for quite some time until Jules finally stopped at a small, two-story building which was as gray as everything else around it, in the meager light of the street lamps.

Inside, they almost felt their way to the second floor, for the light on the first level was not working, and finally came to a stop in front of a door with a doorknob barely hanging from it, held only by one loose screw and some miracle, no doubt. Jules knocked, and stepped aside, as if unsure of what to expect. Yet, as soon as a giant of a man appeared on the doorstep he immediately grabbed him into a bear hug, and Blanche realized that he must have known the people he had brought her to.

"You?" Jules and the other man, who must have been over two meters in stature and possessed a robust built, wouldn't stop slapping each other's shoulders and exchanging the most amicable of chuckles. "No, I positively refuse to believe it! How-?"

As if suddenly remembering about Blanche, Jules stopped himself mid-word and gave the man a warning glance.

"Come in, don't just stand there!" The owner of the apartment flashed two rows of even, white teeth at them and gallantly stepped away, holding the door for Blanche.

She carefully slid past him into a tiny hallway and was almost immediately – and rather unceremoniously – pushed out of the way by a woman who ran out of the kitchen and threw herself at Jules, covering his face with loud kisses.

"Mon petit!" The woman squealed in delight, an emotion which was reflected at once in Jules's stunned face. "I haven't seen you for ages!"

"What are you doing here?" Jules whispered, observing the young woman like she was a newly found treasure. "What happened to your hair? And…"

His gaze shifted to Blanche again and lost some of its excited glimmer. He quickly composed himself.

"I'm Jules," he announced his name to the couple who obviously knew him under some different name.

"Laure." The woman grinned mischievously and shook his hand with theatrical ceremony. "And my much better half, Alain."

The woman motioned them all to the kitchen, and there, squeezed against a wall that sported soiled, peeling wallpaper and a narrow table that was only designed for two, Blanche finally had a chance to see them both clearly.

Both husband and wife were most definitely factory workers, judging by their overalls and the greasy mechanic oil splattered over their garments and still visible under their nails. For some reason, there was something off-putting about the woman, and the more Blanche peered into her face, the more confused she found herself to be.

Laure held herself with a sense of grace and arrogance that was simply uncommon among the class of people she appeared to belong to, and the sneer with which she welcomed Blanche, who was dressed far better than her, was so full of self-assurance and mocking condescension, that Blanche felt just as uncomfortable in her presence as she had felt in the company of a German's mistress, who had been powdering her neck next to her in the gilded bathroom of the restaurant where she dined with Sievers.

Her speech was too refined and elevated for a factory girl, and her hands, though soiled with oil, were too gentle and delicate to reflect years of hard work. Blanche watched her flip her short, shoulder-length dark tresses over her shoulder effortlessly, mesmerized by the cold, ironic expression on her sharp face. Laure discussed something with the two men whose attention she held just as easily as she balanced the worn-out slipper on the tip of her toe. Laure was older than her, Blanche concluded, drinking in the slightly contemptuous pursing of Laure's lips and the squinting of her green eyes as she said something mocking on Jules's account, to which both men laughed. *Was she Jules's former lady friend?* Blanche wondered. *She certainly gave him a rather warm welcome. Why was her husband so happy to see him then? No, something was off here,* and Blanche vowed to get to the bottom of it.

The husband, or Alain, as he was introduced to her, was much more attentive to Blanche than his spouse, who had taken Jules by his hands and led him away to what seemed to be the only other room in the tiny apartment, where their voices soon turned to a hushed whisper as the two spoke of something that obviously wasn't meant for Blanche's ears. Alain, with his intelligent dark brown eyes still twinkling with joy, offered Blanche another cup of tea, which she accepted more out of politeness for it was almost impossible to drink being so bitterly flavored and asked her a few questions about her work with Jules.

"We have only recently moved here," he explained, running his hands through the chestnut mane of his thick hair. "But don't fret; we know exactly what we're doing. Especially *Madame* over there."

He chuckled and motioned his head towards the other room, implying his wife.

"How do they know each other?" Blanche tried her luck and hoped that the friendly giant would supply her with information that Jules would never give her, willingly that is.

"We're all longtime friends," he replied rather evasively and patted her hand. "As I said, don't fret. Soon we'll make this machine called the Resistance work as it should! Time to show those *Boches* what's what."

Blanche nodded several times and pretended to drink the disgustingly bitter tea.

Chapter 12

Father Yves walked up to Augustine's door to offer her some hot tea with honey that Madame Freneau had just made and set up downstairs with Lili's help, but froze in the threshold with his hand ready to knock; out of politeness, of course - as always, Augustine's door was open.

He didn't dare disturb her in such an intimate moment and yet he was afraid to turn around and slip away out of fear of being noticed. No wonder she hadn't heard her daughter's voice when Lili called her from downstairs to invite her to the table. Deep in her own world, oblivious to everything around her, Augustine sat on her bed and caressed an old photograph with gentle strokes of her fingers. Her stooped frame, highlighted by a strand of dark hair that had loosened from the bun at the nape of her neck, and her eyes, so big and full of sorrow and memories, still too fresh and painful, made Father Yves wish for the ground to swallow him there and then, so she would not discover his insolent intrusion.

Despite his discreet motion to move away from the door, she noticed him. She seemed to refocus her gaze, clouded over with melancholy and tears, towards his stiff frame in the black robe, and smiled, gently and so warmly, much to his terror. Less than anyone he deserved her warmth.

"Your husband?" he whispered, just to say something to break the intensity of the silence.

Augustine nodded slowly and shifted on her bed, inviting him to take a seat beside her in such an inappropriate yet sincere gesture. Father Yves contemplated the invitation for a moment and approached her carefully, still hesitant and unsure.

A man in a new uniform smiled brightly from the picture, his dark, handsome features looking even more virile against the typical pastoral background used in most photoshops.

"This was taken just before he went to the front." Augustine's soft voice dug like a knife somewhere at the pit of his stomach. "He didn't want to pose for it, called it a silly idea, said that he was an accountant and not a soldier, laughed at me for my sentimentality... But I talked him into it after all. Like I knew something, knew that he wouldn't come back to me. And he was so sure of himself, said that the war wouldn't last long and he would be back sooner than I knew..."

They both sat, immersed in silence and thoughts until those same thoughts started suffocating Father Yves with the cruelty that only one's guilty conscience could inflict. He had no right to sit next to this widow and listen to her stories when he himself had made countless women widows, back then, when he wore a different uniform and when his guilt was so easy to drown in a canteen of rum. Still, his lips twitched and muttered, almost against his will, "What happened?"

Augustine offered him a sigh and a half-hearted, apologetic one shoulder shrug, in tow with another miserable smile.

"I'm afraid I will never know." Her gaze glazed over again as her fingers resumed their stroking of the man in the photo who would remain forever young. "I was initially told that he was taken as a prisoner of war and sent to Germany. And then one day a German officer – he lodged with a friend of mine in Paris – he told me that my husband is no longer alive. I didn't believe him at first, but he said..."

The words caught in her throat, and she brought her pale hand to it, to regain control of her emotions.

"He said that if my husband was Jewish, the SS had shot him while still in France. They didn't bother taking Jewish prisoners of war to Germany, he explained. I didn't want to believe that... But then it all started to make sense. Why else would he not write to me, not even one letter?"

Her smiling lips trembled, and a dew of tears threatened to fall off her lashes as another ragged breath escaped her mouth.

"It was that German officer who persuaded me to run to the Free Zone together with Lili. He said that if we didn't run now, the SS would eventually kill us all. He said that it was the reason why they closed the border to us: so, they could keep us all inside making it easier to account for us all."

She sat, staring into space again, cheeks glistening with tears and dark brows knitted together. "I had no reason not to believe him. He's German; he knows better, certainly."

"You're safe here," Father Yves spoke, and almost choked on the hypocrisy of his own words.

Safe. Didn't you kill men, wounded and still alive, the same prisoners of war who your commanders didn't want to bother with, asking the most heartless ones to get rid of them? Didn't you laugh after that, together with your comrades, at a game of cards, drinking stolen German rum that you took from the dead soldiers who you killed, cutting more marks into the butt of your rifle, bragging about the lives that you claimed with it?

But those were Germans... Boches... They deserved to be killed.

How do you know that the SS men don't justify their actions with the same words? And you're just like them. Liar. Murderer. Hypocrite.

Augustine's cool palm found his and made him jerk in his seat.

"Thank you, Father. For everything."

That day he didn't find the strength to tell her his story. Maybe those communists would find her someplace to live, and he would never have to see her again... Because he already knew that he wouldn't be able to stand the look that she would give him once he told his truth. It would end him, that much he was certain of. Simone was right after all. The past did catch up with him and demanded they pay its price, and one thing he was wrong about: praying definitely wouldn't help him now. Only redemption would. And he was damned if he knew how to right all the wrongs he was guilty of.

Tommy hissed and cursed, causing Marcel to chuckle. Patrice had silenced them several times already, but that night Marcel was in too good of a disposition to take the communist's threats to tan their hides, seriously. As a matter of fact, he didn't ever remember being in such a boisterous, elated mood. Well, not since he shot that naval officer at least. He stubbornly refused to acknowledge that it had something to do with the cursing and hissing coming from the Brit in his slight accent, barely detectable but so delicious to the ear.

"My father is a Brit, but my mother is French. Can't you tell from whom I got my good looks?"

Tommy squinted mischievously, fixing his hair theatrically and burst out into quiet laughter. Marcel grinned with one side of his mouth and shook his head at the boy. He couldn't stand him in moments like this. He was just too much for him; his eyelashes were too long, his laughter was too contagious, even when he cursed like a sailor and put his sarcastic wit to work; his hands were too confusing when they touched Marcel's, on purpose, he was certain of it...

Tommy was too much. Too overwhelming, and Marcel tried not to even think of him. At all. And then that rascal went and announced that he wouldn't stay home alone and would follow him and Patrice to personally meet the very first parachutist that MI6 was supposed to drop off from their plane tonight. Then he stumbled his way in the dark, catching Marcel's hand to steady himself and didn't let go after. And Marcel couldn't stop chuckling at the cursing next to him, and at the fluttering in his stomach that he desperately wanted to believe was merely due to his excitement about the operation.

"If you two don't shut the hell up this fucking instant, I will tie you both to a tree and go get the guy myself!" Patrice turned around sharply and growled, looking each man in the eye, meaning business this time.

Marcel nodded his understanding. Only, as soon as the communist turned his back on them again, he could hardly restrain himself from laughing: Tommy, being Tommy, made an indecent gesture with his hand and rolled his eyes, indicating how "impressed" with Patrice's threat he was.

It's good that he's a friend of mine now, Marcel thought, a subtle smile playing on his lips.

He'd never had a best friend. A couple of pals at school and the boys who he grew up with; a few friends at the Sorbonne... But no one quite like Tommy. At least something good had come out of this war. Something which had dropped right from the sky and into his hands...

With the compass in Patrice's hand, they had reached the drop-off point twenty minutes earlier. The snow was all but gone, and wet leaves rustled softly under their feet as they shifted from one foot to another, trying to keep themselves warm. March or no March, the forest was still wafting its misty, chilling fog through the growth, turning the men's breath into liquid crystals of moisture. Patrice extracted a pack of cigarettes from his pocket, and all three shared a match, lifting their heads back to the navy-blue sky, full of clouds.

"Not good," Tommy observed, pulling his head into his shoulders and scrunching his nose at the weather. "They will have to fly by their navigation system only. The pilot won't see shit in this fog. They dropped me off on a good night and still missed, bloody eejits!"

"So, we'll have to look carefully then," Patrice conceded, his bad mood all but forgotten.

They heard the plane but never saw it through the thick belt of clouds, when the parachute appeared from the sky and floated slowly and slightly off course, closer to the mountains from where they came from than the forest.

The parachutist was already collecting his parachute when they ran up to him, out of breath from their rush to reach him. Marcel would give him credit if he weren't too busy trying to take control over his heaving chest: The Brit didn't forget to pull his gun on them.

"Are you from MI6 or SOE?" Tommy didn't seem to be impressed with the gun, just like he hadn't been impressed with Patrice's wrath before, and outstretched his hand, palm up, his beaming smile visible even in the darkness. "I'm Tommy, your radio guy. MI6."

"Arthur, MI6. Demolition expert."

The two exchanged crooked grins and handshakes.

"Well, there, mates. Make your acquaintance: your first bomb-making guy." Tommy motioned his head towards his fellow countryman.

Things were starting to look up, at last, Marcel caught himself thinking as everyone introduced themselves. Hopefully, the chain kept working just as smoothly.

Etienne jerked his wrist impatiently and glanced at his watch for the third time in the past five minutes. This was getting ridiculous, the wait. Even his angelic patience had started to wear thin. He had become so used to being a master of his own time back home, in Lyon, that this absurdity of being made to wait for a German official to receive him here, in Vichy, had been a rough awakening, a reminder that even in the capital of the Free Zone they were reduced to nothing more than slaves of their new northern neighbors.

The building, housing a relatively newly elected government (*Elected? Forcefully installed, and quite illegally too, after Pétain and his administration dismissed the assembly*), was just as suspicious and quiet as the quiet spa town itself, like a sky brewing and stirring before a storm. Etienne had noticed a new coat of arms proudly displayed at the end of the long corridor with an endless row of chairs lined up against the wall. The words *"Famille, Travaille, Patrie"* had replaced *"Liberté, Equalité, Fraternité"* and a big portrait of the Maréchal himself had appeared, gazing at the people sitting in the corridor with his usual condescending look. *Changes weren't as prominent in Lyon,* Etienne noted to himself, a shadow passing over his always immaculately shaven face.

Ten minutes later he rose from his chair and approached a secretary who was typing something at her desk.

"I beg your pardon, how long must I wait for? I have a train to catch."

"Herr Oberst is on tight schedule himself, I'm afraid. He's also leaving Vichy tonight so he must see as many people as he can during his short stay. I do apologize for the inconvenience." It was an impassionate and standard reply it seemed.

Etienne could do nothing else but return to his chair.

Finally, he was called in. The German, with a haggard face and a weary look about his black eyes, rose from his chair and offered Etienne his cool, narrow palm.

"I apologize for making you wait, *Monsieur le Sous-Préfet*." His accent was barely detectable. "I won't keep you long. I only need a few things from you, and we can both be on our way. You might want to write them down."

Etienne took the offered chair and pulled a small notepad from his pocket.

"As you know, Monsieur Bouillon, the *Préfet* is busy working on our factories in Bretagne."

The Oberst's slip of the tongue and that word, *our,* didn't go unnoticed by Etienne.

"Therefore, the responsibility for obtaining the necessary information and making it into a report will fall on your shoulders." The German paused and leaned forward, squinting his eyes slightly. Etienne realized that the *Wehrmacht* official was likely near-sighted but refused to wear glasses, perhaps out of infamous Prussian pride or some other ridiculous reason. "You're a very young man to occupy such a post, I must say. How old are you, if you don't mind me asking?"

"I'm twenty-four, Herr Oberst. I assure you, my age will not be a hindrance to state affairs; I would have been a foreign affairs attaché by now anyway, had the war not started."

"A foreign affairs attaché, eh?" The German allowed a thin-lipped grin to appear on his face. "Well, at least Monsieur Bouillon appointed someone with actual qualifications to manage his matters. I feared that you were just some son of a business acquaintance of his. Well, never mind that. What I will need from you, first and foremost, is a full list of Lyon's infrastructure. Factories, farmlands, agriculture production, vineyards – everything that brings profit to the city."

Etienne's cheek twitched against his will.

"Second, I will need a list of your enlisted men, number of the army barracks and everything else that is situated under your jurisdiction. Most importantly, an account of all firearms. Third, I will need a full list of your communists, suspected and convicted; this list should be the easiest one to compile I believe. Take the names from the *Prefecture de Police;* they should have them. And another thing: Maréchal Pétain has already created an office to deal with Jewish affairs, so I will need you to ask them to make a list of all the Jews currently living in Lyon."

"The foreign ones?"

"No. All of them," the German replied in a nonchalant tone.

"May I ask for what purpose you need these lists?" Ordinarily, Etienne would have known better than to ask such a provocative question, but he was irritated by the long wait, the muteness of the city and disgusted with his own government who allowed such a travesty to happen, where everyone dropped everything at the first German's arrival and stood at attention to them, in their own land. "With all due respect, Lyon is under the Free Zone jurisdiction and under the conditions of the armistice of June 1940. It was promised to us that we wouldn't be affected by the occupation."

The Oberst regarded him with a faint smile for quite some time, before replying, "I'm only asking you to bring me the lists. I'm an office worker like yourself, you see. And my superiors pay me to make lists. That's all this is. Paperwork. Don't assign any meaning to it other than that."

Would you really drag me out of Lyon all the way here for some simple paperwork? Etienne incredulously asked himself. Instead, he only lowered his head before the German, compliant and suspiciously silent, like the city of Vichy itself. Outside, a storm was brewing.

Chapter 13

"They're planning something, mark my words," Marcel declared as the group of four – Tommy, Patrice and their new demolition expert, Arthur, sat around the table in the café, their hands wrapped around their coffee mugs.

The owner, also one of their men, had closed down early that evening and was listening to the illegal BBC broadcast in the backroom with the door open.

"If *Chief* said that they demanded the lists from him, then you can say with certainty that things are going south. Literally." Tommy called Etienne by the title they had recently adopted for him; no new men had to know who was really in charge of the southern faction of the Resistance movement.

"You think they're planning to occupy the Free Zone as well?" Marcel glanced askance at the Brit. "But what about the armistice?"

"What about it?" Tommy snorted with his habitual contempt. "They'll do with the armistice paper the same thing they did with the Munich agreement – wipe their *derrières* with it."

"Call me crazy, but from the rumors I've heard from some people in MI6, the Huns are thinking of invading someone all right, but not southern France." Arthur spoke quietly and waited for the coin to drop.

"Surely you don't mean the Soviets?" Patrice pulled back in his chair, chuckling at the impossibility of such a turn of events.

"That's precisely what I mean. Supposedly, our government even warned Stalin of this. I don't think he listened to them though."

Marcel chewed on his lip under his neatly trimmed beard, deep in thought. After Etienne had handed him actual control of the net, he had to be particularly careful in considering and calculating all the options, risks and possibilities presented to them. And this was an opportunity that only a fool would miss.

"In that case, it would be a true blessing for us," he finally determined, causing everyone to murmur in approval. "If the *Boches* take off and head to the east, we'll be able to overpower the remaining forces quite easily."

"Just don't forget to tell your chief not to give the *Boche* the real number of firearms the Lyon barracks have." Tommy gave Marcel a conniving grin.

"Well, the firearms are all long gone from those barracks; hardly a few dozen are left." Patrice snorted under his breath, lighting another cigarette. "The troops handed them over to us as soon as they had to choose between the *Boches* or us. The communists suddenly started to look like mighty trustworthy fellows to them, ha-ha!"

The owner came over to refill their cups and to tell them a joke that he had just heard on the BBC.

"Do you know the latest news? According to *Radio Paris*, last night at 9.20 a Jew attacked a German soldier, cut his heart out and ate it."

The men around the table broke into wide grins as the burly café owner continued. "And that's how you know that *Radio Paris* is the German bullshit-teller: Jews don't eat pork!"

As soon as the men recovered from their laughing fit and dug into the cheese sandwiches that the café owner placed before them, Marcel returned to his serious self.

"I think Arthur is right. It makes sense, them demanding information on our infrastructure and all. They're milking the Occupied Zone for its coal production as it is now; all the produce goes to Germany or their Africa Corps. Naturally, if they decide to attack the Soviet Union they will need much more than that."

"Do we have any connections along the train tracks in both zones?" Tommy inquired.

"Why?"

"Because if we make friends with a couple of the train track workers, I'll be able to transmit the troop movements to MI6 headquarters, and my mate," he nodded in Arthur's direction, "will be able to blow those tracks up."

Arthur didn't even attempt to conceal a predatory grin at such a prospect.

"Do we?" Marcel turned to Patrice, who knew more union workers than he did.

"A couple, but only here, in the Free Zone." The communist rubbed his chin. "I can ask them to make more friends, but I can't promise anything concerning the Occupied Zone. That's all yours."

Marcel immersed himself deep in thought, but in a few moments, his face brightened with a newly concocted plan.

"I have someone in Dijon who is also *a comrade*. He'll know how to talk to them, the workers."

"*Bien*. Let's get to it then."

Blanche studied Laure while the woman read a letter from Jules that Blanche had just delivered. Alain, her husband, was at work, according to her. Blanche had just opened her mouth to inquire as to why she, Laure, was procrastinating at home, but the woman clarified before she even had a chance to do so.

"I work night shifts."

Blanche had nothing better to do but hand her the letter and follow Laure to the small kitchen with the smell of burnt grease that seemed to be forever imprinted into its walls.

From a liaison agent to a delivery girl. Blanche allowed her thoughts to run their sardonic course. Some promotion. *And what did this broad do to appear out of nowhere and overstep her in rank?*

"Don't hold a grudge against me," Laure spoke softly out of the blue, without taking her eyes off the letter. "We all - Jules, Alain and I - have been in this far longer than you."

"It's not that," Blanche said sulkily. "They don't trust me, that's all. None of them. Won't tell me a thing!"

Laure nodded pensively a couple of times and fixed the gaze of her hazel, intelligent eyes on Blanche. "You made mistakes. And in our 'profession' it's better to be safe than sorry."

"As if you never made any mistakes."

"Not really."

"I will prove to Jules, to Margot, to all of you, that I am not some brainless girl, only good enough to deliver your messages to one another. I didn't come to Lyon to work as a postwoman but to..." Blanche made a gesture of frustration. "I want to be an active part of the cell. The only thing I ask for is some trust in my abilities. Someone had to trust in you some time ago to accept you in the cell, didn't

131

they? Why can't you vouch for me now, before Jules, since you're such intimate friends?"

Laure grinned, folded the letter, sliding her fingers sharply over its crease, and placed it in the pocket of her trousers. "You're an ambitious one, aren't you?"

"I want to help," Blanche muttered somewhat defensively.

Laure shook her head slowly, grinning wider. "No. You want recognition and fame. Those are your reasons; not the selfless desire to help. That's why Jules doesn't trust you. We all had to sacrifice a lot for the cell. You, on the other hand, are here to profit from it, no matter how fervently you're trying to persuade yourself in the opposite. You came to us for the wrong reasons, and that's why your superiors are so hesitant when it comes to delegating you something more serious than delivering messages. People do very stupid things when they crave for power. Don't give me such an accusatory look, Lucienne. You know I'm right. And I'm saying all this not to insult you in any way but because there shouldn't be any secrets or half-spoken truths between the members of the cell. I'm only trying to set you on the right way before you slip even further."

"There's nothing wrong with craving recognition," Blanche argued in an odd tone and added the phrase that Sievers had uttered with a strange, dreamy look in his eyes, as if revealing the most sacred of postulates, according to which his people lived: "*One must want more to become more. Don't you agree?*"

Laure's gaze shot up at once, sharp and intent, her green eyes slowly narrowing into slits, scrutinizing the red-haired girl in front of her with newly established interest.

"Which university did you go to, Lucienne?" she asked suddenly.

Blanche's cheeks flared up. She lowered her eyes, clasping both hands on her knees.

"I only finished high school," she admitted reluctantly.

Laure arched her brow in exaggerated surprise. "Is that so? And how long ago did you acquire a taste for nihilism?"

Blanche blinked, mulling over a word she must have heard somewhere but the meaning of which had slipped from her memory.

Laure's grin took on a devious shade as she had likely caught on to Blanche's confusion.

"Do you read philosophy at all?" she inquired.

Blanche grew rather annoyed with the unraveling interrogation. "I don't read philosophy. It's old men's entertainment. Useless ramblings and nothing more."

Laure's eyes shone with a triumphant light like that of a policeman who had just caught a criminal red-handed, but only for a second before her face once again turned into an indifferent mask, as unyielding as a wall. The more Blanche bore her eyes into the woman sitting so close to her that their knees almost touched, the more she admitted to herself that Laure intimidated her. She was intimidated by her relaxed posture, and that superior smirk, which Blanche hated most of all, a look Laure was giving her right now.

Blanche swallowed and smoothed out her skirt over her knees self-consciously, an uneasy feeling taking over her as it finally hit her as to who exactly Laure reminded her of – Jürgen Sievers. Laure was just as cold and mocking, with the same penetrating gaze. Had she been a man, she'd have been a perfect Gestapo agent.

"You travel a lot, don't you, Lucienne?" Laure inquired, a subtle grin playing on her unpainted, stubborn lips.

"Yes."

"Do you talk to station workers at all?"

Blanche scowled, unsure as to where Laure was leading with all these strange questions.

"Not really."

"Time to start then, *ma chérie*. I have a lovely new task for you."

Marcel was cleaning up after all the hired workers had left. As soon as Marcel spotted the Catholic priest ascending the stairs with a dark-haired woman in tow, he quickly wiped his hands on the wet rag that the construction workers kept mainly for this purpose, and smoothed out his hair, in his best effort to make himself look presentable.

"Jules Gallais," he introduced himself, holding his hand out to the tall pastor who had gray, attentive eyes.

"Father Yves." The minister shook his hand and stepped aside so that his female companion could make her acquaintance with him as well.

She shifted her dark, almond-shaped eyes from the priest to Marcel and back as if looking for affirmation of something she was afraid to utter.

"It's all right." Father Yves touched her elbow in the gesture of reassurance. "You can tell him your real name. I'm quite certain it was his comrades who smuggled you across the border and made you your new papers."

The woman chuckled with embarrassment and offered Marcel her narrow palm.

"Augustine."

"Jules." He felt a pang of conscience for having to introduce himself with an alias whereas she trusted him with her true identity, but rules were rules, and in times of war, conscience was something that should be forgotten in matters like this. "And Father Yves is right; it was indeed our cell that helped you. Patrice is the one who's been coordinating everything. I believe he's the one who spoke to you about our little enterprise?"

"I wouldn't call it little," Father Yves replied with a smile, looking around. "This is quite an impressive estate. How did you persuade the government to let you use it as an orphanage?"

"The new sub-prefect turned out to be an incredibly generous man." Marcel grinned.

Well, he wasn't lying exactly; he just failed to mention that the new sub-prefect was the head of the Resistance in the Free Zone. But, Father Yves didn't have to know that snippet of information.

"Would you like a little tour?" Marcel addressed his guests again. "This wing is almost done, as you can see. We started in March, so it took us nearly two months work to completely redo all the floors, to panel the walls and to change the electrics. The wires were so old they were a fire hazard. We haven't ordered the furniture yet; I will be honest, we were hoping that you would help us with that. We don't specialize in orphanages, you see."

Father Yves chuckled with him, nodding his understanding.

"Do you mind Madame Augustine helping me here with the orphans? Your comrades offered her a new place to stay but..."

"I think I will serve a better purpose here," the woman finished for him.

Marcel shifted his eyes from her to the priest and wondered if there was more to their story. Father Yves was a man of the cloth, after all. They exchanged strangely intimate glances, though, especially for a man of the cloth and his charge, who couldn't take her eyes off him.

Not my business, whatever is between them, Marcel quickly decided and rushed to reassure Augustine that she was more than welcome in the new orphanage and that her help would be greatly appreciated.

As they finished their improvised tour around the premises and Marcel diligently put down all of Father Yves' wishes in his notepad, rushed steps on the staircase made the three of them turn their heads towards the entrance.

Much to Marcel's surprise, Etienne appeared in the doorway, still panting from the hurried ascent and positively agitated about something. Used to seeing his superior invariably collected and calm, Marcel felt something in the pit of his stomach clench with worry.

"Oh, what luck!" Marcel managed to say, his change of demeanor almost imperceptible to the couple, or at least he hoped as much. "And here's *Monsieur le Sous-Préfet* himself! I was just showing Father Yves the building. He will be our new overseer. And this is Madame Augustine; she'll be helping him also."

Etienne made an attempt to regain his composure, which didn't escape Marcel's attention, and somehow succeeded.

"Etienne Delattre." He presented himself with the most pleasant of smiles, despite the red spots still marring his pale cheeks. Marcel wondered if it was a result of the run or anxiety. "It is my utmost pleasure, Father. Madame Augustine. Allow me to express my gratitude for agreeing to help us with looking after our poor orphans. I can't tell you how grateful we all are."

"It's our sacred duty, just as it will be our pleasure." Father Yves shook Etienne's hand but eyed him with caution nevertheless.

Marcel guessed that, just like himself, Father Yves didn't trust officials that much. Maybe it was for the better though.

"I apologize for my intrusion, but I'm pressed for time, and I was hoping to speak to Monsieur Gallais about something urgent."

"No need to apologize, *Monsieur le Sous-Préfet*," Father Yves replied, returning his polite smile. "We're already finished here. It was a pleasure to personally make your acquaintance. We'll be on our way, and thank you again for everything you're doing for the poor children."

As soon as the pair disappeared downstairs, Etienne seemed to completely fall apart. He leaned against the freshly-paneled wall, his shoulders hunched and his hand squeezing his eyes tightly. Marcel shifted from one foot to another uneasily, whispering in a barely audible voice, "What?"

"You didn't hear, did you?" Etienne replied in a dull voice after what seemed to be an eternity of silence, finally taking his hands off his face. His eyes were dry but red with anxiety.

"I was with the workers all day... What's happened? One of ours?" Marcel whispered, holding his breath. "Who?"

Etienne shook his head slowly, took a deep breath and started speaking.

"Last night there was a raid in Paris. Ten thousand Jews were rounded up by the Gestapo and local *gendarmes*. They took them to the stadium and from there – to Drancy."

"What the hell is Drancy?"

"Some transit concentration camp, as I was told after I asked around in the prefecture today."

"They're building concentration camps on our territory now?" Marcel's eyes widened with disbelief.

"Apparently. And not only building but housing people there as well." Etienne let out a ragged sigh and patted his suit absent-mindedly, looking for his cigarette case. As soon as he took it out and flipped it open, Marcel saw that, for the first time since he had met Etienne, the case was empty. Even Etienne was staring at it with a frown, seemingly confused with this fact. Marcel's hand dived into his pocket, and he gingerly offered his superior his crumpled pack.

"Only five a day. Moderation and discipline is the key." Etienne's voice was a mere whisper. "My father always taught me that."

He smirked, then shook his head and took a cigarette out of Marcel's pack, muttering, "to hell with everything," under his breath.

"Maybe it's some sort of a... Maybe they just..." Marcel stumbled over his words as if pronouncing his thoughts out loud only made him realize the futility of such hopes. So, he sighed as well and lit his own cigarette.

"You know what the worst part is?" Etienne continued, taking a deep drag and looking out of the window where only darkness and their half-hearted reflections were visible.

"Maréchal Pétain wants to send them our Jews as well, the ones from the Free Zone. As a gesture of 'good will', mind you." He snorted with contempt and looked at the burning tip of his cigarette, shaking his head. "The worst part, my friend, is that I handed him the lists myself. With these very hands, I compiled them and handed them over, served them on a dish for the Nazis to do whatever they please with them. Imagine that, eh? Some Resistance leader I am, aren't I?"

"Stop it." Marcel touched his sleeve, tilting his head in reproach. "You didn't know."

"Oh, I knew. I suspected as much, and don't act like we haven't discussed it, you and I. Didn't I tell you that I didn't like all of those demands about the lists?"

"What choice did you have?"

"Refuse to comply and step down from my position. It's very simple." Etienne sounded almost angry now. "If Maréchal decides to fulfill his promise to the Nazis, all of Lyon's Jews' blood will be on my hands."

He went quiet and rubbed his eyes irritably.

"How will I live with it, Marcel? Knowing that I willingly sent innocent people to their death?"

Marcel smoked next to him in silence for a very long minute.

"At least you won't be the one who pulls the trigger."

"The German that you shot and these people are not the same thing."

"And what did that German do?" Marcel retorted. "Wore a German uniform, in the wrong place and at the wrong time. He was a naval officer, Etienne. A simple serviceman. And I shot him for that. How is that better?"

"We're both murderers then."

"They forced it upon us."

"Excuses."

"No. Bitter truth."

They stubbed their cigarettes in an aluminum can that had been left on the windowsill by the workers and turned to leave.

"Here, take the rest of the pack." Marcel handed Etienne what was left of his tobacco stash.

Etienne didn't reply, only hid the offering in his pocket, trying not to meet his comrade's gaze. Marcel pretended that he didn't notice the tears pooling in Etienne's eyes.

Chapter 14

A lazy afternoon filled with transparent air and the tunes of singing cicadas rolled around them, as they lay on the blanket with a picnic basket beside them. The cotton candy of a single cloud floated delicately in the sky, glowing with a gentle radiance.

"An odd view we make, don't you think? A Catholic priest, a Jew and her daughter on a picnic." Augustine grinned sleepily, lulled by the golden specks of sunlight warming her face through the thick growth of a wide tree, and the red wine from the church that they drank in abundance.

Father Yves observed her relaxed state, the first time he had seen her in such a way since they met. The pain was all but gone from her eyes, her melancholic expression replaced with serenity and, if not oblivion, then acceptance. That would do for now.

"Lili needed it." He refilled his glass, a long-forgotten feeling of a slight buzz and pleasant numbness overcoming him. He'd refused to return to his old ways as soon as he donned his black robe for the first time. He didn't deserve the bliss of forgetfulness that a drunken stupor always brought, just like back in his army days. No; he would have to relive the horrors haunting his memory day after day, sober and clear-headed. That would be his penance.

But today was special. Today he deserved a little peace for all those years of constant inner torment. He didn't know why; he had woken up with a feeling that a rock had finally been lifted off his chest, and all because of her. She had come into his life and brought peace, something for which he'd been striving to achieve for far too long, eventually losing all hope that it was possible.

"She can't sit confined to four walls, learning prayers day after day," Father Yves continued, watching the girl run around the field chasing a butterfly, or a dragonfly, carefree and blithe, just as it should be.

Augustine sighed blissfully, resting on her elbows and following her daughter with her eyes.

"Thank you for taking us out, Father." She beamed at him, glancing up and shading her face with one hand.

He met her eyes and drowned in their depth, suddenly forgetting that he was still wearing his church robes. Today, with the wine bottle in his hand and her by his side, the thought of it was ridiculous. He wasn't a priest; he was a former soldier who had lied when he walked into the seminary for the first time. They lay so close to each other that he could easily lean towards her wine-stained lips and kiss them greedily, like he had kissed so many women before, during the war too, before picking up his rifle and setting on his way to claim more lives.

He turned away quickly. She cleared her throat, shifting away from him ever so slightly as if sensing the vulnerability of their common situation.

"Do you think I should tell Lili?" Augustine asked quietly. "About her father."

"I think you should. It's cruel for the both of you to keep this ruse going. It probably hurts you as well, hearing her say all these 'When Papa returns...' phrases."

"I'll tell her then. She needs to let go."

Did you? The words almost broke off and fell from his lips before he bit them back and gulped his wine down just to distract himself from the lavender smell of

141

her hair. She insisted that regular soap was fine, but he paid a ridiculous amount of money for some of Blanche's insanely overpriced cosmetics that she carried with her on her trips. Blanche had given him a mighty strange look when he had tentatively asked her if he might buy the soap from her...

And for what, all of this? He could never be with Augustine. He would never tell her about his feelings, only suffer silently by her side, and let her go once she was ready to.

"I wish I could shake that German officer's hand," he confided so softly that Augustine barely heard him. "The one who saved you. Who told you to run."

"I thought he was lying at first, imagine that. I thought he only wanted to get rid of Lili and me because the woman who he lodged with took us in, and it was all of us under one roof: Kamille, the German, his adjutant, and us two Jews. I thought he was afraid someone would discover us. But those poor people in Paris! He was telling the truth, after all."

"You have nothing to fear now, Augustine. You're safe now."

"Thank you for letting me stay with you."

"You can stay as long as you want."

Her subtle smile and how she closed her eyes, settling for a nap beside him, was all he had needed all these years, he realized that now. Father Yves looked up at the azure sky and prayed, with gratitude and sincerity pouring out of his heart, for this woman's happiness above all.

Villas like this only existed in the glossy interior magazines that she saw on the newsstands, Blanche thought. She sat rigidly in the burgundy velvet chair that the gentleman across from her had offered, her back unnaturally straight, hands clasped on her lap, and glanced up at Standartenführer Jürgen Sievers, lounging leisurely in the chair opposite her, with the relaxed poise of a resting lion. What was she thinking, coming here in the first place? Blanche pulled her legs under the chair, shrinking from his steely eyes which penetrated to her very core. Why did she call him again, when she shouldn't have done so the first time?

The truth was that Blanche was tired of all the nauseating, sleazy men and their continuous insinuations that she had had to deal with lately, and all thanks to the high and mighty *Madame Laure,* whom Jules had appointed as Blanche's superior so unjustly. After reading Jules' letter which had apparently been full of instructions, Laure ordered her to make connections with platform station workers, ticket booth tellers and even porters, who worked in the first class waiting rooms. Anyone who would be sympathetic to their cause and interested in helping a pretty girl out with some information, while Alain would work on recruiting union workers who worked on the railways.

The plan was good, there was nothing that could be said against it, except for one thing only: all the tellers, porters, and platform station workers she approached had seemingly, and unanimously, decided that their information should come at a price. Blanche shuddered with disgust in her padded chair at the thought of all those disgusting, sloppy kisses and cheap feels she'd had to endure in so many back rooms over the past couple of months, so many that she had eventually lost count of them. All the while, Laure sat on her high horse and commanded. Now, Blanche just wanted to enjoy a tiny sliver of respite among the people she craved to be surrounded with. So, she was now in the company of the most feared of them, someone certainly possessed of enough power to not only put Laure and the likes of her in their place but squash them all without mercy. Blanche swallowed the dark thought like liquor and felt it warm her lungs from the inside.

"I see that something's bothering you, *herzchen*." The unfamiliar term of endearment that rolled off his tongue made her cheeks light with a warm glow. Sievers tilted his head to one side, observing her with curiosity. "Must be something serious, if you refused dinner."

"I'm sorry. I wasn't hungry."

He had invited her to the same restaurant as before, but she wouldn't have been able to talk to him there, so she was secretly thrilled when he had casually invited her to his house. She didn't know if she could find the strength to speak to him at all, so she spent time attempting to collect her thoughts. All the while he sat there patiently as if he had all the time in the world. He probably did.

"Let me pour you some brandy." Sievers got up and, passing her by, patted Blanche's shoulder slightly. She heard the clinking of glasses behind her back. "It always seems to do the job."

Blanche wanted to express her protest and say that she didn't drink, but he had already lowered the glass into her palm, toasting his with its rim.

"Prost."

Blanche gulped down the amber liquid and nearly choked when it burned her throat. Sievers chuckled and soon returned with a glass of soda. Blanche washed down the bitter, burning brandy with relief and froze in her seat as he lowered his hand on her shoulder again.

"What happened to my sweet little sales girl? Did anyone offend you?" He sounded almost compassionate.

Blanche worried that he knew all too well what exactly she'd been up to and was now simply grooming her into openly admitting it.

She shook her head slowly, trying to resist the hypnotizing look of his.

"What is it then? Money? Some scheming, no-good salon owner refused to pay you? Just tell me, *schatz,* and I'll send my men to shake all of your money out of them right in front of your eyes."

Her eyes lit up with unexpected mirth at such a prospect, sending her into a fit of chuckling. Suddenly, Sievers caught her by the chin and turned her face towards his.

"What is it, Lucienne?"

He was so close to her that she could smell his aftershave on his immaculately shaven face; his unmoving eyes fixated on hers without blinking, hypnotizing, terrifying, and reaching for the biggest of her secrets.

"Lucienne," he drawled in a sing-song voice, a teasing grin playing on his vicious mouth as he traced his finger on her lips. "Tell me the truth. There is nothing that I can't help you with."

Yes. He definitely knows.

Blanche shuddered. "You'll get mad at me."

"I only get mad when people lie to me, Lucienne." Sievers stroked her cheek with his finger, with a tenderness that never reached his predatory gaze.

"My name is Blanche," she uttered, at last, not knowing what she shivered more from – the fear or his seductive touch.

Sievers grin became even wider, a triumphant light dancing in his conniving eyes.

"Schatz." He cupped her cheek, leaning even closer. "You're an even bigger treasure than I thought."

His mouth closed on hers, his hand holding the back of her neck firmly as if he had expected resistance. Blanche was mortified and elated at the same time, failing to make any sense of her own emotions with her wildly beating pulse muting everything besides the taste of him. Her first kiss. Who would have known that it would be with a Nazi, the most formidable of them, who could devour her alive if it came to his mind?

Margot had made her into something suitable, attractive, into this Lucienne persona. Because of her origin, boys had only mocked her or ignored her completely, and, besides, she had always worked from dawn till nightfall, and such a schedule didn't leave much time for romance, not that anyone showed interest in her anyway.

Blanche caught herself thinking that while she didn't consider physically resisting him, her hands were still pressed against his cross-marked chest, like a barrier which referred to her instinctual modesty, until something different, much darker and much more feral replaced it, fueling the hunger with which she responded to his demanding mouth.

But, just as her hunger urged him on, he pulled away as unexpectedly as he had kissed her. "And now be so kind as to tell me: why did I just kiss you instead of breaking your neck, *schatz?*"

His palm, still grasping the hair on the back of her head remained in place, only now it wasn't from passion anymore, but like a hardly veiled threat. Blanche swallowed a lump in her throat.

"I can be of use, I promise!"

"What use can I possibly make of one silly girl who plays around with the Resistance? Why don't I just kill you instead? A public execution, let's say, just to teach everyone a lesson?" He grinned again, his forefinger pressed against his chin in play-pretend decision making.

Blanche's eyes froze in terror, which seemed to amuse him even more.

"I can give you all the names of all the connections that I'm working with."

"They will be fake names. Just like yours was. As soon as my people arrest one, the rest of the cell will scatter, and I will never find them."

Blanche raked her thoughts feverishly, in the hope of finding something that would save her life, now potentially hanging by a thread. "I can give you the names of my superiors."

"You don't know them."

"I can find out."

"They will never let you."

"I can sabotage their operations then. I can inform you of everything that they're planning, and you will be able to arrest them on the spot."

Sievers squinted his eyes slightly. "Maybe you're not as silly as I originally thought. Good thinking, *schatz*."

He finally let go of her hair. Blanche breathed out with relief.

"Why did you get involved with them, Blanche? Someone else in my place might not have been so charitable with you."

"It's a long story, Monsieur Sievers."

"We have plenty of time. You came here to talk, didn't you? So, go ahead. Talk."

He stood next to her with his arms crossed over his chest, smirking slightly, looking like a typical Gestapo interrogator. What was she thinking, imagining him as being noble and gallant, able to save her from her imaginary foes, when the real one was right in front of her?

As if sensing Blanche's hesitation, Sievers stepped forward and lowered his palms onto her shoulders, sending a jolt of electricity into her chest.

"Do not be afraid of me, Blanche. I can be your worst nightmare or your best friend, and it's up to you to decide which one it will be. I only need honesty from you, my sweet, little Blanche. Truth. Do not lie to me. Understand?"

She nodded readily several times.

"It's all because of the circumstances of my birth."

"Must be fascinating circumstances if they got you involved in the Resistance." He sneered and squeezed her shoulders slightly.

"My father was a German soldier."

Sievers pulled back at once, the Cheshire cat's smile returning to his face.

"Is that so? Fascinating indeed. So, you're half-German? Why such hostility to your compatriots then?"

"Because since I was born all I was called was a *Boche's* bastard. Had that soldier not raped my mother, maybe I would have respected his kin better," Blanche blurted out with unexpected defiance.

Sievers, much to her surprise, only shook his head and laughed.

"I see. Your mother probably told you and her neighbors, and most certainly your Papa – there was a French Papa, who had returned from the war and was very much surprised with such a turn of events, wasn't there? – this incredibly sad and tear-jerking story. Some luck she had, getting pregnant from the only time she'd been with that German fellow, passing her town by, eh?"

Blanche scowled, observing the mirth crinkling the corners of his eyes.

"What do you mean?"

"I mean, some women take years to produce a child, and your Maman, according to her, went and won the lottery getting big-bellied from one single occasion. Must have been some fertile German seed, if I do say so myself!" He burst out laughing.

"I don't see how it's amusing." This time Blanche folded her arms on her chest.

"Don't take offense, *herzchen*. If your poor Maman indeed got raped, that would have been truly tragic, and I would wish to find that despicable excuse of a man and execute him personally. Only, I regret to disappoint you, but she made this story up for her reputation's sake, and to escape some good trashing her husband would most likely give her. The German was probably stationed nearby, fancied your Maman, offered her some rum and sausage, and there you have it – he was more than welcome in her household. Why rape anyone if the soldiers had women go with them more than willingly? Their men were at the front, too, and nature and desire are such that one can't go against it. And when they bring food and rum with them on top of it... Trust me, my little Blanche, she lied to you and turned your life into hell just to make her own life easier. So, it's your French folk you should hate, *schatz,* not the Germans."

Blanche sat quietly for some time, her hands folded on her lap, recollecting all the rumors that she had heard from the neighbors concerning her mother and her *Boche-lover*. A lover, they said, not a rapist. Not that it made her life any better, but her mother could have at least not blamed her for her sins. As if it was Blanche's fault that her mother had gotten pregnant.

"Come, cheer up, *maus*. You're half-German. That has to account for something. At the least, I like you even more now." Sievers lifted her chin again, making her look him in the eyes. She was confused, about good and bad, truth and lies, light and darkness, and finally let him decide for her, entrusting her very life into his hands, even it be the biggest mistake she could possibly make. "Now, how about that dinner? Still not hungry?"

She nodded and took his gallantly offered hand. *Yes, let him decide. He knows better.*

Chapter 15

Dijon, Occupied Zone, June 1941

Marcel paused in front of the familiar door with the broken doorknob, removed his cap to smooth out his hair and caught a glimpse of a mischievous smile on Tommy's face. The British rascal had somehow wormed his way into what was supposed to be Marcel's trip to Dijon, alone, throwing the most unbecoming, fake temper tantrums until Marcel finally gave up and allowed him to tag along. It was pure madness, taking Tommy across the Demarcation Line, and even though he spoke perfect French and his papers were in perfect order due to MI6's impeccable efforts, Marcel spent the entire trip on pins and needles, breaking into a cold sweat every time an inspector in a German uniform entered the train car. Tommy, on the other hand, couldn't have been more at ease, humming something under his breath and breaking into the brightest of smiles at somber looking conductors while handing them his papers – like a kid on a holiday trip. Marcel cursed inwardly the whole time on the train; but then, Tommy fell asleep and dropped his head on Marcel's shoulder, and Marcel didn't move for two hours straight, so as not to disturb his comrade's slumber, suddenly forgiving him everything he'd put him through.

Marcel knocked, and the door opened almost instantly. No wonder, taking into consideration how small the apartment was. He was immediately scooped into an embrace, and Marcel happily returned the affectionate hugs and kisses on both cheeks, finally turning to Tommy and introducing the leader of their Dijon cell to him.

"Tommy, this is my sister, Giselle. You know her as Laure, just like everyone else in the cell. Giselle, this is Tommy, our radio guy from MI6."

"The famous Mademoiselle Legrand." Tommy bowed down and kissed her hand most graciously. "It is my honor to finally meet you in person. I couldn't wait to make your acquaintance after everything your brother told me about you."

"Kind sir, your impeccable British manners are a breath of fresh air for me after all the riff-raff I have to deal with daily," Giselle replied, playfully squinting her green eyes.

The tall man with dark features, who stood behind her back, cleared his throat with intentional loudness.

"Oh, don't take offense, Philippe. I wasn't talking about you."

Marcel grinned at the skeptical look Philippe shot his "wife". Leaving them both in Paris last November, Marcel could never have imagined that these two would have been able to coexist at least somewhat peacefully for even a few days, given that Philippe – or Alain, as everyone knew him now – was a hardened communist, while Giselle was a firm believer that money ran the world. Yet, they somehow managed to not only restrain themselves from murdering each other in this sorry excuse of an apartment but worked seamlessly together.

"Tommy, this is Philippe, otherwise known as Alain to everyone else," Marcel quickly corrected himself as the two men exchanged their handshakes. "He saved my skin when I deserted from the army."

"Almost exactly a year ago," Philippe confirmed, his warm brown eyes smiling warmly at the memory. He went on to explain. "Marcel was such a terrified mess of a boy; I felt sorry for him. So, my comrades and I took him in, even though, at first, he was almost as afraid of us as he was of Germans. And now look at him, the right-hand man of Lyon's *Résistance* leader, the infamous Ghost as the *Boches* call him. Just that name makes them shake in their boots."

"Giselle created the Ghost, actually." Marcel grinned crookedly at his older sister, who returned the smile at once and added a playful wink to it. "She and her *Libération*, the newspaper that started all this."

"I read all of your articles when I can get my hands on them." Tommy beamed at Giselle. "I can't even tell you how much I admire your writing. Not as much as I admire the way you finished off your Nazi fiancé, I must admit. Poison – this is so... noir!"

Tommy's eyes sparkled with excitement, despite Marcel's attempts to shush him.

"Well, technically speaking, she didn't poison him. She strangled him with her bare hands; that's what the poor fellow died from," Philippe remarked, looking at his nails and barely hiding his grin. "Although, the poison would have killed him in the end anyway."

"Trying to get back at me for calling your comrades riff-raff?" Giselle threw him a glare, much to Tommy's delight, who was obviously enjoying the couple's banter.

"Oh, please, do tell me the whole story! It is so exciting!"

"You've heard it a hundred times from me," Marcel pointed out, trying to shift the Brit's attention away from the morbid subject. Tommy harbored a strange fascination with murders, bombs, and guns – basically, all things that Marcel tried to stay away from.

"Maybe another time." Giselle winked at Tommy and gestured for the men to settle around the small table, moving two additional stools from under it. "Sorry about this; our living arrangements leave a lot to be desired, as you can see. Between this shit-hole and the factory I'm working at, the idea of going to the prefecture and giving myself up to the Gestapo is starting to look more and more attractive."

Tommy snorted with laughter, gratefully accepted an aluminum mug containing steaming chicory coffee, took a gulp and scrunched his nose in the most non-aristocratic manner.

"Disgusting, I know," Giselle stated flatly, taking a sip from her mug. "That might be another reason why I should give myself up to those uniformed gentlemen."

"Stop complaining," Philippe chided her, with surprising mildness, Marcel noticed. "You should be happy no one has caught us yet."

"Caught us?" Giselle smirked. "*Chéri*, look at my face. I'm covered in soot most of the time, while I bend my back at that damned-to-all-hells armament factory; I haven't plucked my eyebrows in over two months, and my hair hasn't seen a perm in even longer than that. I wear mousy brown shirts and men's pants all the time, so, trust me, no *Boche* in his right mind would want to look at such a disgrace of a woman as I represent in my current state."

Philippe regarded her for some time, then shrugged and smiled a little bashfully. "You look fine to me."

Giselle merely waved him into silence and crossed her arms over her chest. "Well? Let's talk business, shall we? I suppose you didn't come here just to drink this poor excuse for coffee and listen to me fighting with Philippe."

Marcel produced a notepad, writing down the numbers from his memory. "This is what we got from our latest radiograms. MI6 agreed to supply us with weapons to store for now, but they need to know if we have a safe place for them."

"I thought you were going to use that orphanage you were rebuilding for just that purpose?" Giselle frowned slightly.

"Yes, we are, but that's for the Free Zone. The British want us to store weapons in the Occupied Zone as well, so we can be prepared when the signal comes to attack."

"That won't happen anytime soon," Philippe remarked gloomily, chewing on a nail.

"Did you manage to make any connections with people who work on the train tracks?" Tommy shifted forward, now fully in work mode.

"I did." Philippe nodded. "But there's a problem with them."

"What kind?" Marcel inquired.

"They're all members of the Party, you see. Which means that whatever the Party says, they do."

"Well? Why won't the Party tell them to kill some *Boches?*" Tommy was seemingly confused with the inner working of the Communist part of their cell.

"Because the Party, with Comrade Stalin as its leader, signed the non-aggression pact with the Germans if you remember. Which means, we aren't allowed to attack our Nazi 'allies'."

"Well, that's some first-grade bullshit, if I do say so myself!" Tommy huffed, crossing his arms over his chest.

"Yet, they refuse to do anything for now." Philippe shrugged.

"So, all these weapons and bombs, are all for nothing?" Tommy's light brow moved into a scowl.

"Not for nothing, but…"

"We'll have to wait." Giselle looked into her mug. "Fill up the storages in the orphanage for now, and then we'll start bringing the weapons here when the time comes."

"Bloody commies," Tommy muttered under his breath, shaking his head in disbelief. "No offense, Philippe. I didn't mean you. You, obviously, are one of the few rare ones who doesn't lack common sense."

"None taken. And yes, you're right: *bloody commies*," Philippe repeated the last words in perfect English, mimicking the Brit. The latter grinned in response.

The evening ascended without anyone noticing, immersed in their lively conversation which was quite often interrupted by bursts of laughter. Giselle took a bottle of cheap red wine out of the cabinet, but no one seemed to care about such petty things as to its quality that evening. The golden rays of the sun, melting away at the horizon, colored Tommy's amber eyes with precious rhinestones, reflecting in Marcel's hazel ones when the Brit turned towards him and asked Marcel what he thought of Giselle's kind offer to spend the night in their apartment instead of catching a night train. Marcel didn't think anything; there was no space in this tiny place, only one sofa in the other room, and he still had no idea how Giselle and Philippe managed to share it.

"We'll sleep on the floor." Tommy shrugged without a care in the world. "It will be fun. Besides, my behind is still sore from the train's wooden seats; spare me another night of that torture, I beg of you!"

Marcel chuckled, felt his cheeks blush for some reason, but agreed of course. He knew all too well that it was impossible to fight with Tommy, for Tommy invariably won. What was so special about him that Marcel couldn't force himself to say no to him? He cursed like a sailor, had the worst temper that Marcel had ever encountered, and defied any form of authority as it seemed. How did his MI6 superiors put up with him? But how could they not? He was made of the finest things, this boy with a halo of hair made of the finest silk, and eyes the color of molten gold; a sharp, brilliant mind and charisma that no one could help but fall in love with. Even Giselle liked him, and Giselle didn't like anybody. *Fat chance she would let Blanche stay in her apartment for the night,* Marcel noted to himself. And now, look at her: arranging their sleeping nook with the affection of a sibling towards a British boy she'd just met, even asking him which way he wanted his pillow to face – the front of the room or the back.

"The way Marcel wants his," Tommy threw back nonchalantly, taking a drag on his cigarette. Something broke inside of Marcel after those words; a chord ripped and reverberated within his ribcage, sending the strangest waves of tingles all over his skin.

Marcel pointed towards the window silently. They settled down, at last, Tommy's warm back pressed against his, for Marcel had turned to face the wall right away, the further from the Brit, the better. In their place in Lyon, each had his own bed and therefore there were never any awkward moments like this. Marcel, even though he was exhausted from the trip, couldn't possibly fall asleep because his body was so strained with tension, that even breathing became a chore.

The air, hot and stifling even at night, didn't seem to circulate through the opened window. Marcel lay wide awake, feeling streaks of sweat travel down the small of his back. And then Tommy turned towards him, pressed his hot body against his, threw his arm around Marcel's stomach, which transformed into a rock at once, and completely smothered him with his unbearable heat and his even breathing, burning Marcel's wet skin on his neck.

Marcel swallowed with difficulty, his parched throat not listening to him after he tried to take shallow breaths as Tommy's hand slowly moved down his belly. Marcel caught it and held it firmly, feeling the Brit chuckle soundlessly somewhere into his hair. Even before that, he knew somewhere deep inside, in the very pit of the stomach, now fluttering with a million butterflies, that Tommy wasn't sleeping.

"Stop it," Marcel whispered through gritted teeth as Tommy's leg moved on top of his, like a snake slowly hugging its victim.

"Why should I?" The answer came together with soft lips pressing to the base of his neck.

"Just stop." Marcel was terribly afraid that their whispers, no matter how quiet they were, would awaken Giselle or, even worse, Philippe. But more than anything, even though he tried not to admit it to himself, Marcel was afraid that he would give in to the intoxicating embrace.

Tommy crossed all borders when he traced his tongue around the back of Marcel's neck, licking droplets of sweat from it. Marcel shoved him off rather rudely and kicked him in the leg that was draped still around him. Tommy chuckled again, but turned away, at last, giving Marcel some room. Soon, he started snoring softly. Marcel lay awake with tears streaming down his face – a bittersweet concoction of bliss and torture, and everything else he simply didn't comprehend.

————————

The next morning, the train platform represented a swamp of green-gray uniforms, an ocean of concerned faces, constantly moving in waves, shifting towards the trains and disappearing in their cars.

"What's going on?" Marcel muttered, more to himself than to anyone in particular.

Giselle stood next to him, boring her eyes into the green-gray crowd in front of her with an odd gleam shining in them. Philippe pulled his cap lower in an effort not to attract any unwanted attention to his hulking frame; however, the Germans were too busy to pay any heed to the tall communist. Even Tommy wasn't his usual lighthearted self that morning, observing the Germans and seemingly immersed in appearing to be just as brooding as the Germans themselves.

"All trains for the civilians will resume their schedule after the troops depart!" a train platform worker shouted out from the megaphone, repeating the same message as he walked along the length of the station.

"What happened? They're ending the occupation?" someone joked behind Marcel's shoulder.

"Hey, *kameraden! Hallo! Kameraden!*" Tommy called out to the Germans suddenly before Marcel had a chance to clasp his hand over the Brit's mouth. But Tommy was already waving to a group of privates, who were smoking nearby, his beaming smile being the perfect weapon against any repercussion. "Where are they sending you this time?"

"Russia," one of the soldiers shouted back, stomping on his cigarette with disgust on his face. "The war started last night."

"With the Soviets?"

"*Ja.*"

The Germans huddled together, agitation and worry written all over their faces.

"Well… Good luck to you then!"

"*Danke.*" The soldiers waved Tommy goodbye and started moving closer to the next train car, which would take them to the endless steppes, from which only a few of them would return. Even the French were strangely quiet and weren't gloating, as Marcel would have expected. Even he didn't feel like gloating.

Suddenly, Giselle pushed Marcel out of her way and rushed forward with the urgency of a person who had just seen an old friend boarding the departing train. Marcel traced her gaze and noticed a familiar face as well, gasping in worry and rushing forward to catch his sister before she made the mistake of attracting the man's attention. Philippe turned out to be faster, though and caught his "spouse's" wrist before she could make another step.

The officer, who stood on the train's step and watched the troops under his command board the train, locked eyes with Giselle – much to Marcel's horror. He saw how the young German raised his hand in greeting, but then stopped abruptly and let it drop to his side, allowing only a shadow of a smile to light up his face.

"Who's the Hun staring at your sister?" Tommy's whisper burned Marcel's ear.

"An old..." *Friend?* Marcel stopped mid-sentence and shook his head slightly. "An old acquaintance of hers. Ours. Helped me get out of the jail back in Paris. It's a long story."

Giselle gave in to Philippe's subtle pulls on her hand and followed him back into the crowd of civilians, with visible reluctance. Marcel watched her yank her wrist out Philippe's hand and leave the platform altogether. Philippe sighed and followed her after a moment's hesitation, waving his farewell to Tommy and Marcel. The latter's face visibly clouded over; Giselle had to be truly upset not to even say goodbye. He knew that Giselle had used her female charms on the German, which helped hers and Philippe's plan to get him out of jail, but who knew what the real story between the two was? At least Marcel liked this German slightly better than his sister's late fiancé, Karl. Maybe she had harbored some feelings for the young fellow back then, in Paris, and now seeing him leave to meet his almost certain death, somewhere in the cruel steppes of Russia, had conjured up old flames of the past in her mind...

Even Tommy shook his head and squinted against the sun.

"Rotten business, the war. Have to feel bad for the poor lads. They should have told their Adolf to go fight Comrade Stalin himself if he's such a feisty guy. A shame, they're sending them all to slaughter. *Ivans* will end them all, you'll see. And for nothing, too. They're privates only. All of the generals will sit on their behinds and discuss strategy while boys like us will be murdered in the thousands. Rotten business, I tell you."

Marcel only chain-smoked his third cigarette in silence, glancing in the direction in which his sister had disappeared. *Yes. Rotten indeed.*

Chapter 16

Father Yves walked along a hallway that seemed endless, connecting two wings of the orphanage: one for the boys and another for the girls. Naturally, he was in charge of the first wing, while Augustine oversaw the second. Several nuns had arrived with children, all speaking with the distinctive accent that was ridiculed unmercifully by the general population. They arrived from the mostly German-speaking Alsace, from which the occupying troops kept forcing them out to free up space for the *real Germans*, and not some German-speaking French folk. So, both the nuns and the children struggled with their identity - French by origin and yet mockingly called *"ya-ya's"* by their kin for their German-accentuated speech. *How strange it was, how much hatred people could harbor in their hearts for the most defenseless of people,* Father Yves pondered, his fingers moving the beads of his rosary absent-mindedly.

He descended the stairs and almost ran into two men, carrying a heavy wooden box towards the open door of the basement. No one had given Father Yves the keys for it, and Jules had reassured him that there was nothing down there besides working equipment, left from the reconstruction of the building.

"Can I help you, gentlemen?" Father Yves inquired, eyeing the strange couple with suspicion.

"Just move out of the way, Father. Please. This damn thing weighs a ton." One of them shifted the box in his strained arms.

"What's in it?" Father Yves still blocked their way, refusing to let go of the matter without proper explanation.

"We don't know. *Monsieur le Sous-Préfet* told us to store it here. It's his property, so he can store whatever he pleases in his basement I suppose," the same man retorted, clearly getting annoyed with the priest's interrogation. "Now, be so kind to move away, please. We can't hold it the whole evening."

Father Yves stepped aside, at last, letting the men through. They came out a minute later, locked the door after themselves and tipped their hats before disappearing as fast as they had arrived. Father Yves decided that he had not been meant to see them at all. Had his class not been substituted by one of the nuns, for he had to leave to attend to a dying man from his parish, he wouldn't have seen them at all. No one would.

Father Yves walked outside and narrowed his eyes in the direction in which the odd couple disappeared, wondering how many of such comings and goings had been taking place behind his back, and what exactly it was that *Monsieur le Sous-Préfet* desired to store in his basement with the utmost secrecy.

He all but forgot the occasion, his mind busy with much more pressing matters and the orphans' needs, when one night, heading downstairs to lock the orphanage for the night, Father Yves caught Augustine's daughter, barefoot and dressed in her long-sleeved nightgown, placing a plate and a folded blanket next to the cellar's door.

"Lili?"

The girl gasped and straightened out, her black eyes widening against her will.

"I'm sorry, Father. I was just leaving."

She darted toward the rickety staircase when Father Yves stepped forward, blocking her way.

"You were supposed to be sleeping two hours ago, Lili."

"I know, Father. I was just..." She shot a look at the items that she had left behind and shifted her gaze back to the priest, chewing on her lip in worry.

"Who are you leaving the food and blanket for?" he asked in a mild voice, tilting his head to one side curiously.

"The gnomes that live in the cellar," the girl replied assertively as if it was the most obvious answer in such a situation.

Father Yves chuckled. "Aren't you a little too old to believe in gnomes?"

Lili shook her head giving him an innocent smile.

"I think your new friends from Alsace can use the food instead of the gnomes, no?"

"The gnomes need to eat too," she argued in a quiet voice, her eyes as serious as before.

"Lili." Father Yves crouched in front of the girl, adopting a new tactic. Something was very off about the whole scenario, and he didn't want to let go of the matter before he got to the bottom of it. After all, this was not just some child he had only met, but Augustine's daughter and he didn't want the girl to become involved in any kind of trouble. "You know that whatever you tell me I won't tell anyone else, right? Let's just think of it as a confession, shall we?"

"But I'm not Catholic."

Lili is far too smart for her age, he noted to himself with a smile.

"But you believe in God, don't you?"

She nodded after a moment's hesitation.

"Well, I'm one of God's servants, and whatever I promise in his name I have to do. And I promise not to tell anyone your secret, whatever it is. You know that you can trust me, right?"

"And you can trust me too, Father. I'm not doing anything bad," Lili announced, sounding strangely adult for an eight-year-old child. "*The gnomes* need their food and a warm bed just as much as the children upstairs."

"But Lili, the cellar is locked. How will the gnomes unlock it to get the food and the blanket?"

"They aren't there now. They come after midnight. Monsieur Jules brings them and locks the door after they go downstairs, and lets them out in the morning. But we shouldn't talk about them." Lili pressed her finger to her lips, making a gesture as if she were sealing them.

"Monsieur Jules hides someone down there, doesn't he?"

"Loose talk takes lives, Father. I know; one German officer in Paris used to hide *Maman* and me too. That's how we survived. If you want the gnomes to survive as well, let them be, Father. *The gnomes* are friends."

"Does Maman know about the gnomes?"

"No. Nobody does. I saw them by accident one night. Since then I started bringing them food and blankets for the night. Monsieur Jules said it was all right."

"Well, if Monsieur Jules said so." Father Yves also pretended to seal his lips, causing Lili to break into a wide grin. "You and your *gnomes'* secret is safe with me."

He stepped aside, letting the girl go. "Now, run upstairs before you catch a cold. And don't sneak out at night anymore; I'll take care of your friends."

"Make sure they don't see you though, or they'll get scared."

"They won't. I'll make sure to leave the food before midnight."

Lili beamed before running upstairs. "Good night, Father!"

"Good night, Lili." He watched her disappear into a dark hallway and added quietly, "Brave little girl".

————————————

Giselle quickly wiped her tears away at the sound of the front door unlocking, and busied herself with her cigarette, looking out of the opened window from the windowsill on which she was sitting.

"Look what I managed to get at *le Marché Noir* today! A whole chicken!" Philippe sounded so proud of himself that Giselle forced herself to turn her head and smile at the beaming man holding a dead chicken by its neck, still with its feathers. Apparently, her smile came out so pained that his also disappeared at once. "What happened? Are you still upset over that *Boche* that you saw on the station?"

"Don't call him that," she reproached him softly. "He's a good boy. He helped us save Marcel from jail."

"Unwittingly."

"Still…" She took a long drag on her cigarette – a disgusting, cheap brand she despised, together with everything else surrounding her – and looked away again, scowling.

Giselle heard Philippe fumble with the bag that he had brought. He apparently wished to busy himself with something – anything – just so he didn't have to talk to her.

He left to the kitchen, but then walked, in his resolute step, back into the living-room and asked, with a strange note in his voice, "Do you love him?"

Giselle held his gaze, a slow, contemptuous smirk showing itself, just as in old times, on her otherwise arresting face.

"No. I don't love anyone. Never have. Never will."

"Ah. The nihilistic, sentimentality-denying, post-war generation. I beg your pardon; I forgot." The sarcasm disappeared from his voice as soon as he heard her stifle a sob. "Hey, Giselle, no, please, don't cry! I'm sorry! I didn't mean it..."

She almost laughed at how his attitude changed in a fleeting moment. He had already outstretched his hand to rub her back in comfort, but then pulled it away and just stood near her, agitated and vulnerable, not knowing what to do. *The big feared communist leader,* Giselle sneered, wiping the annoying tears away with the back of her hand.

"No, Philippe. I don't love him. He just reminded me of my former life, that's all. When everything was normal. When I wrote my books, wore expensive perfume and dined at *Maxims* at least once a week. When chicken wasn't a luxury, when my nails weren't broken and black from the machine oil no matter how hard I try to scrub them off. When I wasn't on the Gestapo's most wanted list, when—" She stopped mid-sentence, took a ragged breath, raking her hand through her chestnut hair.

"When you were engaged to its chief," Philippe finished her thought.

"Go ahead, ask me if I loved *him*," Giselle threw over her shoulder, sounding positively sardonic.

"Clearly not enough to keep him alive."

She allowed a mirthless chuckle to escape her lips.

"You know, I used to think that he was a misguided, lost soul that didn't have any chance for redemption. And now," she sighed, frowning at the red glowing tip of her cigarette, "now I think I'm the one."

"Don't say that. You did the right thing."

"Did I really?" Giselle pulled her knees towards her chest and rested her chin on them. "Remember which book used to be my favorite?"

"Of course. 'Crime and Punishment'."

A shadow of a smile appeared on her pale face. "I hate it now. It haunts me like it haunted Raskolnikov in it. I see *him* in my dreams sometimes. Or, shall I call them nightmares, perhaps?"

She snorted softly and rubbed her forehead.

"Who? Karl?" Philippe inquired.

"Yes. Karl." She glanced at him after a pause. "Do you think I'm going insane?"

"No. I think it's normal after what you did. You'll keep thinking about it for quite some time. It's unnatural for humans to take another human's life, so we suffer greatly if we go against this law of nature."

"Very logical explanation. Just the way I like it." Giselle grinned.

Philippe grinned too. "Wake me up next time you have a nightmare."

"I sleep while you're at work, Philippe."

"I can ask to switch my schedule so that I'll be working night shifts together with you."

"I'm a night owl. You're a morning person. You won't last long during the night shifts."

"I'll manage," he promised confidently.

Giselle stubbed her cigarette on the brick outside the window and threw it on the ground. The street was littered as it was; what did one more cigarette butt matter? Her whole life was now one big garbage pile; she lived in it, she worked in it, and now she had a sudden, moral qualm, that had awakened in her several months ago, something she never suspected she would experience. What was happening to her? She was becoming like her father right after he returned from the Great War, the righteous, honorable Monsieur Legrand who tried to teach her things that weren't meant to be taught, as it appeared. One had to live through them to understand the true value of things, and Giselle hated all of the new revelations that came to her in this swamp of a street.

"Do you want me to pluck the chicken?" Philippe's mild voice distracted her from her musings. "I assume you wouldn't know how to do it."

She reached out and pressed his hand ever so slightly, much to his surprise.

"Let's do it together, *comrade*. I need to learn a few things, now that I'm stuck here with you."

Philippe's eyes lit up as he recognized the old, feisty blonde in this shell of the former Giselle he used to know. *No, the new life didn't break her then; merely burned mercilessly but soon, like the Phoenix, she'll come out of this even stronger, and maybe then…*

Philippe stopped at the door, gallantly allowing her to go first. *Maybe then she'd look at him with different eyes.*

———————

Paris, July 1941. Bastille Day.

A tender July night covered the city with its velvet embrace. The circle of the moon spilled its liquid silver onto the streets – the only source of illumination left in the city after the blackout law had professed its power. People lurked in the darkness, although Etienne knew well enough that they shouldn't be; not after the curfew at least. He doubted that these small groups, throwing wary glances his way as he passed them by, had an *Ausweis* allowing them to be out in the after-curfew hours.

Another couple passed him by, the young man's shoulder nearly brushing Etienne's as the two rushed along *Place de la Concorde*. Etienne scowled but decided not to pay heed to the students, who the couple most likely were, with serious yet agitated sharp faces, glancing straight ahead of them. Etienne strode unhurriedly towards *l'Arc de la Triumphe,* a bittersweet, melancholy mood overtaking him again at the ungodly sight of all the swastika flags and banners marring the capital, their crimson draperies turning deceivingly black at night like the SS troops' uniforms. Lyon had been spared such humiliation, so far. Today was Bastille Day, and like any proud French citizen, Etienne wanted to at least pay his respects to the monument of the Liberty, even though honoring Liberty under the enemy's occupation seemed like a mocking charade. Naturally, the local *Kommandantur* strictly prohibited any gatherings and parades celebrating the biggest national holiday; strangely enough, the Parisians grumbled their displeasure but obeyed.

The official reason why Etienne had traveled to Paris was to attend a security meeting on behalf of the ever-absent Prefect of Lyon, Raimond Bouillon, to reassure the Germans of their "most willing cooperation" in surrendering any Allied parachutists and Resistance members that the *gendarmes* of Lyon encountered. Etienne barely concealed a smile thinking how astonished and furious the Germans' faces would become if they only knew that it was him and his cell members who were hiding Allied parachutists in the cellar of his orphanage. However, there was another reason, an unofficial and much more dangerous one: tonight, Etienne was to meet with the man who was currently collecting information about all functioning Resistance groups to later deliver his report to General de Gaulle in London. The man's name was Jean Moulin.

He knew nothing about the man, well, not enough to form any opinion at least, besides what Marcel had told him before arranging the meeting. Supposedly, Patrice knew Moulin, and strongly advised *the chief* to meet with him. Etienne managed to collect little snippets of rumors from here and there before setting out on his trip, and had acquired an official document which stated Moulin's "crimes". Etienne knew well enough by now that crimes nowadays meant one thing only: a refusal to collaborate. Moulin had seemed to take it even further than that, actively defying the Germans while he still held a position in the administration. This resulted in his incarceration and endless torture by the Gestapo, who more than anything loved teaching the disobedient French what a mistake their refusal to collaborate was.

Moulin tried to cut his throat with a piece of glass that he found in his cell. Fate, however, had another plan on his account; Moulin not only survived and managed to escape his captors but swore to fight against the Germans until he drove every last one of them out of his land. With more and more resources falling into his arms from the sky thanks to the generous MI6, Etienne thought it would be simply foolish not to offer help to his counterpart, whose connections encountered more obstacles towards obtaining weapons and explosives than the Resistance in the Free Zone did. The meeting was to take place at midnight in one of the conspiracy apartments Moulin's people used. So, Etienne still had time to pay his silent respects to the defeated French Liberty and vanish into the night.

Loud singing and shouts burst through the night air like a thunderstorm, unexpected and startling with the sheer insolence of its force. Etienne stopped in his tracks but, following natural human curiosity and completely ignoring a heightened sense of alertness hammering insistently in his brain, telling him to go back, he rushed in the direction in which the students had previously disappeared.

The view that unraveled in front of his mesmerized eyes when he turned the corner was truly fascinating. Over a hundred, or maybe even two hundred, young men and girls, dressed in the colors of the national flag, were marching along the street laughing with intentional boorishness, shouting derogatory slogans against the Germans and acting with such reckless fearlessness that Etienne found himself holding his breath in, instinctively, enthralled by the utter madness.

Apparently, the Parisians grumbled their discontent only during the day, turning the night into a true nightmare for the local *feldgendarmes*, a few of whom now watched the improvised student parade with their mouths agape, looking entirely unsure of what to do as the numbers were obviously not in their favor. It was a breathtaking celebration of life in the darkest of hours, a celebration of defiant youth over the authority which had been forced on them, shouts over imposed silence, and laughter over gunshots.

The gunshots, and not metaphorical ones, followed far sooner than Etienne had hoped. Not even ten minutes passed before reinforcements, in the form of the German military, arrived, dispersing the crowd the best they could by shooting into the air. Only, the young mob, drunk on wine and fearless patriotism, turned on their aggressors, much to their surprise. Some soldiers ran; one almost knocked a stunned Etienne off his feet, but smaller brawls soon broke out between the students and the soldiers, some of whom found themselves surrounded near their military cars, now shouting their last warnings to the enraged youth, pointing their machine guns in their direction instead and not into the air. Etienne hoped that the students would think rationally and burst into a run as well. He also wisely decided not to stick around to see what would come out of all this and joined the small group running past him.

All he could hear was loud footsteps, heavy breathing, and meaningful silence. No one exchanged excited exclamations or banter to cheer each other up, as they escaped through the smaller Parisian streets. They ran like a very organized group led by a single mindset: *tonight, we showed them what we're worth. Tonight was only the beginning. Tonight is when our fight for liberty begins.* Etienne felt electrified air filling up his lungs with each labored breath, their collective determination pushing them forward, back to the shadows where they belonged – for now.

Only several hours earlier he had been shaking hands with the men who were chasing him now, and in an hour, he would meet the man who would soon unify the entirety of the Resistance in the Occupied Zone, and if he accepted his proposal, would soon unify the Resistance in the whole of France. Etienne's eyes gleamed in the dull light of a narrow alley, to which he darted after breaking away from the running crowd. He resumed his regular walk at once, willing his breath to calm. He fixed his tie, checked if his hat sat perfectly straight on his head, and soon appeared in a brightly lit square, walking right into the muzzle of a German machine gun.

Etienne quickly scanned the street, visible in the yellow light of the military car's headlights, noticed one soldier propped against its hood who was eyeing him with malice while holding a bloodied handkerchief to his nose, and several students sitting cross-legged against the wall with their hands above their heads. He raised his, just in case.

"*Papeire!*" the German, who held him at gunpoint, barked out.

"I'm a Vichy government official," Etienne offered, keeping his tone purposely respectful, and slowly reached into his inner pocket so as not to provoke the soldier. At least one of his comrades had already suffered at the students' hands judging by his broken nose, which could have made them all much more trigger-happy than they originally were. "Here is my passport and my *Ausweis*."

The German lowered his machine gun and moved closer to the car to study Etienne's documents. After thoroughly perusing them and exchanging a few remarks with his men, the German glared at Etienne.

"What were you doing here at night?"

"Evening, not night," Etienne corrected him politely and allowed himself a warm smile. "I was just now dismissed after meetings with the *Kommandant* of *Groß-Paris* and the rest of the officials, and merely wanted to take a walk along the streets of the city when all this hell broke loose. I suppose I happened to be in the wrong place at the wrong time, *Mein Herr*. Surely, you can tell I'm not one of these unruly young men who came out looking for trouble tonight."

"Collaborating pig," one of the students immediately snorted under his breath, looking away from Etienne in disgust. One of the Germans kicked the big-mouthed young man with obvious pleasure, now having a good reason for it.

Etienne only tilted his head to one side and offered the German another humble smile as if apologizing for his compatriots' behavior.

That, and the scorn with which the rest of the students regarded Etienne was a decisive factor in the soldier's decision-making. He grinned in response, handed Etienne back his papers and even courteously saluted him.

"If I were you, I'd go straight home, *Herr* Sub-Prefect. The streets are still full of these scoundrels. It'll take us some time to round them all up. Would be a shame if one of our particularly ardent comrades rounded you up together with them."

"What will happen to them?" Etienne probed carefully, making use of the German's shifting attitude towards him, and motioned his head in the students' direction.

"What *Herr Kommandant* ordered. Prison, and in some cases – execution."

Etienne threw a last glance at the group of brave young men and women - who didn't grace him with even a single look – and fought off a surge of repulsion as he shook the German's hand, and set off on his way, deep in his brooding.

Chapter 17

Lyon

Blanche critically appraised her reflection in the mirror. It was one of the first things she had bought for her new apartment. The priest, who took over Father Yves' congregation after the latter moved to a city-funded orphanage (which was odd to begin with, as Blanche never pictured him as a person who loved children that much), didn't take too kindly to her living under the church's roof and had sternly advised her to move out at the first chance. Blanche shrugged indifferently and went to pack her meager possessions. She had nothing left there anyway. And as for Father Yves, whom she had adored with such passion just mere months ago? She didn't deem him a second glance after he wished her farewell and left with his black-eyed Jewess in tow. *Very well; good riddance to them both.*

Blanche selected the thickest needle from her sewing kit, wiped it with rubbing alcohol carefully, disinfected her earlobe with the same cotton pad and then, without giving it a second thought, drew the needle through her tender flesh.

She had someone better now, someone who paid attention to her, even though most of the time she questioned the very motive of that attention. But as soon as those doubts started gnawing on her thoughts, Blanche chased them away with the same determination with which she had just pierced her ear, observing the result with a twisted smile. Standartenführer Sievers had presented her with pearl earrings during their last meeting, and Blanche had every intention of wearing them. The fact that her ears hadn't been pierced didn't deter her from such a decision in the slightest.

Sievers demanded information from her with the ruthlessness of the most merciless of the interrogators; yet, he didn't forget to award Blanche with these small gifts even when she had nothing else to tell him, just like a master awarding his dog with a treat for a seamlessly followed command. She sketched the whole scheme of her cell for him, and even though Sievers visibly cringed at the vagueness of it, he had at least seemed satisfied with what she supplied him, for now.

"My primary supervisor in Lyon is Jules," Blanche had told him two weeks ago while sitting at the mahogany dining table, bent over a sheet of paper with a pencil in her hand. Sievers hovered somewhere over her shoulder, sharp gaze trained on the paper, the usual glass of brandy in his hand. It was strange how his presence both terrified and excited her at the same time. Blanche cowered a little lower above the paper before writing down the first name. "I only know his first name, not his surname. He's young, about my age, maybe a little older. Short brown hair, hazel eyes; he has a beard, and wears glasses. He's a communist."

Sievers grumbled his approval, left the room without speaking another word and soon returned with a stack of files, which he threw on the table in front of her.

"Look through the pictures. Those are all communists, registered with the *Prefecture de Police* of Lyon."

Blanche wondered how many of those files he had in his study, in which she was not allowed, and started shuffling through the multitude of mug shots. Ten minutes later she admitted her defeat.

"He's not among them."

Sievers only raised his brow, the cynical smirk she feared so much pulling the corner of his mouth upwards.

"Which means he's either not a communist, or not from Lyon, *schatz*. You can't even confirm this little bit of information?"

The somewhat sadistic disappointment in his voice slashed her strained nerves like a scalpel.

"But the description—"

"He can grow out his hair, shave the beard and dispose of the glasses, Blanche." Sievers sighed tiredly, swirling the liquor in his glass. "Moving on."

Blanche felt her cheeks heating up and tried her best to keep her composure.

"There's this woman, Margot, she works in the *photo atelier,* in which they make all of the documents for new agents and runaways. Here's the address." Blanche hurriedly wrote down the name of the street and the number of the building. "She's tall, large, somewhat crude looking, with dark hair and brown eyes."

"That's all fine and well, but my interest mainly lies with the Occupied Zone. You see, my dear Blanche, I can't just take my people and barge into the Free Zone to arrest some *résistants*. That's why that zone is called Free, for we have no authority over it. Now, the Occupied Zone and your connections here is something *feasible*. Give me something I can use, *herz*."

"My supervisors in Dijon are a couple – husband and wife. Her name is Laure and he is Alain. They appeared sometime around late March-early April, and Jules wouldn't tell me where they came from, but I don't think they're from Dijon. I'd been working with an entirely different man there before they came along."

"The names are fake, most certainly, but... Husband and wife, you say?" Sievers lowered onto a plush chair next to her, rubbing his chin pensively. "Interesting. What do they look like?"

"She's older than me, maybe in her late twenties-early thirties. He's about the same age, and he's very tall. About two meters, I would say. He's quite handsome, with brown hair and brown eyes, and he has a charming smile."

"What about the wife?"

"Brown, shoulder-length hair, green eyes. Sometimes they seem hazel; it depends on the lighting." Blanche shrugged with sudden irritation. "She's a factory girl. Looks as pale as death. Smokes a great deal. Wears men's clothes. Very full of herself for an unkempt woman."

Sievers broke into a fit of chuckles. "That sounds like jealousy, Blanche."

"Why would I be jealous of her?" Blanche jerked her shoulder.

"That's what I'm curious about. Why do you say she's full of herself?"

"Because she is. Arrogant and stuck-up, like she some *society dame*, and not a union worker."

Sievers narrowed his eyes, sudden interest shining in them. "How does she talk, this mysterious Madame Laure?"

"I didn't hear any accent..."

"No, that's not what I mean. How is her speech? Choice of words? The manner of her talking?"

"She sounds... educated, I suppose," Blanche conceded at last, grudgingly. "And she always talks down to me, like she knows it all."

"Educated like *you*, or educated like *me?*"

Blanche bit her lip, trying to ignore the jab. "Like you."

"What about the husband?"

"He talks... normal. Not condescending, like her. He's definitely a communist; he told me that himself."

"But he's not from Dijon, so that poses a certain difficulty. He could have come from anywhere." Sievers tapped his finger on the rim of his glass several times. "Do not fret. We'll find out who they are eventually. And for now, sit tight and play along with them. Report every task they delegate to you, of course."

"How long shall I pretend before you arrest them?" Blanche inquired gingerly.

She loathed the thought that she would have to go back to "befriending" more train station workers, but Sievers didn't seem to care for her feelings on this account. He rose from his chair and lifted up her chin, holding her head firmly in place.

"For as long as *I* tell you to. *Hast Du verstanden?*"

She nodded, swallowing her pride. She wasn't in a position to question him, and, besides, he treated her far nicer than any other man had or could. Not that she had much to compare to, but Blanche thought that the new silk and Crepe-de-Chine dresses that he bought for her accounted for something, just like the fact that he would take her out from time to time.

And now, he had given her the earrings, telling her to wear them next time he took her to the opera.

"We need to educate you too, don't we? Then you won't have to envy Madame Laure." He grinned.

Blanche nodded happily and impulsively kissed the hand on her face, that was so generous to her. Sievers only pinched her cheek in response; Blanche tried to ignore the condescension in his gaze, the same look that she had seen so many times in Laure's.

———————

Father Yves fumbled with the impressive lock on the door, leading to the cellar, his brows drawn together in utter concentration. Tonight, he was determined to get to the bottom of the whole conspiracy and what exactly the communists, who Monsieur Jules Gallais oversaw, could possibly be hiding in the Sub-Prefect's new orphanage, right under his nose. Crouching by the door, his gaze fixed on the precise, almost professional movements of his hands, Father Yves heard the familiar click of the lock giving in to his efforts at last when suddenly a voice spoke right above his ear.

"Father? What are you doing?"

Caught red-handed, he turned to Augustine and offered her a timid smile instead of an answer. She was supposed to be sleeping now, yet there she stood, looking puzzled and alarmed, tugging the ends of her shawl to cover her bare arms and the upper part of her simple cotton nightgown.

"Did they teach you that in the seminary? To pick locks?" Augustine tried to smile back at him, but worrisome thoughts still wrinkled her forehead.

"No. Of course not." He lowered his head, chuckling softly. He couldn't quite tell her that a fellow marksman with a shady past had taught him during their service together when the two would break into abandoned houses. So, Father Yves lied to her, just like he had lied about so many things before. "I'll admit that I have a rather shameful fondness for crime stories. In one of them, the process was described quite explicitly, so it wasn't particularly difficult to follow the 'instructions'."

"I see." Augustine seemed to be satisfied with such an explanation. "What are you hoping to find inside?"

"It's what I'm hoping to not find." Father Yves got to his feet and dusted off his black robe mechanically. "I'm afraid our communist friends might be hiding something illegal down there."

"Illegal like what?"

"Weapons, for one example."

His nonchalant reply, or maybe the tone that he used, brought a frown back onto Augustine's face.

"Why would they? There aren't any Germans around," she spoke quietly, hugging herself with both hands under her shawl.

"Not yet," Father Yves remarked and cursed inwardly at once, seeing her reaction.

Augustine had just lost her husband to the SS a year ago, and, had one decent German not warned her of the upcoming raids, she would have long been gone as well, to Drancy or even worse, to one of those ill-famed Nazi camps in Poland, from which no one had returned so far. And, here he was, lacking the common sense not to tell her that they might very well come to the Free Zone as well.

"You shouldn't be afraid of them," he said softly, stopping himself from reaching out and touching her shoulder. "You're not Jewish anymore, according to your new passport. Your papers will protect you, and little Lili too."

"I hope so," she murmured, lowering her big black, liquid eyes.

Father Yves hesitated before pulling the cellar door open.

"Why don't you go back upstairs?"

She pondered something, eyeing the door with suspicion.

"No. I want to go in with you."

"As you wish."

He flickered a small flashlight that he had brought with himself and started descending into the darkness, barely seeing two steps ahead. Augustine clasped his shoulder midway, after nearly losing her footing. Father Yves straightened out rigidly but didn't say anything against the fingers that remained on top of his robe. *He didn't want her to stumble, did he?*

Liar. Her palm warmed him like the most euphoric of blessings in the middle of the darkest witching hour. When she removed it, as they stepped onto the concrete floor, Father Yves sensed its absence as if his own limb had been taken away from him.

"What do you think, are there rats in here?" she whispered behind his back.

"No. There's nothing for them to feast on here." Another lie. But, even he be damned, he only wished for her to be safe, and to feel safe, above all.

She took his hand, still throwing fearful glances under her feet. He bit his lip and clasped her palm tightly.

"Come. There are some crates over there."

He led her towards one of the supporting columns near which wooden boxes were stacked, resembling the one that he had seen in the communists' hands. Setting his flashlight on top of one of the boxes, he let go of Augustine's hand, warning her to stay near. To his luck, the first crate that he decided to inspect wasn't closed properly or had been left open on purpose by the communists, for easier access. *Not that they expected anyone to snoop around in their cellar,* he guessed.

Father Yves removed the bulky top and sighed. Just as he had suspected: the cold, unmistakable glimmer of dull gray metal shattered the rest of his hopes. Old memories caught in his throat at once, and his hand outstretched towards one of the rifles that lay in a cozy bed of straw. The heavy weapon felt natural in his skilled hands, like that of a killer, and Father Yves grinned crookedly against his will, instantly immersed into the old world of endless trenches and no-man's land, pockmarked with countless wounds from artillery shelling. He inspected the gun almost with reverence, gliding his fingers along its length, put the wooden butt to his shoulder with a practiced move... and only then noticed Augustine's gaze, shifting her eyes from his face, which no doubt displayed blissful forgetfulness, to the rifle in his hands, and back.

"Do you know how to use it?" she asked in a flat, impassionate tone.

Father Yves lowered the rifle slowly, together with his guilt-ridden eyes, and nodded.

"Have you ever... used one?" Her words were a mere whisper.

He only nodded again.

"How many times?" she asked so softly that he barely heard her.

"Three hundred confirmed ones. After that, I stopped counting."

She caught her inaudible gasp with her hand, now covering her mouth.

"You fought in the war, didn't you?"

"Yes. All four years. I was a sharpshooter." He snorted softly, shaking his head at himself. "But I suppose you guessed that much already."

Augustine's eyes looked even brighter despite the meager light; two pools of the most tantalizing darkness he'd ever seen, in which it was impossible to read anything.

"Why didn't you tell me before?"

"Come now, Augustine." He tilted his head to one side with a reproaching smile.

"No, I understand that you're not supposed to... I mean... How did they accept you into the seminary?"

"I lied to them, of course."

She made a small step towards him, much to his surprise.

"You could have trusted me though. I would have kept your secret."

She sounded almost wounded by his mistrust. Father Yves smiled the warmest smile, radiating from his very tormented soul.

"Augustine, I didn't tell you not because I didn't trust you. I didn't tell you because I was afraid that I would lose your trust."

"For being a soldier?" She offered him a tentative smile as well.

"No. For taking lives without any remorse."

"Judging by the minister's robe that you've been wearing for over ten years now, I don't think anyone would dare reproach you in not having any remorseful feelings."

"I'm not even a real priest. I lied to become one. Do you think it counts?"

"Good intentions, that's what counts."

Simple as that.

She moved a little closer, stood on her tiptoes, cupped his face gently and placed a kiss on his cheek. She waited as if for him to interject something, to push her off, but he stood as still as a statue, his knuckles turning white on top of the rifle's butt. Augustine moved closer again and kissed him on the corner of his mouth, her black eyes peering into his with an unspoken question in them.

She gasped when he grabbed her by the waist, making her body crash into his as he covered her mouth with his, a hunger present that would ordinarily have frightened her. Now, however, she seemed to crave his suffocating embrace and demanding lips like a starved person that had just gotten to his first meal, in the most inappropriate of settings, with the most inappropriate of men.

The rifle fell from Father Yves' hand, its dull thud going unnoticed by both. Augustine's shawl joined it soon as Yves' fingers – he would never call himself Father again after that night – closed on her ample breast, pressing it insistently through the cotton cloth. She didn't offer the slightest resistance when he lifted her on top of a crate and yanked the hem of her nightgown up, his hands pushing her legs apart with an unmistakable urge raging in his steely eyes. Augustine only opened her mouth to his again, breathing heavily from his ruthless caresses and hands that felt almost rough on her tender breasts and thighs.

He relieved her of her underwear with a practiced move, pulled his robe up and pushed her down onto the crate. Augustine blinked her eyes open when he froze suddenly, shaking his head and stepping away as if doubting his own strength if he had stayed near her.

"What? Is it something I did?" she muttered, sitting up and covering her bare legs in sudden shame.

"No. It's not you. It's just..." He shook his head again and let out a ragged sigh. "It's wrong, Augustine. It shouldn't be this way."

"But you said it yourself that you aren't even a real priest." She couldn't bring herself to look into his eyes now.

"It's not that," he began softly, picking up her shawl, and handing it to her. He stepped away again, away from the biggest temptation he'd ever faced – a black-eyed witch that captured his soul. He didn't mind; God wouldn't want it anyway. "I can't do this to you. Not here, not in some dirty cellar, like two thieves..."

She hung her head, tucked a loose strand of dark hair behind her ear, her dejected look almost painful to him.

"Augustine..."

"I think I'm in love with you," she proclaimed calmly out of the blue, her hands lying limp on her lap.

"I'm quite certain I'm in love with you, too," he replied with a lopsided grin.

Her head shot up, her mouth twitching slightly as if she couldn't decide whether to cry or to smile.

"Let's go back upstairs." Yves offered her his hand. "I need a good night's sleep before I can demand some answers from Monsieur Jules tomorrow."

Augustine enclosed her palm into his and slid off the top of the crate, stepping closer to him than he wished.

"Don't tempt me. I can't promise that I'll be able to stop next time," Yves warned her, narrowing his eyes, a gleam in them that rendered it impossible for Augustine to decipher whether he was joking or speaking seriously.

Chapter 18

Suburbs of Dijon, July 1941

A match flared in the almost absolute darkness, highlighting the faces of two German patrolmen who cupped their hands to shield their cigarettes from the wind. Five pairs of eyes followed their steps as the Germans moved further along the train tracks, back to the station, away from the people laying still in the midst of the tall grass, alert and vigilant despite the late hour.

"The good thing about them *Boches* is how regimented they are," a voice murmured, even though the soldiers were well away from hearing distance. "They come here every night at the same exact time. I've been watching them since June."

A man lifted his head and slowly got up on his knees, still following the patrol, his eyes shining in the darkness.

"Philippe! Lay down for Christ's sake!" a woman's voice hissed at him. "Of all of us you have to be the last one to get up, with your height!"

"They're gone. Besides, without a flashlight, you can't see squat here." He straightened out completely, and the rest of the group soon followed suit. "Come, let's go!"

Philippe trotted in the front, a man in grimy road worker's overalls trailing after him step by step, followed by Giselle, Marcel, and Arthur – the British demolition expert. As they stepped onto the train tracks, Arthur squatted down and lit a dim yellow flashlight, checking the rails and the wooden beams connecting them while the rest of the group shielded him. The whole inspection took less than fifteen seconds, after which the Brit turned off the flashlight and hid it in his pocket.

"Just like I thought. Standard construction, nothing fancy. Is this the only route that they use?" Arthur turned to Philippe's comrade, who stood nearby with his hands in his pockets.

"This is the only *eastern* route that goes straight through Alsace and towards the Eastern front. There are other rail tracks, *bien sûr*, but those will slow them down for at least a day or so, and during the war, a day without needed supplies can be decisive for a victory. Now that the Soviets are at war with the *Boches*, the Party demanded that we help the Red Army with all we can. I say blowing up the tracks that they need to cater to their celebrated *Wehrmacht* will do exactly that." The man smirked from under his mustache.

"Will you be able to do it?" Philippe turned to the British specialist again.

"With the right amount of explosives – no doubt. The only problem is, all my supplies are in Lyon. How are we going to get them here?"

"How much do you need?" Giselle inquired.

"Well, if you want me to just cause a minor derailment and some track damage – half of one standard case, which is how MI6 drops them. If you want me to blow this thing up so that they couldn't repair it for a month at least – two cases."

Marcel whistled quietly. Giselle chewed on her lip, deep in concentration.

"How are you going to get two cases of explosives through the Demarcation Line?" Philippe's comrade asked the question that occupied the minds of everyone.

"Standard route?" Giselle suggested to Marcel.

The latter shook his head. "Impossible. They arrested our guy in May, and we are afraid to try and find a new one. Someone from the Occupied Zone tried that, and the fellow who promised them safe passage turned out to be an infiltrated Gestapo agent. Everyone got shot on the spot."

"Merde," Giselle cursed out loud, and shook her head, with its neat French braid holding her hair together.

"Wait, we do have a perfectly suitable courier with an *Ausweis,* don't we? That Lucienne girl." Philippe's expression brightened at once. "Why doesn't she transport the explosives for us? No one will ever suspect her; just an ordinary girl and two suitcases. We can fit those explosives into regular travel suitcases, right?"

Arthur nodded pensively. "Yes, only she will have to be very careful transporting them. MI6 packs them a certain way and drops them off with small parachutes so that the crates don't get damaged in any way. If that stuff starts leaking, one single kick into that suitcase will send the whole train flying."

"I don't think it's a good idea." Giselle folded her arms on her chest, looking skeptical. "Telling that girl about the operation."

"Oh, Giselle, give it up!" Philippe snorted with amusement. "You didn't take to that girl from the first moment you met her, for no apparent reason."

"Say whatever you want, but I don't like her."

"You don't like anyone," Philippe retorted, laughing.

Giselle shrugged nonchalantly. "True, but it has nothing to do with our current situation. Didn't I tell you that she quoted Nietzsche to me when she seemed to have no idea whose words they belonged to? Do you know who always used to quote him? Karl. The Germans built their whole worldview on his '*Will to Power*'. Where do you think she picked up such quotes from, if not from some *Boche?* Do you think it's a wise idea, to trust her with something so serious? What if she's seeing one of them? Who else would teach an uneducated girl philosophy?"

"It's all conjecture," Philippe declared, shaking his head. "That's merely your opinion, and we all know that, as a writer, you have quite a wild imagination. I met the girl, too; she's a little too impulsive but she seems a good girl nevertheless. She'll do just fine."

"Besides, we won't tell her what she's transporting," Marcel suggested. "She knows better than to ask questions about the tasks we give her. She's been moaning for months that we haven't delegated her anything important. Well, we'll just tell her this is something utterly important, and that she shouldn't ask a thing about it."

"Sounds like a perfect plan to me." Philippe shrugged.

"She's not stupid; she'll want to know what's inside the suitcases," Giselle argued. "I know I would. So, how do you know she won't open them?"

"We'll get her ones that can be locked. We'll buy them here, and you'll have the keys." Marcel pointed at Philippe and Giselle. "And once she drops them off, you'll open them and get them ready for Arthur."

"Why can't someone else transport them? Someone else with an *Ausweis?*" Giselle shot Philippe a glare as he rolled his eyes at his stubborn "spouse".

"We don't have anyone else with an *Ausweis* except for *Chief* himself, Tommy, Arthur, and myself," Marcel spoke quietly. "My face is on the wall of every prefecture of the Occupied Zone and I risk capture by crossing the Demarcation Line. The *Boches* hardly check anyone who travels without luggage, like me; if I traveled with suitcases it would be pure suicide. As for *Chief*, Tommy, and Arthur, we can't risk any of them being arrested in case some damned *Boche* decides to check their suitcases. *Chief* is in charge of everything, and he's our only link with Paris, now that he's finally had a chance to meet with Moulin. Tommy is our only radio operator, and Arthur is our only explosives expert; we can't risk losing them either. If Lucienne gets arrested, it's collateral damage; if these two do, we'll get in big trouble."

"I guess that leaves us no other choice," Philippe concluded. "Lucienne, it is."

"I still don't like this idea," Giselle muttered, sighing.

Marcel put his arm around his sister, smiling at her. "Hey, what can possibly go wrong?"

Mountains of Lyon, July 1941

"They're late again." The annoyance in Tommy's voice was evident.

A faint, purple glow had long disappeared from the sky replaced by the opaque ink of the night.

"You shouldn't have been here in the first place," Marcel grumbled in response. "*The Chief* strictly prohibited us from taking you anywhere near the drop-off point. You're our only radio connection with London. We can't risk your safety. Why do I always give in to your ridiculous demands?"

"Because you like having me around." Tommy nudged him with his shoulder, not even bothering to hide his mischievous grin.

Marcel jerked his shoulder irritably and moved away. "No, I don't. It's just that I find it easier to give in to your demands than deal with your outbursts whenever something doesn't go your way."

The two sat, leaning against the moss-ridden trunk of a tree, waiting to hear the familiar low grumble of the British plane engine. Marcel wouldn't take his gaze off the sky, anxiously fighting the doubts that had been bothering him all the way to the mountains. This was the first message that he had received and decoded all by himself, with Tommy standing near of course, but with him using the only pair of headphones, so it was impossible to tell if he had decoded it correctly. *Maybe it was his fault they hadn't heard the plane yet, and he had misinterpreted the time of the drop-off?*

"Can I have your cigarette?" Tommy asked, already holding his hand out.

"What happened to yours?"

"Left them at home."

Marcel thought of reaching into his pocket and giving him a fresh one, but then, for some reason, gave the one that he was smoking into Tommy's fingers. The Brit took a long drag on it and let out a satisfied sigh.

"Have you ever had a girlfriend?" Tommy asked abruptly.

Marcel hesitated before replying, but then only shrugged his shoulder uncomfortably. "No."

"Why not?"

"I had no time for girls. I had to study."

"The lamest excuse I've ever heard." Tommy snorted. "Have you ever slept with a girl?"

"Why do you care?" Marcel shot back, feeling his cheeks getting hot and thanking the darkness of the night for keeping his emotions invisible from the nosy rascal.

"Just curious. It's a simple question which demands a yes or no answer. No need to tell me the details."

"Yes. Happy?" Marcel snapped at him again for no apparent reason.

A second later he heard Tommy sniggering under his breath. "A working girl?"

"Why does that matter?"

"Did you like it?"

"I'm not going to discuss it with you." Marcel folded his arms on his chest and turned away.

"Apparently, that's a no." Tommy didn't even try to keep the amusement from his voice. "Have you ever kissed a guy?"

"No, and I am not planning to."

"Why such anger? Maybe you'd like it better than with a girl."

"Piss off."

"Oh, come now, don't be such a prude."

Tommy was laughing, his breath so soft and enticing near Marcel's chin, where the Brit's velvet lips caught him as he turned his head away at the last moment. Marcel shoved him in the chest and jumped to his feet, breathing heavily from anger... or was it because the damned Brit had made his heart beat so wildly against his ribcage from one simple, playful kiss that Marcel feared it would break his ribs any second now.

"Try that again, and I'll put a nice shiner on your handsome face!"

He could see an impish gleam in Tommy's eyes even in the darkness, as he got up as well, with the grace of a feral cat, and moved towards him. "So, you *do* think I'm handsome?"

"Piss off, I said!"

"Make me."

Before Marcel knew what was happening, Tommy flicked the cigarette away and moved towards him with unexpected agility. Marcel threw a punch which missed its aim and soon found himself in a deadlock, struggling with the Brit's surprisingly strong arms. Despite all the fight that he was trying to put up, Tommy overpowered him laughingly, tripped him with yet another move that Marcel never saw coming, and he found himself being placed almost gently on top of the soft moss beneath them, his arms completely restrained behind his back.

"Now what are you going to do, tough guy?"

Marcel desperately tried to worm himself out of the Brit's iron grip but to no avail.

"Nice attempt." Tommy was definitely having the time of his life, laughing at his futile efforts to release himself. "I'm from MI6, mate. They trained us for months in moves like that."

"Let go." Marcel swallowed with difficulty at the strange look that appeared in Tommy's eyes.

"You don't really want me to." Tommy grinned softly, pushing his knee in between Marcel's legs.

"Please." Marcel's voice sounded so miserably full of weak pleading that he felt disgusted with himself.

"Well, if you're asking nicely."

Of course, he didn't let him go; instead, he only pressed his chest against Marcel's, caressing his lips with his mouth. Marcel shut his eyes tight and tried not to breathe, so utterly perplexed with the strange emotions inside him, that changed with the speed of light, thrilling him, but confusing him all the same. Tommy's lips were so soft and gentle, in contrast with the steely clasp on Marcel's wrists, that had started to go numb under the weight of their bodies, and Marcel finally gave in to the most delicious sense of twisted pleasure. The sensations of pleasure coursed throughout the depths of his body, and he opened his mouth to allow Tommy to do whatever he wished to him – giving in to Tommy as he nearly always did.

It was wrong, unnatural and frowned upon – criminal even – yet Marcel couldn't possibly comprehend how something so wrong could suddenly feel so very right. Tommy's hot mouth searched his with unrestrained desire, the Brit's teeth sunk into Marcel's bottom lip, catching it with his lips to suck on it gently, and his hands were pressing Marcel's hips into Tommy's. Marcel hadn't even realized that the Brit wasn't restraining him anymore and that it was his own hand that was entangled in Tommy's golden hair now, pulling him closer, breathing hard with him, helping him pull his shirt from under his belt... His whole body screamed in protest when Tommy suddenly moved away.

"Shit! The plane!" Tommy added a few elaborate expletives under his breath and almost yanked Marcel back to his feet. "Come on, hurry up!"

Running behind the Brit, it was still a mystery to Marcel how he had heard the plane at all. All he, Marcel, could hear now, was the sound of his own blood pulsating in his ears. His skin still burned like fire, despite the brisk gusts of wind swiping at their faces, as they dashed towards the nearest clearing to see where the plane would drop its cargo.

As the small white parachute opened not too far from where they stopped, Tommy grabbed Marcel by his hand, pulled him close, laughing, and planted another loud kiss on his mouth.

"Well, what do you say? Better than with a working girl?"

Marcel caught himself grinning back gingerly.

"I'll take that as a yes." The same feral look was back in Tommy's eyes, but this time Marcel found himself craving its contagious power. "Let's go get our parcel and then we can discuss it further once we're back home."

Something caught in Marcel's throat again, and he took a tentative step back without realizing it. Tommy didn't pursue him this time, much to his surprise.

"Don't be afraid of me," the Brit spoke with unexpected tenderness in his voice. "I'm sorry for having to hold you before. I promise I won't do it again. I won't do anything that scares you."

"*You* scare me," Marcel admitted in a hoarse whisper.

"Why?" Tommy cocked his head, an impish grin back in its place.

"I don't know," he admitted with painstaking honesty, looking for answers in Tommy's amber eyes. "One day I'll figure it out."

It took them less than five minutes to reach the white cloud of the parachute covering the precious cargo that they had to carry all the way to the abandoned forest overseer's hut. The next morning Patrice and one of his comrades would bring a truck to pick it up and deliver it to the orphanage. The carefully developed plan seemed to be working seamlessly so far.

They quickly found the standard wooden crate in the folds of the white cloth, cut the parachute's restraints carefully wrapped around it, and folded the parachute, hiding it under the unearthed roots of a near tree. The forest and the mountains surrounding them were all but abandoned; no one even hunted in these areas anymore, for the war efforts had commandeered all available horses, so there was no fear that the concealed evidence would be discovered.

It was a long way to the hut, and Tommy finally signaled Marcel to put the heavy crate down and rubbed his numb arms.

"What the hell is in this bloody thing?"

"Guns. Mills grenades. Or plastic explosives, judging by the weight." Marcel handed Tommy a cigarette he had just lit for him and lit one for himself. "They're always heavy. By the way, if it's the second item, we probably shouldn't be smoking near it."

Tommy shrugged indifferently and slumped down on top of the crate with a devil-may-care look on his face which always fascinated Marcel for some inexplicable reason. Feeling particularly brave himself, with a strange sense of excitement overpowering his common sense, Marcel also sat on top of the crate.

"You don't care that we can blow ourselves up, do you?" Marcel asked him quietly, hiding a grin.

"It's such a beautiful night," Tommy replied with cynical dreaminess in his voice, squinting at the darkness enveloping them, "that I don't mind dying before the dawn."

A sudden burst of light blinded them, together with a shout and the unmistakable sound of a rifle being cocked. "You two! Hands up!"

"Well, bugger me," Tommy hissed, spitting out his unfinished cigarette and rising from the crate with his hands up in the air. "It turns out that the proverb about fearing one's desires for they tend to come true turned out to be full of sense."

Marcel got up warily, unnerved by the fact that he couldn't see their captors.

"Do you have any weapons on you?" a booming voice pierced the silence.

Before Marcel could open his mouth to try to negotiate with the *gendarmes,* and he suspected that was exactly who they were, Tommy had already spread his arms in the sincerest of manners, the most innocent of smiles playing on his face, and said, "*Bien sûr non, Monsieur!* We're just ordinary citizens, not some *vigilantes.* Besides, isn't carrying arms prohibited by the armistice?"

"Shut it, smartass!" a second voice shouted rather rudely. So, there were at least two of them, armed, against Marcel and Tommy and their bare fists. "No ordinary citizens would lurk around in the middle of the night in the mountains! What you got in that crate?"

"I'd be cursed if I know." Tommy's confident answer came before Marcel's, who had his hands pressed against his heart in a theatrical manner. "We just found it."

"You found it?" The skepticism on the part of their interrogator was palpable.

"That's right. We tried to pry it open but it wouldn't budge. So, we decided to take it home and see what's in it. We're hoping it's some good quality English whiskey."

"Why would there be English whiskey in it?" The voice betrayed a hint of interest this time.

Tommy took a deep breath as if pondering something and then looked at the blinding light of the powerful flashlight again, shielding his eyes from it.

"I'll be honest with you, Monsieur. We conduct a little trading on the side. Times are tough on everyone you see, so we started a small business to support ourselves."

"Le Marché Noir?"

"It pains me to admit it, but yes, my law-enforcing friend. We found out that the Brits drop whiskey in similar crates in the south of France when they can't reach their troops in Africa – we have a similar business in Marseille too – and our business associates pick them up and sell the same whiskey back to the Brits. Sometimes even our French lot don't mind picking up a case or two if they have the means, *bien sûr*. We sell it to them. And today we walked around to see if we can set up some traps to catch some rabbits to sell – you won't believe the demand there is for them now! – and we noticed this thing. Naturally, we didn't want to drag it to our house in the middle of the day, so we waited for night and came back for it. It's most likely whiskey, I tell you. If it were something else, those *commies* would have picked it up by now."

Marcel felt a surge of awe at Tommy concocting such a credible story, that even Marcel almost found himself being persuaded by it. The other party seemed to ponder his words as well until the flashlight jerked to one side.

"Move away from it."

Both Marcel and Tommy readily obliged, as the second flashlight lit up while the first one stayed trained on the crate. Both *gendarmes* - and it was indeed them, Marcel was fortunate enough to catch a glimpse of the uniform – discussed what to do about the crate while Marcel took several discreet steps back, pulling Tommy by the wrist.

"Hey! Stay where you are, I said!"

"We just wanted to give you room," Marcel replied, trying to sound as genuine as possible. "We aren't going anywhere. We told you, we're ordinary merchants."

"You're still under arrest for dealing goods on the black market. Don't even think that we'll let you go without charging you."

"By all means, do what you feel is right." Marcel lifted his arms in the air again, carefully faking compliance.

As the two poked and probed the top of the crate, Marcel chewed on his bottom lip, his eyes glimmering feverishly.

"Try shooting at it," he shouted, trying to keep a tremor out of his voice and stepping back some more. "That's how we always open it when a crowbar doesn't work."

Tommy stepped further away as well, catching onto Marcel's plan.

The two *gendarmes* kicked and hit the crate with their rifle butts a few more times before admitting defeat. Marcel held his breath as one of them aimed his rifle at the top of the crate. They stood so close to it that the rifle's muzzle nearly touched the wood. Marcel glided even further away, catching Tommy's wrist again. A shot pierced the silence, and then a deafening explosion took both Marcel and Tommy off their feet in its wake. Marcel landed on top of the Brit, shielding him from the debris with his body. A sharp pain shot through his thigh and back as several wooden splinters pierced his skin. Marcel hissed and immediately felt Tommy push his body away.

"No, not on my back!" Marcel screamed out, and Tommy's arms caught him at once, holding him up in a sitting position.

"Are you hurt? Where?" Tommy's hands shook slightly, despite his firm voice.

"Back and legs, I think. Splinters from the damned crate. They didn't go deep. I'll live. Just help me get up."

Tommy held Marcel by his elbows, helping him to a standing position.

"Can you walk?"

"I have no choice. We just killed two *gendarmes,* Tommy." Marcel shifted from one foot to another gingerly, trying to assess his condition. The shock would probably help him walk for some distance at least. After that... After that, they would just have to improvise.

Tommy glanced in the direction where the two flashlights had danced a mere minute ago. The darkness around the flickering embers of the crate contents remained opaque and silent now as if swallowing two lives didn't matter one bit to the night.

"Why did you do that?"

"You heard them. They would have taken us in," Marcel muttered.

"No, I'm not talking about that. Your idea was excellent by the way. I'm asking about why you jumped on top of me? You could have died, you know, if one of the nails from the crate went through your neck."

"I don't know. I didn't think, I guess."

"Fair enough. Well... Thank you anyway."

"It's nothing."

"It's my life. I suppose it's yours now." Tommy breathed softly, put Marcel's arm around his shoulder, and the two started making their way back home.

Chapter 19

Giselle lay on the battered sofa, wide awake despite feeling severe exhaustion from the night shift. She curled and uncurled her toes in an effort to return some feeling to them, inwardly cursing the day when she'd donned men's working boots for the first time, replacing and discarding the patent leather shoes she used to collect. With disgust, Giselle studied her feet and the never-healing sores and blisters on them, recalling the times when she had flipped through the pages of a literary magazine, drowning in the softness of a leather chair, while a salon girl painted her toes burgundy red – to match her fingernails and favorite lipstick. *Oh, what she wouldn't give to have her pedicure done now!* Giselle groaned her frustration, rubbed her eyes and cringed at the smell of the oil on her fingers of which she never seemed to rid herself of. And to think of it, just a few months ago those fingers were taken care of with commendable thoroughness, for those precious fingers typed the novels for which Michel Demarche, the owner of the publishing house that bore his name and who had become her most intimate friend, paid her ridiculous money. *What happened to all her bank accounts after she had fled Paris,* Giselle wondered. The Gestapo had seized them all most likely. She doubted that they would leave them be after she had killed their chief in cold blood. Not so much cold, as it had turned out...

Giselle tried to banish the image of *his* face from entering her thoughts; the face that seemed to haunt her ever since her fingers had coiled around his throat with ruthless determination. She didn't have to kill him with her hands; he would have died eventually anyway, after consuming a lethal amount of strychnine which she had doctored his wine with. She could have just left him in that secluded place; but with his relentless willpower, who knew if he would have crawled to the nearest road, and it would have been just her luck that some of his fellow countrymen might have picked him up.

The image stood so vile and tangible in front of her unblinking eyes that Giselle shuddered involuntarily, just as she had when she awakened from yet another nightmare earlier that morning. In her dream, she was strangling him again, but this time, instead of dying, he broke into a grin that grew wider and wider and soon burst out laughing as if her whole murder scenario was one big joke. Giselle had blinked her eyes open and nearly fell off the narrow sofa, finding herself lying right next to the man she had killed. Karl was sleeping next to her, his features hardly distinguishable in the graying morning light outside; austere and somber, dark-haired and strong-chinned, handsome and dead, and yet breathing by some miracle. Giselle had pulled herself upwards on one elbow, peering into the face she could barely make out in the meager light of the dawn and breathed out in relief when the veil of the deranged delusion fell off her eyes. It wasn't Karl anymore, but Philippe, sweet old Philippe, her *comrade* as she teasingly called him and which irritated him to no end.

Giselle sank back into the flat pillow and fought the urge to smoke. She tried losing herself in sleep again, but familiar charcoal black eyes peered into her closed ones and the voice with its slight German accent, that she would never forget, mocked her, putting ideas into her mind that she had struggled so hard to relinquish. *So, my beautiful Gisela, how do you like waking up next to a communist? Is that the life you wanted for yourself? Was it truly worth it, killing me for it? You disappoint me, herz. I thought you were smarter than that, superior, my kin. But you turned out to be nothing but one of those weaklings we both always despised. What happened to the Gisela I met in Paris, on that stifling June day in 1940? She was a brilliant woman, a cynical, practical writer who defied the very notions of morality and sentimentality. She was a veritable Nietzsche scholar, one who understood every word he expressed and lived according to those postulates of his. Remember what remarkable debates we had about him, Gisela? You out-argued me on most occasions, being the sharp, brilliant conversationalist that you are... Or used to be, should I say? What do you talk to this Neanderthal about? Diversions and communism? Has he converted you to his faith yet? How long will it be before you start discussing the postulates of Marxism and Leninism with him, Gisela? My little comrade, eh? Ha-ha-ha! My little comrade; I think it's hysterical, don't you? The renowned novelist Giselle Legrand, who used to spend thousands of Franks in the casinos in Riviera, who drank Dom Perignon for breakfast and typed her groundbreaking, rebellious novels wearing silk robes in her ridiculously overpriced apartment in the Champs-Élysées. Did you really find writing for your little underground newspaper more important and satisfying? Running around with your new friends from the Resistance? Trading me for that excuse of a man who wouldn't even know what to do with a woman like you? We could have been so happy together, Gisela... You could have been home, in Paris, with me now. And I would bring you something better than a chicken as a present. I would wrap pearls around your neck, Gisela... But, apparently, you like chickens better.*

'Shut up! Philippe had to turn the whole city upside down to find that chicken for me. And no, we wouldn't have been "so happy together", Karl! You were this close to uncovering the cell that was behind *La Libération*. You would have only thrown me in jail together with the rest, so don't even start on that account. You keep tormenting me because you can't let go of the fact that I outsmarted you and killed you first before you got the chance to kill me. And you would have done it; without batting an eye, you would have done it.'

Why do you feel so guilty then?

'I don't.'

Liar.

'Go away.'

I can't; you won't let me.

Giselle forced her eyes open but, on the verge of the dream losing its power over her, she still heard his voice. *You're wrong about me. I'm not angry that you outsmarted me and killed me first; I would have been very disappointed in you if you didn't. But there are much more dangerous enemies out there, Gisela. I'd watch your back if I were you...*

The drapes were tightly drawn together to block the sunlight that had finally emerged in the growing morning hours, throwing green shadows over her face. Philippe was still snoring softly next to her, unsuspecting and undisturbed, his arm under his head and another one resting on his stomach. Giselle carefully sat up musing over Karl's last words, and reached for a cigarette pack that lay on a small three-legged stool near their sofa – *their bedside table* – she thought with a disgusted sneer and lit up one.

She had always prided herself on having a sharp, analytical mind and a cool head when it came to any decision. She never believed in ghosts or any superstitious or religious nonsense, as she had called it from her early teens. Yet, following that voice's advice, the voice that sounded far too real for some reason, she stood up resolutely, stubbed the cigarette in a small, tin ashtray and tiptoed to the kitchen, throwing a shirt on top of her undershirt and grabbing her pants from the back of the chair. In the kitchen, she took several bills out of the stack that she and Philippe stashed in a can, put them in her pocket, paused on the threshold of the door for a moment to throw a last glance at the sleeping communist, and silently slipped out of the door. He'd try to stop her if he knew, try to bring up some argument, logic, psychology even, against what she planned to do, try to reassure her once again that the voice wasn't real and it was only in her head... No, she'd rather leave now and deal with him later. He'd thank her afterward, she was certain of it.

Giselle walked to the nearest clothing store, mulled over the idea of throwing away such a ridiculous amount of money on a dress she would probably wear only once in her life, then took a deep breath and walked inside. A salesgirl glanced askance at her but still inquired as to what *Madame* desired today.

"Whatever fits me and costs the cheapest. And a pair of shoes, please. And the cheapest handbag you have," Giselle responded in a flat tone, Karl's amused chuckling still audible in the back of her mind.

The salesgirl cast another apprehensive glance but soon returned with the needed items. Giselle cringed inwardly at the floral pattern on the simple cotton dress but headed to the fitting room, reminding herself that now wasn't the time to indulge in vanity. She looked herself over critically and decided that this would have to do, hid her clothes in her new canvas bag together with her old work boots, threw the bills on the counter and walked out of the store, heading towards her destination point – the train station.

———————

Blanche pressed her temple against the window-pane and felt her eyes closing as the monotone rocking of the train gently lulled her to sleep. The first train car, which she had started riding in ever since Jürgen Sievers became something more than just a feared name but a means of protection, was cool and almost empty, for most of the troops had left for the front a little over a month ago. Both Blanche's seat and the one across from her were empty, except for the two heavy brown suitcases, standing near her feet. Sievers had promised her that his men would meet her at the station in Dijon and bring her to his office so he could see for himself what the fighters were transporting. She didn't know and didn't care, what was in them, so long as Jürgen was happy.

Oh, and he was more than happy with her, calling her a *prinzessin* and his *herzchen,* while caressing the bare skin on her neck, right under her hair, causing her thoughts to melt away, disappearing except for one: the sensation of his fingers on her hot skin.

"You will be forever faithful to me, *ja?*" he had whispered in her ear once, sending waves of euphoric shivers down her spine. "You will do exactly what I tell you."

Blanche nodded fervently, her eyes gazing adoringly into his, cold like Arctic ice, with unspoken promises in them.

A subtle smile curved Blanche's lips. Her closed eyelids slightly twitched as she immersed deeper into her daydreaming. If there were something worthy of his time in those suitcases, maybe he would invite her into his bed at last. Oh, how much she desired him!

"Salut."

Blanche sat bolt upright, startled, and blinked several times trying to figure out if the woman in front of her was a part of a dream that she hadn't shaken off, or if she was indeed here, sitting across from her with a cynical smirk in its place.

"I thought Jules forbade you from riding in the first car."

No, she was real, all right. She was even dressed like a lady, with her chestnut hair pinned from both sides, the gentle waves of her tresses barely reaching the tops her shoulders. But it was the eyes, those cat-like devious eyes that were narrowed on Blanche as if she were nothing but prey, which persuaded her that it was indeed Laure.

"What are you doing here?" Blanche straightened in her seat, her face taking on a guarded expression.

"Let's just put it this way: I was feeling uncharacteristically charitable and decided to relieve you of your burden."

Only now, after throwing a frantic look under her feet did Blanche notice that the suitcases now stood near Laure's feet.

"You didn't have to do that. I'm perfectly capable of bringing them to Dijon myself." Blanche started feeling nervous under the brunette's cold, unmoving gaze.

The train was already slowing down, approaching one of the transit stations. The slower it went the more predatory Laure's grin became. Blanche ground her teeth in helpless fury, knowing perfectly well that there wasn't a chance in the world that she could make a scene without giving them both away to the Germans now moving towards the exit. Judging by the triumphant look in her eyes, Laure knew it as well. She rose from her seat gracefully, picked up both suitcases and presented the most radiant of smiles to an officer, who immediately offered her to carry her luggage.

"Go home, Lucienne. Before it's too late," Laure threw over her shoulder, and disappeared out of view, together with the broad-shouldered German.

Blanche sank back into her seat, hit her head on its back several times in despair and cursed under her breath. *Now, how was she supposed to explain her failure to Jürgen?*

Etienne paced in front of the entrance of the new orphanage, checking his watch for the third time in two minutes. The orphanage was their weekly meeting place under the perfect guise of the Sub-Prefect inspecting the premises when in reality he was getting a detailed report from his second in command. Marcel was never late; as a matter of fact, his punctuality rivaled Etienne's, and yet today, out of all days, he had to be so very late. Etienne spun on his heel upon hearing steps behind his back, and nearly grunted in disappointment when he saw the priest's black robe.

"Monsieur le Sous-Préfet." Father Yves acknowledged him with a bow of his head. "A pleasure to have you here. Can I be of assistance?"

"As it is mine, Father." Etienne inclined his head as well. "Pay me no heed; I'm only waiting for Monsieur Gallais. He promised to give me his report concerning the construction of the new playground for the children in the back. His men are still working on it, as I understand? Is everything to your satisfaction so far?"

The priest folded his hands behind his back, a hint of a knowing grin appearing on his face. He looked at his feet for some time as if pondering something and then raised his eyes to Etienne.

"May I have a word, *Monsieur le Sous-Préfet?*"

"Of course."

Father Yves gestured for Etienne to follow him inside and led him straight to the door of the cellar, Etienne's uneasiness growing with every step.

"Are you aware of what is being stored down there?" the priest said innocently. "Your construction men never gave me the key, I'm afraid."

Etienne held his gaze and spoke in a voice that didn't betray the slightest of emotions. "Construction equipment, I suppose. They didn't give you the key because they're communists and don't trust priests. Don't take it personally; it's in their doctrine, or so I heard."

"It's rather brave of you, hiring communists nowadays."

"They're good, honest workers."

"They might be good, but they sure as hell aren't honest."

Etienne's brows moved into a scowl upon hearing the word that would send any other priest crossing himself fervently and whispering prayers under their breath. Yet, Father Yves stood tall and unmoving, his steady, gray eyes narrowed in a manner that seemed mocking to Etienne.

"I beg your pardon, Father?"

"I said, your workers have been bringing a lot of items downstairs recently. Lots and lots of very dubious-looking crates that piqued my interest."

"I have already told you, it is most certainly construction equipment," Etienne asserted, with a barely concealed warning in his voice.

Father Yves made a dismissive gesture with his hand. "Construction equipment? Is that so? Why lock it then? No one is going to steal it; it's an orphanage, for Christ's sake."

"You surely say a lot of unseemly things for a priest," Etienne remarked coolly, trying to change the subject.

"You surely cover up a lot for your communist friends," Father Yves countered, unfazed.

"I don't understand your allegations, Father."

"I'll ask you straight then: why are there so many weapons and explosives in the cellar of your orphanage that it would be enough to level the whole city to the ground? And who are the men whom Monsieur Gallais brings here for the night?"

It took Etienne exceptional self-control not to react to the provocation. He regarded the priest silently without so much as a twitch of his mouth, even though his thoughts were dancing in a frenzy.

"How would you know what's in the cellar, Father?"

"I picked the lock. And it was me who's been leaving out food and blankets for your Allied parachutists, or foreign agents or whatever they are, all this time. They never saw me, *bien sûr*."

Etienne regarded him warily. Something was off about this black-clad man, so very off that he needed to tread as carefully as possible.

"Interesting. Well, even if you did find the aforementioned items in the cellar, I'm afraid I can't help you regarding their origin. I merely sponsor the orphanage. I know nothing of any comings and goings, and I certainly know nothing of any Allied parachutists."

"I suspected you would say something of this sort."

"What are you going to do? Report me to the authorities?"

"*You* happen to be the authorities, conveniently, *Monsieur le Sous-Préfet*."

Etienne sighed, admitted to himself that he had been cornered, and inquired tiredly, "What do you want? Money?"

The priest chuckled softly. "I'm a man of the cloth, Monsieur. Do you really think I have a use for worldly possessions?"

"You don't seem like a man of the cloth to me, Father, with your interesting choice of words and skills. You're a rather unorthodox priest. Hence my question."

Father Yves shook his head with a slight smile, fumbling with something in his pocket. "I don't need your money. I only need your word."

"My word?"

"Yes. I have a cross, you see."

"I would think so."

"No, you don't understand." Father Yves grinned crookedly and extracted something from his pocket, holding it out to Etienne. "It's a different type of a cross."

Etienne studied the military award carefully. *Croix de Guerre, 1914-1918*, with two crossed swords – for valor.

"Yours?"

The priest nodded. Etienne returned the award and cocked his head, regarding the man in front of him with interest.

"What do you want?" he repeated his previous question with increased curiosity.

"I used to be a very skilled fighter, you see, but I killed far too many men. As soon as the war was over, I swore to myself that I would never take another life and have spent my life in penance. But something happened which changed my mind."

Etienne stood quietly, taking in his story.

"You remember Madame Augustine, who helps me with the orphans?"

Etienne nodded his acknowledgment.

"She's Jewish. But you most likely know this, because it was your communist friends who made her new papers and brought her here; for which I will be forever grateful." He paused as if collecting his thoughts. "She has a little daughter, Lili. Augustine lost her husband during the war. The Germans shot him, for being a Jew."

"I'm sorry to hear that," Etienne muttered instinctively.

"I'm telling you all this so that you'll know how much I do not want the same to happen to them. But it will, as soon as the Germans march in here." Father Yves lifted his heavy gaze to Etienne. "I want to be prepared when they come. I want to be able to protect them, in case I have to. And I want your word that you will let me."

Etienne glanced at the door leading to the cellar. "You want to be a part of the cell?"

"Whatever you call it. I want to fight together with your men, communists or not; it doesn't matter. I just want to get rid of the Nazi lot if they show their faces here."

Etienne rubbed his chin, looking the priest up and down with his eyes slightly squinted, appraising him. "We might have another use for you, even though it doesn't involve actual fighting yet."

"Whatever it is, I'm ready."

"Can you get any more of those black cassocks?"

"Why?"

"There are some 'fathers' out there, who got shot down above our zone and desperately need to get to their 'flock' across the Pyrenees. It's them, whom you've been feeding this whole time. You won't have to march with them all the way, just up to the mountains. We don't have a good cover for them, and your attire would be perfect."

Father Yves held his hand out, a satisfied grin on his face. "Consider it done, *Monsieur le Sous-Préfet.*"

"What about your penance, Father?"

"It'll have to wait until the end of the war."

Chapter 20

Dijon, August 1941

"Well, at least we now know what was in those suitcases." Blanche watched as Sievers methodically tapped his finger on top of his sleeve while keeping his arms folded on his chest. "Our armies were advancing so rapidly towards the crumbling Soviet capital, and now one of our major coal supply routes has been blown up to all hell. Berlin has called me more in the past few days than all other times combined since I started my career. I have promised them results and what have I got? The Resistance sabotaging supply routes in the city that has been entrusted me. Fascinating. Fascinating indeed."

His unemotional tone terrified her more than any screaming would. Even if he was indeed furious with her for failing him, he still masterfully concealed his true emotions.

"Blanche. I trusted you. I gave you a chance to work with me because I assumed that you would do anything to prove yourself to me, as a representative of the Reich, your country by blood let me note because you would want to become a rightful citizen eventually. I assumed, and mistakenly as it appears, that you possess a superior intelligence because of your birthright, that you would effortlessly outplay your former countrymen, to show them what you're truly worth so they would regret ever scorning you. Now, I'm starting to wonder if I have any use for you at all, Blanche?"

"What can I do?" she pleaded in a whisper.

Sievers arched his brow in mock curiosity.

"What could you do? Let's see. Not sleep on the train for starters so that no *résistants* can steal your suitcases from under your nose?"

Now she could detect hardly contained fury in his voice. Blanche shriveled under the icy glare of his eyes, lowering her head into her hands.

"I never thought *she* would appear out of nowhere, and especially in the first train car…"

"But she did. Why? Because obviously, she has more brains – or guts – than you. Because it was something important to her, and she wasn't afraid to risk her life for it. Because she's crafty and brave – everything I thought you were. But you're not, and that's why you hate her so, Blanche."

Every word of his hit worse than a lash, lacerating her very heart with their sadistic coldness. Blanche felt hot tears pooling in her eyes and applied all her will towards not allowing them to spill over.

"I'd love to meet her one day," Sievers declared with a strange dreamy note in his voice. Blanche lifted her head and, through the tears distorting her vision, she saw him smile as he stood by the window, looking out at something in the distance. "*Ja,* she seems like a formidable foe, your *Madame Laure*. How I would love to get my hands on her."

"So, do it," Blanche muttered, wiping her eyes angrily. "Go ahead and arrest her. I told you where she lives."

Sievers cringed and looked at her like she was an annoying insect that had ruined his enjoyment of the weather with its incessant pestering.

"You're such a stupid girl, Blanche." He didn't hide a disappointed sigh. "I need to arrest them all at once, on the spot, while they're preparing another diversion. If I arrest her, and even her husband, now, the rest will disappear without a trace, and I'll be left empty-handed again."

"She'll tell you where to look for the rest of them if you..." Blanche bit her lip, a strange gleam appearing in her eyes. "If you interrogate her intensively."

"You mean torture her, *herz?*" Sievers' nostrils twitched ever so slightly. "She won't talk. Women like her don't talk."

"You don't know that," Blanche argued sulkily, fidgeting with the hem of her dress.

Sievers grinned, traced his fingers on top of the windowsill, scowled at the dust that collected on them and took out his handkerchief to wipe them in an irritated manner.

"I'll give you one more chance, Blanche. Only one more. Bring me to her, when she's red-handed and vulnerable. So that I can have her friends and loved ones to threaten her with. So that I have all the cards up my sleeve, you understand? So that she won't be able to back away."

Blanche felt her cheeks flare up at the unconcealed passion in his voice. He sounded like a hunter who would give his life to claim the king of the jungle as his trophy. Apparently, with Sievers, the mere scent of blood excited him, and no matter how twisted and perverse it sounded, Blanche was almost envious of this new obsession, even though the obsession would die as soon as he laid his hands on Laure. With her, all he did was cringe and mock her impotence. Blanche nearly wished to switch places with Laure; for Laure, he felt at least something.

And what if I don't put her in your hands? She had just opened her mouth to say as much but met his gaze, which made her shudder inside. *He wanted that damned Laure. Very well then. She'd bring him to her, and watch him kill her, and laugh.*

Lyon, August 1941

Marcel inhaled sharply as Tommy pulled another thread from his back. He had refused stitches at first, but Tommy was more than insistent on tending to Marcel's wounds in a proper manner. The Brit was cautious when he was cleaning his wounds and stitching the two deepest ones, that much Marcel had to give him. He was just as careful when removing them, or maybe it was because Tommy pressed his lips gently next to each wound that made Marcel's breath catch in his throat.

"I sent a message to London, told them to hold off all on all drops until we scout a new place."

Laying on his stomach in their apartment, Marcel thought of how different Tommy's words and actions were. He kissed him one moment and discussed MI6 matters at the same time as if such behavior was normal. Marcel thoroughly tried to ignore the kisses.

"It'll take us some time," he mused out loud.

"Who cares?" Tommy was his usual nonchalant self. "We have enough supplies for now. A few weeks of not getting any won't do us harm."

"What's the news from London?"

"They asked me if we had anything to do with the Dijon diversion."

"What did you tell them?"

"The truth."

"What did they say?"

"They asked me if we can do another one anytime soon."

Marcel broke into a fit of chuckles together with the Brit and turned his head to face him. Tommy outstretched his hand and brushed the hair away from his face. Marcel turned away at once and heard Tommy sigh inaudibly.

"Did you hear the latest news in regard to our untimely departed forest friends?" The Brit decided to change the subject.

"The gendarmes? They found them? Are we in trouble?" Marcel shifted on his elbow, visibly concerned.

Tommy grinned and shook his head. "Not at all. Apparently, it seemed like an open and shut case to them, whoever led the investigation. The papers also unanimously decided that all the blame went to us, the Brits, who dropped 'all that nonsense' from the sky, which, instead of helping the French folk, killed them. They thought the gendarmes found the case while patrolling the forest, tried opening it and – a very unfortunate accident happened. No one suspected even for a second that someone else could have been with them."

"Lucky us," Marcel commented, lowering back down onto his bed.

Tommy nodded in agreement and returned to his task of tending to Marcel's wounds.

"It was a very admirable thing what your sister did. Stealing those suitcases from under that girl's nose."

Marcel was relieved when the Brit changed the subject.

"Yes, it was. Giselle doesn't trust her. Neither do I."

"Why did you hire her then?"

"It wasn't me. *The Chief* did. There were circumstances... Well, let's just say, he had no choice."

"Hm," Tommy grumbled his disapproval and started rubbing something cool which smelt of herbs on top of Marcel's healing wounds. "She's a great girl, your sister. A real tough cookie."

"She likes you too." Marcel smiled, trying not to melt under the gentle strokes of Tommy's fingertips. "And she doesn't like anybody."

"I don't like anyone either. Except for you." Marcel tried to let the insinuation pass. Tommy snorted softly and added, "And your sister. She talks in her sleep, you know."

"How would you know?"

"I couldn't sleep that night we spent at their place. She kept repeating the same name again and again."

Marcel kept his face buried in the pillow without acknowledging the Brit's words.

"You're not going to ask me the name?"

"I know it already." Marcel's voice was muffled by the pillow. "Karl."

"Sounds German."

"That's what he was."

"A lost love?"

"More of an exorcised demon."

"What a fascinating comparison," Tommy noted. "Only, not so exorcised, if she keeps talking to him in her sleep, eh?"

Marcel was quiet for some time, before speaking so quietly that Tommy could barely hear him. "Some demons have to be killed twice, I suppose."

Dijon, September 1941

Dijon still smelled of summer, warm asphalt, and an earthy breeze. The local *feldgendarmes* were busy supervising the prisoners who were entrusted with the task of removing all of the *V* letters that had been marked on the walls of the city during the brave act of sabotage executed by the *résistants*. The sabotage was praised not only in local underground newspapers but even on the prohibited BBC radio channel. Skinny, unkempt children eyed the prisoners from around a corner, only to put more *V*'s on walls with white chalk as soon as they had moved to a new spot, together with a cross that had become the national symbol of the Resistance.

Giselle's mind, however, seemed to be a thousand miles away for she failed to notice all this, or at least it appeared as such to Philippe who was walking next to her. He wondered why he had to almost drag her out to the street for a Sunday stroll; before, she used to love being outside. Lately, she'd been far too quiet and subdued, and surprisingly unwilling to leave their apartment.

Her hand caught his suddenly, pulling him close.

"Can you do something for me?" her urgent whisper murmured next to his ear. "Stop right now, stand before me, put your hands on my waist, kiss me and look above my head right after, but do it discretely, will you?"

Philippe was more than surprised with the unexpected request but complied nevertheless, stepping in front of her and hugging her just like she had asked.

"You see anyone suspicious?" Giselle's whisper caressed his neck.

Philippe pressed his mouth to her hair, smelling the lavender soap he had bought for her for ridiculous money on the black market, and slid his gaze over the street as inconspicuously as possible.

"No."

"Anyone at all?"

"No. No one."

Giselle let out what sounded like a disappointed grunt. Philippe released her as if sensing her mood, and the two resumed their stroll.

"Who was I supposed to see?" Philippe inquired, noticing a scowl creasing her brow.

"I don't know. No one, I hope."

He caught her hand and pressed it gently as if asking her to trust him with her doubts.

"I'm just paranoid. Don't pay attention to me."

"I can't. Now that you told me this, I'll be paranoid too," Philippe replied jokingly.

They walked in silence for some time, until she pulled him into an alley by the canal, where the trees formed a shadowy natural arch above their heads.

"I've had this feeling for some time now," Giselle resumed the conversation, not forgetting to glance over her shoulder once again. "Like someone's following me all the time. I swear, I feel someone's presence near me, right behind my back, like a constant pair of eyes are boring into my back as soon as I step out. But no matter how carefully I look, I can't seem to notice anyone who could possibly be following me. Do you think I'm slowly going insane because of all this subterfuge, that I'm only imagining Gestapo agents dogging my every step?"

Philippe felt an urge to throw a glance behind them as well but willed himself not to. Giselle had never been a particularly overly-cheerful person, and was prone to dark, melancholy moods; but back in Paris she had at least been a society dame, a celebrated novelist with high standing friends and well-established connections, which in its turn allowed her to be much more carefree, laughing off all dangers in an admirable manner. Ever since they fled Paris, Philippe hardly saw her smile at all. She smoked a lot, bit into her stained, broken nails angrily and waved off all his attempts to penetrate the walls around her private world that she had so carefully erected.

"It's just the money issue, *comrade*," she even mocked him intentionally, just to disguise her true feelings. "I grew up in poverty, and I swore to myself that I would never be poor again. And look at me now, even worse than when I was a student at the Sorbonne and as poor as a church mouse. At least back then I had a dream. But why do I even bother saying this to you? You wouldn't understand anyway, with your *everything-for-the-masses* ideas."

She would shake her head bitterly, take another drag on her cigarette, cough and look out of the dirty window. Philippe would only sigh and leave her alone.

"How long have you had this feeling?" Even if she was paranoid, Philippe decided to indulge her with his question.

"A couple of months."

He frowned. For some reason, he had expected her to say, *ever since we came here from Paris*. This didn't seem like paranoia anymore; more like a gut feeling, and gut feelings were something Philippe had learned to trust, ever from the moment he had enlisted in the International Brigades during the Spanish Civil War.

"What about when you're at home?" he asked her.

"I feel safe at home. Especially when you're there with me."

He couldn't suppress a radiant smile from appearing on his face. He should be used to Mademoiselle Giselle Legrand always being full of surprises and the most unpredictable of mood shifts - which, no doubt, had enthralled far too many men in Paris - yet, she never ceased to amaze him.

"I'm with you now," he replied softly.

"I still feel someone staring at me."

This time Philippe turned. The emerald alley stood empty and silent.

"There's no one there, Giselle."

She made a dismissive gesture with a graceful flick of her wrist. "I told you I was only paranoid. Don't listen to me then."

Philippe lowered his head and followed her in tense silence. Neither of them noticed the man who stepped from behind a tree trunk, fixed his hat and disappeared back into the shadows.

Chapter 21

Lyon, October 1941

Etienne sipped his sherry, nodding his agreement to everything Raimond Bouillon suggested. He had to nod, and with as much enthusiasm as he could muster; after all, if he faked enough compliance and the fervor of a collaborator, there would be more chance that the Prefect of Lyon Bouillon would leave the whole enterprise in his hands without any additional supervision. Sabotaging it would then be a piece of cake.

"The *Wehrmacht's* advance slowed down considerably when they were almost at the doors of Moscow." Bouillon swirled the liquor in his glass, his sapphire cufflink sparkling with every movement of his wrist. "Our German partners need our support more than ever now. You assured them not too long ago in Paris that they can count on our assistance as soon as they ask for it, and now is the perfect time to put ourselves at their disposal. With our support, they will take the Soviet capital, they will make the Soviets sign the capitulation, and I have already been promised – but it's a secret matter so far, so, please, I ask you not to discuss it with anyone until everything is settled – that the permit to open the new Bouillon Works will be granted to me on the territory of a newly conquered Soviet protectorate. If you help me achieve this, you'll get your share in the whole business affair, of course. The Germans are very generous when it comes to their partners, and there are so many business opportunities in the Soviet protectorate, that we will both be swimming in money."

Etienne concealed the expression of his blue eyes with his long, dark eyelashes and looked down at the table nonchalantly. No need for Bouillon to notice even a speck of defiance in them. Instead, he looked at his immaculately polished black shoes made of the finest patent leather, stroked the soft material of the tailor-made pin-striped suit that he was wearing, took in the elegant luxury of the drawing room of his family house, in which he had invited Bouillon to, for he wasn't sure that he could bear to witness the travesty of what this *nouveau-riche* had done to his family friend's mansion a second time, and calmly admitted to himself that he didn't mind losing it all, as long as his conscience was clean. That was the difference between them: Etienne had been raised with morals, with an almost romantic idea of sacrificing himself for the better cause, with the aloof serenity of a future martyr – it didn't matter whether he was a diplomat or an officer. Raimond Bouillon loved his money and would spring a rope for anyone who threatened to take it away from him.

Etienne took another sip from his crystal glass. "You can fully count on me. How exactly can I be of service?"

Bouillon beamed, his round cheeks reflecting a healthy, pink glow from the fireplace that had been lit up early that year. The autumn was particularly cold, but Etienne couldn't help but gloat when reading the news on the Eastern front in the newspapers. In Russia, the snow had already fallen, catching the whole of the German army, in their summer uniforms, unaware.

"Splendid! They need wooden planks for their tanks. The dirt and muck on the Soviet roads are so deep that they get stuck, and, what's worse, when all that mess freezes overnight, the heavy machinery freezes in its tracks as well. I need you to supervise the first shipment of wood that goes to the front from Lyon. Fill up the whole train, all the freight cars you can use. I want them to see that we won't spare anything for the victory."

For the victory, bien sûr. All the while, our French citizens are chopping up their furniture to warm their houses, Etienne thought. He gulped more of the finest Spanish Madeira after raising his glass in a toast.

"I'll go see Morel from Morel Woodworks first thing tomorrow morning. I'll tell him that not a single wooden board will leave his premises until he fills up our train to the brim."

"And please, mind the route you choose, I beg of you. After what happened in Dijon... The Germans can offer some of their men to watch the tracks. All you have to do is ask."

"No need. Nothing will happen to their precious wood, you have my word," Etienne promised, hiding his eyes once again.

"I knew I could count on you, Etienne." Bouillon held out his hand, and Etienne shook it firmly, trying not to show his disgust. "And know that you can count on me also. I never forget favors, and I return them gladly."

"I'll keep that in mind."

They were getting closer to the mountains, Yves could tell. Gusts of wind tore into their black robes, flapping the cloth against their legs, which were numb from exhaustion, and slowing them down with each passing hour. They had been on the road since early morning, after getting off the last station the train reached. The rest of the way had to be on foot.

His new charges, five sturdy airmen that Jules had entrusted into his care at the orphanage, some of whom didn't even speak French, trailed patiently behind him, dressed in black cassocks. The enthusiasm that they had displayed when Yves first met them, had long been exhausted. Even as they neared the escape route that would take them back home, their spirits didn't seem to lift.

Yves stopped and checked his compass. This was his second expedition, and he was grateful for the military training that allowed him to easily navigate his way through unknown terrain; nevertheless, he preferred to double check his coordinates now and then to ensure that they didn't veer off the correct path.

"How much longer?" one of the downed airmen asked in English, his comrade translating his words to Yves.

"About four hours."

A collective groan echoed through the group.

"Can we take a break at least?"

"In this cold?" Yves raised his brow, regarding the youngest of the pilots with skepticism. "Do you want to catch pneumonia? We need to move without stopping, son. When we get to the hut, you'll get a nice warm meal and a very hot iron stove to warm yourselves by. So now, man up and stop your whining. You're shaming your celebrated air force with your nancy-boy attitude."

The young pilot blinked a couple of times, clearly not expecting a dressing down from a priest who spoke more like a drill sergeant back in his base, and mumbled a quiet *"yessir"* out of habit. They resumed their walking when the same British fellow, who could not communicate in French, said something excitedly. Yves shifted his gaze to where he was pointing and understood everything without translation. A military car had appeared on the horizon and was approaching them quickly, the Vichy police markings soon revealing themselves, much to everyone's horror.

"Don't move and don't say a word, any of you," Yves warned them quietly, clasping his hands in front of him and stepping towards the vehicle. "Let me do all the talking."

"We all have guns," the young boy whispered, while the car slowed as it approached them. "There's only four of them. We can outshoot them."

"And then what?" Yves hissed, barely moving his lips, watching the patrolmen getting out. "We're in the middle of nowhere, four hours away from the nearest shelter. If they don't come back to their base within a couple of hours, their comrades will send a reconnaissance mission, and we're all done for. Shut up and let me do the talking, I said. And don't you dare do anything stupid."

The four Vichy gendarmes held their weapons in sight, with visible hesitation. Yves took on a compliant expression, calmly waiting for their leader to approach their group. The leader's gun pointed to the ground, he noticed. Maybe their good Catholic faith would do him a favor that day; the men were clearly apprehensive to point their weapons at a rather peaceful looking group of priests.

"Good day, fathers."

"Good day, my son," Yves replied in the soft manner he always adopted while listening to confessions.

"May I ask as to where you're heading, fathers?" the leader, a man in his early forties asked, giving each man of the cloth an evaluating look up and down.

"They're not fathers yet." Yves motioned his head to the young men behind him, huddling together meekly. "They're merely seminary students. I'm the only ordained minister here. It's almost their graduation, but before that, they must pass their last test to show their dedication to the Lord. They need to spend a week in silence, away from civilization, and that's exactly where we're heading – to a hut near the mountains. If upon completing this final task they feel that the strength of their faith has grown, they will become ordained ministers as well. For some, such a demand can be too much, and they return to their civilian life. I hope you forgive them for they cannot talk to you for the reason I just explained."

The leader of the Vichy police squad looked at him askance. Yves patiently waited for him to allow them to pass.

"This route is known among the *résistants,* who take downed British airmen through the Pyrenees to Spain and from there back to Britain, Father. That's why we patrol it."

"I assure you, I haven't seen any *résistants* or any British airmen here." Yves allowed himself a little smile.

The policeman grinned as well, but only with a corner of his mouth.

"Let them go, Jacques." One of his comrades beckoned the police leader, stepping forward. "They are priests, can't you see?"

Jacques, however, didn't seem persuaded, much to Yves's annoyance.

"And how can I be sure of that?"

"I've never seen résistants dressing up as priests," the second policeman continued, catching his comrade's sleeve. "Leave them be."

"Maybe it's a new ploy that they've adopted," Jacques said, looking Yves squarely in the eye. "Would explain why the boys can't talk. Maybe they're Brits."

"Test me then." Yves held out his small, leather-bound Bible with worn out corners to the leader of the squad. "If I really am a Resistance fighter, I won't be able to quote the Bible. Open it on any page and ask me what a certain passage says. If I reply correctly, you will have your answer as to what we are: men of the church or partisans."

Jacques looked at the Bible in Yves's hand for a few moments, then shrugged and took it in his.

"*Bien,* Father. Let's see." He flipped the yellowish pages. "Genesis 4:7. What does it say?"

"If you do what is right, will you not be accepted? But if you do not do what is right, sin is crouching at your door; it desires to have you, but you must rule over it." Yves looked at his feet with a subtle smile.

The leader of the police squad nodded his appreciation and opened a different page.

"James 1:2-4."

"Consider it pure joy, my brothers and sisters, whenever you face trials of many kinds because you know that the testing of your faith produces perseverance. Let perseverance finish its work so that you may be mature and complete, not lacking anything."

"Leviticus 26:6?"

"I will grant peace in the land, and you will lie down and no one will make you afraid. I will remove wild beasts from the land, and the sword will not pass through your country," Yves quoted, regarding the leader of the police with a strange gleam in his eyes. "God truly works in mysterious ways, don't you find? How befitting those passages are to our current situation."

The leader of the squad scowled as the second policeman took the Bible from his comrade's hands and handed it back to Yves, bowing his head before him. "Forgive us, Father."

"You don't have to apologize, my son. You're only doing your job." Yves took the Holy Book from him.

The leader of the squad gave him a last appraising look, then tipped his hat and turned around to leave. "Have a safe trip, Father."

Yves nodded and drew a sign of the cross in the air. The leader's comrade whispered "thank you" and hurried away after his friend. In a few minutes, the truck disappeared in the same direction from where it had come from.

"That was close." The youngest of the airmen wiped his brow which was now covered with sweat, despite the cold temperature. "Are you really a priest then?"

"No. Just a sharpshooter with a photographic memory." Yves grinned crookedly and started walking towards the mountains once more, the pale sheen of their peaks barely visible in the distance.

Dijon, October 1941

Clouds of cigarette smoke lingered heavily in the living room where the five *résistants* sat in a tight circle around a map of the city, an overflowing ashtray pressing the southern part of it down.

"Right here we'll hit them." Arthur pointed to an object on the map.

He, Marcel and Tommy, who refused to stay in Lyon and miss another diversion, had just returned from the place that they were currently studying on the map and were meeting with Giselle to discuss their next move. They had gone there in the daylight, strolling casually with their hands in their pockets, and walked right past the uniformed German patrol without causing any suspicion... After all, what Resistance fighters in their right mind would scout the future location of a mission in broad daylight?

"Will you have enough time to leave after you place the bomb?" Philippe asked the demolition expert.

"The bomb will have a pencil-timer detonator, so yes. Don't worry about my well-being. I promise, getting killed by my own bomb isn't in my plan." The Brit chuckled good-naturedly.

"Did we agree on the day when that big shipment of wood will be passing through? What does *the Chief* say about that?" Giselle turned to Marcel.

"*The Chief* says, blow the whole thing up." Marcel shifted his position and winced at the pain that shot through his thigh, which hadn't completely healed yet. "The greater the damage, the better."

"Isn't he worried, after we blew up the tracks the last time?" Giselle lowered her voice.

"I suppose he knows what he's doing." Marcel shrugged. "That's why he's *the Chief*."

"That wood shipment couldn't come at a better time." Arthur tapped his pencil on top of the map. "The Huns will never know what hit them."

"And *where* it will hit them," Tommy said with an impish grin.

"The Gestapo are all over the train tracks." Giselle slid a finger along the top of the narrow railroad on the map. "They will definitely send agents there several days before *the Chief* sends that shipment."

"Let them send them." Arthur winked at her. "Better for us."

"Do you think it'll work?"

"It'll work. The plan is perfect," Philippe reassured her.

"Are you going to use that same girl to bring the explosives into town?" Arthur inquired. "That... What's her name? Lucille?"

"Lucienne." Philippe nodded. "Yes, we'll use her. And this time Giselle will be so kind as to not intercept the suitcases."

Giselle seemingly ignored the pointed look Philippe shot her. Instead, she got up to her feet and addressed Tommy with a smile.

"Will you help me with something in the kitchen, Tom?"

"It'll be my pleasure." The Brit courteously bowed his head and followed her to the kitchen, where she stopped near the window.

Outside, it was raining torrents, streaks of water sliding down the dusty glass, leaving muddied traces in their wake.

Tommy's wide grin disappeared as soon as he saw a deep scowl settling over Giselle's pale face as she contemplated something. Tree branches were clawing at the leaded windowpane dangerously close to her face, illuminated from time to time by bursts of lightning.

"What is it?" he whispered, abandoning his usual playful persona as he stepped closer to her.

"Can I ask you for a favor, Tom?"

He didn't like the cold, determined look in her green eyes.

"It depends."

"I can see you care for my little brother a lot." She adopted a new tactic, and her grin was immediately reflected on the young Brit's face. Giselle caught his fingers and Tommy gladly returned the gentle press of her hand, reading definite approval in both her smile and the intimate way in which she held his hand. "You wouldn't want anything to happen to him, would you?"

"Of course not."

Giselle nodded and leaned towards his ear, making use of the background noise provided by the violent storm outside. Not one of their comrades could hear them conspire together. "Then do what I will ask you to. No one else will be able to do it except you, without him suspecting something."

"Does it have anything to do with our plan?"

Giselle fell silent for some time but then placed one hand on top of Tommy's shoulder and whispered something in his ear, his frown deepening with each word.

"Are you sure?" he demanded breathlessly after she stepped away. He refused to release her hand as if it would stop her from executing her suicidal plan.

The resolute look in her eyes was his answer. He lowered his gaze, chewed on his upper lip angrily and then suddenly brought her hand to his lips and kissed it; for his Marcel, for all of them.

"Thank you," she said with obvious relief.

"No, thank you," Tommy said, imprinting her face in his memory. Who knew if he would see her again, after this day.

Chapter 22

Blanche kept twisting the end of her coat belt in her gloved hands, feverish anticipation growing in her with each passing minute. Another train station disappeared from behind the window, the third one she had passed in the Occupied Zone. They had crossed the Demarcation Line a long time ago, and Blanche couldn't help but throw a plain-clothed man sitting on the bench across the aisle a helpless look when no one appeared in the doors of their train car after yet another stop. But, the plain-clothed man, who Sievers had sent to accompany her, appeared to be much more patient than she was.

She has to show up. Blanche clenched her hands into fists to prevent them from trembling and bore her unseeing gaze towards the view outside, counting the minutes until the next station.

Twenty minutes later the train started to slow down, and Blanche's breath caught in her chest, the air tingling in her lungs with every short, shallow breath. She clenched the suitcases between her legs and refused to let her gaze wander away from the doors.

"Salut."

Blanche jumped at the familiar, mocking voice. She had surprised her again, damned Laure, who had come to her from the direction behind her and slid onto the bench right next to her this time. Who knew for how long she had ridden on the train; maybe she'd even sat behind Blanche's back and delighted in her nervous shifting and the way she had craned her neck each time the train made a new stop. Blanche pinched her lips in fury, while Laure studied her reddening face with her usual sardonic expression. *Don't worry; soon he'll wipe that arrogant grin off your face,* Blanche thought to herself and sneered.

"What a pleasure it is to see you again, Laure. I was counting on this meeting."

"Oh, I have no doubt that you did, *ma chérie*. How could I possibly disappoint you?"

Blanche laughed vacantly, noticing the time on the small watch with a golden face that Sievers had given her for her birthday. The train would leave in five minutes sharp; Laure would most likely try to get off with the suitcases right before it did. That left them some time for talking, and, oh, how many things Blanche had to tell her!

"You think you're so smart, don't you?" she began in a low voice, as Laure calmly pulled the suitcases out from under her legs and arranged them by her own feet. "You think that you're better than everyone else."

"No. I think I'm smarter than you, but not better. If we had had more time to become acquainted, you would have soon come to the conclusion that I'm not a good person."

The reply, offered in an impassive, leveled tone, infuriated Blanche.

"You're not smarter than me, Laure. And do you know why? Had you been, you wouldn't be sitting here next to me right now. Isn't it the first rule that Jules teaches every recruit? Predictability kills. One always has to strike where it's least expected. I'm surprised that you, being such good friends with him, or whatever it is that you are to each other, didn't pay attention to such wise words. They might have saved your life."

The train's whistle shrilled, the conductor announcing that it would leave in three minutes. Laure, for some reason, didn't rush towards the exit. Instead, she remained in her place with a mysterious grin on her face.

"Remember the last time I told you to go home, Lucienne?" she said. "You should have listened to me. You should have gone home while you could."

"You're not in a position to threaten me, Laure," Blanche started haughtily.

"Do you still think you will be able to get out of the mess you put yourself in?"

"I'm not afraid of your friends either." Blanche gave her a dismissive shrug.

Laure shook her head slowly, with a look about her that shattered Blanche's newfound confidence, much to her dismay.

"It's not my friends who you should be afraid of. You should be afraid of the one who recruited you. The one who gave you all those pearls, and that new coat, and your new golden watch."

Blanche pulled away from her, scowling. *How could she possibly know?*

"Oh, I knew all along. Would you like to know the very first thing that gave you away? You shouldn't have repeated quotes, the origins of which were unknown to you. And the rest... The rest was far too easy to guess. I'm a woman too; you think I didn't notice the very first golden bracelet, that you, a poor *girl-résistante,* started sporting all of a sudden?" Laure cast a knowing look in her direction. "I was engaged to one of them. They can be very chivalrous, the Germans. And very generous; when they need something, that is."

"He loves me," Blanche hissed.

"He was only using you, you silly thing." Laure got up, picked up both suitcases and turned around. "You better pray that his people kill me first, Lucienne. Because if they don't, I'll come back for you, and it won't be an easy death."

Blanche laughed with intentional loudness, but mirth was absent from her voice. She watched the plain-clothed man follow Laure to the exit, watched Laure step off the train, and rushed to the window across the aisle to press her face to it in excitement. Several uniformed men appeared out of nowhere and surrounded the woman. Blanche couldn't contain an elated gasp when she noticed Sievers himself among them; he had most likely ridden on the same train so he could be personally present during the arrest. Blanche hurried to the platform to stand by his side.

Laure didn't appear taken aback by the ambush and stood in place with a tranquil half-smile on her face. Blanche carefully observed Sievers as he approached Laure, scrutinizing her with greedy fascination.

"Madame Laure Vignon, I suppose?" He spoke in a mild voice, tilting his head slightly. "SD Standartenführer Jürgen Sievers, at your service, Madame."

He clicked his heels. Laure placed both suitcases at her feet and held out her hand to him. Blanche watched in amazement as he took it, almost with reverence, and shook it gently. The surrealism of the scene seemed to confuse his men as much as it did her; however, they didn't betray their incredulity in any way, likely too used to fully trusting their commander's judgment.

"It is my pleasure to make your acquaintance, Herr Sievers. May I ask if there's a problem?"

He beamed, seemingly delighted with her, and eyed the suitcases with interest.

"Would you be so kind as to open your luggage for us, Madame Vignon?" he asked her in the most courteous of manners. "I'm afraid my informant has labeled you as a known Resistance fighter. It is my duty to my country to check every such lead. I hope you won't hold it against me."

Blanche's stomach twisted and churned when he didn't grace her with even a single look, but merely flicked a wrist in her direction. *An informant. Was that all she was to him?*

Laure glanced at Blanche with a hard, triumphant look. *Didn't I tell you so?* It read in her green, cat-like eyes.

"Not at all, Herr Sievers." Poised and dignified, Laure extracted the keys from her purse and held them out to Sievers. Her hands were steady.

He motioned one of his men to open the luggage, nearly holding his breath in anticipation, and then suddenly burst into laughter upon seeing the contents. Blanche stepped forward, not believing her eyes. Both suitcases were full of men's clothes.

Having gotten his laughter under control, Sievers pressed one hand to his heart, nodded several times and started clapping. Laure merely lowered her head, trying to conceal her smile. Blanche went completely pale observing them both.

"Madame Vignon, I must say, you're a fascinating opponent, the likes of which I've never met in my entire career."

"*Merci*, Monsieur Sievers. I'm truly flattered."

"You wouldn't be so kind as to inform me of the whereabouts of the real suitcases? The ones with the explosives?"

Laure shook her head with the same sweet smile. "I'm afraid I don't know what you're talking about."

"Of course, you don't." Sievers stepped aside, gesturing Laure towards the exit. "Won't you come with me, please. We have a lot to discuss."

Laure followed him without any display of resistance. Blanche trailed after them; her nerves were strained like a guitar cord.

Inside his car, Sievers continued to ignore her, condescendingly telling Blanche to ride next to the driver in the front while he slid into the back seat together with Laure. Blanche glared at them through the large rearview mirror.

"Would you like some cognac perhaps? I'm sorry, I don't have any glasses."

Sievers offered his silver flask, with an eagle holding a swastika wreath engraved on its face, to the woman next to him. She regarded the offering for a moment, took it in her hand and took a hearty swig from it, much to his pleasure.

"Danke, mein Herr."

Sievers beamed.

"You speak German, Madame?"

"Just a little."

"I've been watching you for some time."

"I know."

"You noticed my man?" Sievers cocked his head curiously. "No one has ever noticed him before. He's one of my best assets. We call him 'The Shadow'."

"No, Herr Sievers; I never saw him. I felt him though. And, besides, your little *informant* was careless enough to display all of the presents you awarded her with for her service. It wasn't hard to guess where it all was coming from. The French are all poor nowadays. Only you, *Herren,* have money."

Blanche turned around to defend herself, but Sievers shot her such a glare that she thought better of it.

"I would like to know your real name, Madame Vignon." His tone softened at once as soon as he addressed his captive.

"Laure Vignon," she said with assured confidence.

"Laure Vignon," Sievers mimicked softly. "And you know nothing of the suitcases with the explosives."

"I'm only a poor working factory girl, Herr Sievers. What would I know of such matters?"

"Oh, no, you're by no means a factory girl, Madame Vignon. Your speech, the manner in which you hold yourself... You're one of us, Madame. Part of the upper class. Not one of the masses." The admiration in his voice was apparent.

"Those whose lives are impoverished, the weak, impoverish life even more; those whose lives are rich, the strong..."

"...enrich it," she finished after him. *"The former are life's parasites, the latter its benefactors... How is it even possible to confound them?"*

"I knew you would know your Nietzsche, Madame. Now you truly have my utmost respect."

"I knew a man who used to quote it quite a lot," she replied pensively. "Sometimes we had night-long discussions about Nietzsche's philosophy."

"A German? Anyone I know, perhaps?"

"Could be. He's no longer with us, I'm afraid. Died of a rather unfortunate accident." She turned to the German, her eyes sparkling emerald green with emotion. "Unfortunately, you won't be able to win with me. We're both strong people, Herr Sievers. So, where does that leave us?"

"I wish to have you as a friend, Madame Vignon, not my enemy. Work with me. Say the word, and together we'll be unstoppable."

"A very alluring proposition, Herr Sievers, and especially in my current situation. However, I'm afraid I must decline."

"Why? Patriotic duty? Morality? Ethical reasons? But they are signs of weakness, and we have just spoken of how we are both strong, Madame! Only the strong survive, those who don't burden themselves with such notions, those who crave power, those who deny the very notion of altruism and self-sacrifice..."

"What if you're mistaken on account of my reasons, Herr Sievers?" She squinted her eyes, an enigmatic smile playing on her lips. "What if I have no morals in me whatsoever, and no desire to do my patriotic duty? What if I only want to prove myself as *the strongest*, and kill you all?"

"But you should recognize when it is time to admit defeat then, Madame. Because your fight is all but over."

"I'm afraid to disappoint you, but I think it is *you* who are defeated. You still don't have the suitcases you so desire and know nothing of the place where, let's say, a possible diversion might happen."

Sievers laughed softly. "You are one fascinating woman, Madame Vignon. Please, tell me where the suitcases are. I'll grant you a pardon; I give you my word."

"I can't tell you something I know nothing about."

"For some reason, I suspect that I will be hearing the same reply from you for the next forty-eight hours. *Ja,* I saw you note the time on the station clock. Forty-eight hours during which you will exert your willpower, to allow your men to proceed with their operation and disappear without a trace. Do you think you'll be able to hold out for so long? I would hate for anything to happen to you."

"Don't torture me then."

"I have never laid a finger on a woman in my life, Madame, and never will. My men, however, are an entirely different case."

"It will be a very long forty-eight hours then," she murmured with strange aloofness.

"As soon as we arrive at the prison, or at any point in your interrogation, just say the word, and it will stop. I'll come and get you, we'll sit upstairs in my office, have some coffee, and you'll tell me everything, in a civilized manner. No need to sacrifice yourself, Madame. I already know that you're targeting the tracks. I have my men all over them. Your friends will only end up getting arrested and executed, together with you. Save yourself, Madame. Accept my offer, I beg of you."

"You're very persuasive, Herr Sievers. Now I see why this silly girl in the front seat fell under your spell."

"Just say the word, Laure." His words came out in an almost seductive whisper.

She regarded him, took in his icy-blue eyes with fire dancing in them, outstretched her hand and grinned at him crookedly. "Can I have some more of that fine cognac of yours?"

Sievers handed her the flask and watched her gulp it down, admiring her exquisite profile and the silent desperation in which her throat moved with every new gulp.

Blanche sobbed silently in the front seat, wiping bitter tears away with the back of her hand, as if it was her who was heading to the Gestapo prison.

Chapter 23

Giselle stole a last glance at the simple white clock above the entrance of the narrow corridor, its walls painted green, smelling of fear and death. They'd driven for a miserable twenty minutes only, which meant that for forty-seven hours and forty minutes she would have to endure whatever the Gestapo agents' sick, inventive minds were capable of. The worst part of it all was that she wouldn't be able to trace the time anymore; inside the damp, concrete cell, smelling of old rot, to which they had brought her, there was no such luxury as wall clocks. Only desperation and agony, imprinted into the silence of it; into a single chair in the middle of it, with iron cuffs designed to hold the prisoner in place; into a small tank of water, still bearing the metallic scent of blood left from the previous occupant; into the small table laden with metal thongs, a hammer, a blowtorch, and God knows what else, laid out neatly on top of a pristine white cloth. Giselle commended the meticulousness of the Germans but clenched her teeth as hard as she could while they cuffed her to the chair, telling herself not to start openly shaking, so she might save face and keep her dignity for another useless minute.

Sievers stood in the door with his arms folded on his chest, observing the preparations with a deep scowl. As soon as one of his agents picked up a hammer, he stepped towards him and said something quietly in German. The agent replied with a curt nod and the usual *"Jawohl"* and placed the instrument down. Giselle looked stubbornly in front of herself, counting seconds in her mind with feverish obsession, just to distract herself from what was going on around her. Noticing that her fingers dug into the handles of the chair against her will, she forced herself to relax them.

She wasn't good with handling pain and knowing that fact didn't help at all. The memory of Karl's stern, handsome face flashed through her mind, as consciousness itself nudged her and began pushing her off her intended path, whispering its weak and disgusting solutions with its shaking voice. *'Accept Sievers' offer. Karl merely played with you back then, hardly bruised you, if he did at all, and you were screaming bloody murder from that single touch. Do you really think you will be able to endure hours of torture? You're too weak. Surrender all this Resistance business. You're a writer and should have stayed one. You write about fighting and heroes, but you aren't one. You're only a woman and a woman who can't handle pain. He'll release you, you'll see. He recognized a kindred spirit in you. Maybe he won't even ask you to work against your countrymen. Maybe he'll just keep you around for his pleasure, instead of that silly Lucienne girl. He's not too fond of her, and you know it. How is it different from securing a well-connected lover back in peaceful times? Agree, for now, play with him, deceive him later how you deceived Karl... Kill him maybe, when the chance presents itself.'*

Because I will need to answer his questions first. Because my safety will mean that Marcel, Philippe and the rest of our cell will get arrested and executed. And I would never be able to live with that on my conscience.

She caught Sievers' gaze on her. *Just one word,* he implored her silently with his attentive, pale-blue eyes. Giselle forced a lopsided grin to appear on her face in response and shook her head slowly.

He looked at his feet for a moment, turned on his heel and headed towards the exit. At the outer door, he paused, said something to his men, again in German, and walked out without looking at Giselle. The door closed after him, and Giselle's eyes met the heavy gaze of a tall, uniformed agent, who stepped towards her. The second one lit a cigarette, having perched on the edge of the table nonchalantly.

"Herr Standartenführer gave explicit directions not to touch your face," he announced in perfect French. "Which means I will have to work with other areas."

With those words, he grabbed the collar of her dress and tore it open, a thin cotton slip under it following suit.

"Can I borrow your cigarette, Helmut?" He turned to his comrade.

"By all means."

Giselle inhaled a full chest of hot, sticky air and held it tight, while the man in front of her blew on the cigarette tip, heating it even more. Her scream reverberated through the walls of the cell but nothing could overpower the sickening sound of searing ashes burning through the skin on her chest. Only forty-seven hours and thirty minutes left.

The man on Philippe's doorstep smiled pleasantly, even after flipping his military ID open and announcing in a calm voice, "SD, Amt IV."

No name, only the organization he worked for. *The Gestapo*. Philippe rubbed his eyes, red from lack of sleep, and assessed the man from head to toe. The German, dressed in an immaculately tailored dark navy suit under a black cashmere coat, appeared to be alone. He stood patiently, waiting for an invitation to be invited in. Philippe shrugged, realizing that he didn't have much choice, and stepped aside, gesturing his guest inside.

The German, who didn't bother introducing himself, had a face that was pleasant enough yet he seemed to possess indistinguishable features which would be impossible to remember or to describe. He was of a medium height and build, and his age could be anything from early thirties to late forties. He was clean-shaven, poised and, so far, extremely well-mannered. Philippe offered him a seat in the kitchen, and the German accepted it with grace, seemingly not deterred or offended by Philippe's more than humble living quarters.

"Monsieur Alain Vignon, if I'm not mistaken?"

Philippe barely detected an accent in his voice.

"Yes. How can I help you?"

"Oh, I think it's me who quite possibly can help you, Monsieur Vignon." The German offered him another subtle smile, and placed his hat on his lap, folding his hands next to it. "Would you care to guess why I had to pay you a visit today?"

Philippe had returned from his night shift earlier that day, after waiting for Giselle for over an hour next to the factory's entrance and slowly came to the painful realization that she had disappeared again, likely pursuing another reckless plan which she didn't wish to share with him. First, it was that rotten affair with Karl that landed them here in Dijon with false papers; then the suitcases and Lucienne... Philippe was afraid to think what she could have possibly involved herself with this time. He had arrived home to smoke one cigarette after another, pacing around their apartment and hoping that the door would open any minute and she would come in, and mock him for his worrisome nature. Instead of her, though, a German had appeared, and that fact alone wasn't a good sign. The suitcases, which Lucienne was supposed to bring to their place, were also absent, together with Lucienne. As to Marcel and Arthur's whereabouts, Philippe preferred to not even think.

"Do you mind if I smoke?" he asked the German, patting his pockets in search of his pack.

The German noticed his futile attempts to locate his cigarettes and generously opened his cigarette case to Philippe.

"Where is your wife, Monsieur Vignon?" It was a simple question, spoken in a mild voice, but it made the blood rush to Philippe's head at once.

"I don't know," he replied, at last, not knowing what else to say.

"Would you like to know?"

Philippe swallowed with difficulty, got up and went to the sink to fill a metal, enamel mug with tap water. He downed it all and turned back to his guest, who was observing him with mild curiosity.

"Yes. Very much."

"You care for her, don't you?"

They didn't know they weren't really husband and wife then. At least their identities were still safe. Philippe breathed out with relief. "Of course, I do. She's my wife after all."

"*Gut*. This simplifies my task. You see, your wife was arrested this morning by our people. We have been watching your cell for quite some time, and are aware of the diversion that you have been so carefully preparing."

Philippe listened to him silently, without denying or acknowledging anything.

"Madame Vignon is being interrogated as we speak," the German continued, carefully watching Philippe's reaction.

Philippe clasped the mug in his hand with such force that if it were made of glass, he would have probably crushed it. He kept his face impassive.

"You've come to arrest me then?"

"Arrest you? Not yet. You see, I prefer persuasion to blunt force. I decided that maybe you, being the sensible man that you are, would want to listen to my proposition first. I can always arrest you later."

Philippe returned to his seat with reluctance. "I'm listening."

"A girl from your cell was supposed to deliver you suitcases packed with explosives so that you could use them for your planned diversion. Madame Vignon tried to take those suitcases from her to secure the delivery I assume." The German drummed his fingers on the table several times, his look pensive. "Only, much to everyone's surprise, when our people opened the suitcases, there were no explosives inside."

Philippe frowned. The German caught onto his confusion and grinned. "You have no idea what was in the suitcases, do you?"

"No, I don't," he finally admitted.

"Men's clothes." The German chuckled softly.

Philippe narrowed his eyes, not appreciating mirth in a situation like this.

"Is this some kind of a sick joke?" he demanded with barely concealed anger in his voice.

"It certainly was, one that your crafty spouse played on all of us." The German was still smiling, as if more delighted than upset by this fact. "I'll admit, heading to your place, I hoped that you would be able to tell me where the real suitcases are, but I see now that you're in the dark just as much as I am. Oh well, every problem can be resolved if one is dedicated enough to finding a solution; don't you agree?"

"You already said it yourself; I don't know where the suitcases are. I have nothing to offer to you."

"Oh, but you do. You can tell me where the diversion is to take place. We know that you want to blow up the train tracks to sabotage a major wood supply heading to the Eastern front, but the tracks are long, and we don't know the exact place. We also know that they will put the explosives down tonight, closer to the morning, with a timing mechanism – just like last time. Now, if you could just point out the exact place for me, and we can arrest your friends before they do any serious damage, then I can personally guarantee that Madame Vignon will be released immediately. And, you will both get a rather mild sentence only. Two, maybe three years in jail, here in France. It's the deal of a lifetime if you ask me."

"What about our friends?"

"I'm afraid I can only guarantee a pardon to you and your wife, and only because I'm acting on the orders of Standartenführer Sievers. Ordinarily, you would all be executed; but he decided to grant you both life. Your friends will have to face the firing squad I regret to inform you. What kind of Gestapo we would be if we released all of the diversionists?" The German spread out his arms with a smile.

"You surely do have a reputation to mind," Philippe grumbled sardonically, not entertained by the joke in the slightest.

"We can argue about our methods all you want, my dearest Monsieur Vignon, but keep in mind that every minute spent in such polemics prolongs poor Madame Vignon's sufferings," the German said in the same pleasant tone, however this time the coldness in his voice revealed itself, intentionally no doubt.

"If you touch a hair on her head—" Philippe started with a threat in his voice, to which the German only waved his hand dismissively.

"They already did, Monsieur Vignon. Standartenführer Sievers was kind enough to offer her a chance to tell him everything willingly, but she refused. He was certain that she would start speaking within minutes, but... It's been several hours, and she hasn't spoken a word. That's what brings me here to you, Monsieur Vignon. I really need to get to those explosives before your comrades get a chance to do something irreparable."

Philippe could barely contain himself from jumping up from his chair to throw himself at the grinning German and beat him until he stopped breathing. The thought of Giselle in the hands of those monsters made his blood boil, but the German was right. Philippe was caught between a rock and a hard place, with two choices that he wouldn't wish on his worst enemy: save himself and Giselle, but lose Marcel and

Arthur, or keep quiet and try to save his comrades with his silence, but lose Giselle and quite possibly his own life.

"Well? What is it going to be, Monsieur Vignon?" The German tapped his finger on top of his hand again. This time he wasn't smiling.

Philippe squeezed his temples with both hands, resting his elbows on the table, not caring one bit that the German would see his despair. *What was it going to be? He'd be damned if he knew.*

"Think of your wife, Monsieur Vignon." The German's disgustingly sweet tone seemed to get right under Philippe's skin, making it crawl with hatred. "Quite possibly, one of our men is currently holding a hammer in his hand, getting ready to break her beautiful little toes. It's rather painful and can leave a person limping for the rest of their lives. The longer you play mute, the graver her injuries will be. You don't want that, do you?"

Philippe clenched his jaw in fury, raked his hand through his dark hair, and rose from his seat. The German remained in his place while he returned with a map, threw it on the table and pointed at a place on it.

"This is it. Now call your people and tell them to stop hurting Giselle immediately!"

The German smiled gleefully, got up, folded the map neatly and placed his hat back on his head. "I'm sorry, I'm afraid I won't be able to stop it until we secure the suitcases and arrest your friends. Who knows, you might have lied to me."

Unable to control himself, Philippe swiftly moved to the countertop, pulled a kitchen knife from the stand and turned around, ready to cut the German into pieces, only to find him calmly standing in place and pointing a gun at him.

"I would advise against it, Monsieur Vignon. If I don't return within an hour, your spouse will die a very painful death. Surely, you don't wish such an unfortunate outcome for her."

With those words, he hid the gun in his pocket, bid his farewell, bowed his head slightly, and proceeded to the exit.

"Oh yes, one more thing. I don't have time to bring you in right now because I need to organize an ambush for your comrades, so I would greatly appreciate it if you took yourself to prison without my assistance, and gave yourself up. Our people are waiting for you already. Good day, Monsieur Vignon!"

"I will find you, and I will kill you," Philippe hissed through gritted teeth, still holding the knife tightly, but the German was already gone.

Chapter 24

Lyon

"How could you do this?!"

Tommy blocked another blow, even welcoming the pain that reverberated through the bone of his forearm where Marcel had struck him countless times. He had expected such an outburst, and mentally prepared himself for it, having set his mind on meekly accepting every single hit until Marcel ran out of steam. He soon did, lowering his hands with balled fists, but Marcel's eyes held such hurt in them, from the betrayal that he had never expected from one who he trusted the most. That caused Tommy more anguish than any physical pain ever could.

"Marcel, listen to me, please." Tommy moved closer, but Marcel only raised his hand again. "You can hit me all you like, but you will have to listen to my explanation at some point."

"What kind of explanation can you possibly give me that will make me change my mind and not shoot you like the backstabbing rat that you are?!"

"Don't scream, please. The neighbors—"

"To hell with the neighbors! You went behind my back; you drugged me; you stole suitcases from me, you and Arthur! You both put my sister's life in danger. Why?!"

"Because she asked me to."

"And you listened!"

"Yes, I did. It was the only reasonable thing to do. She was being followed. They both were; her and her husband. The whole operation would have been compromised, and all of us would have been arrested. This was the only chance we had."

"And my sister's life is a fair price to pay, you mean to say?! We should have just called it all off! Why didn't she tell me anything?"

"Because she knew that you would have tried to stop her. She was under constant surveillance; she had no place to run anyway. Besides, we don't know if she was arrested or not. Maybe they saw that the suitcases didn't contain what they were looking for, and let her go."

"Do you even believe what you're saying?"

Tommy released a ragged sigh and lowered his head. "I'm sorry, Marcel. I did it for you. She didn't want anything to happen to you, and neither did I. I love you…"

"Go fuck yourself with your love!" Marcel shoved him hard in his chest.

Tommy stumbled backward without even trying to protect himself. "You have every right to be angry. But with time you will understand—"

"If something happens to Giselle, I'll kill you. I swear to God, I'll kill you!"

Tears were streaming down Marcel's face as he hurled his threats at the Brit. Tommy wanted to cry himself, but at least one of them had to remain strong.

"Arthur is already in Dijon," he spoke quietly. "He'll wreak such havoc among them, the likes of which they have never encountered before. And all because she gave us all a chance, Marcel."

"At what price? Her own life?"

"She was under their surveillance as it is. They would have arrested her anyway. Now, we all have a chance at least. A chance to disappear and reinvent ourselves under new names, in a new city. For us, Dijon is done for. But the fight will continue someplace else. She sacrificed herself to save us all, Marcel. Now, we all owe her for that. We owe her more German deaths than the Huns ever imagined. We will avenge her, I promise. I will fight along with you till my last breath until we kill every last one of them…"

Marcel's eyes clouded with tears, full of hatred, and the pressure on his chest prevented him from talking.

"No, Tom. I don't want to fight alongside you. You lied to me, and your lies will cost Giselle her life. I don't care what arguments you bring. It won't change a thing. I hate you. I will never forgive you. I don't want you near me. Now, get your things and get lost. Tell your MI6 we'll find ourselves a new radio operator. One who we can trust."

Tommy took his verdict with stoicism, nodded his head several times in understanding, sighed with difficulty, and said, "You saved my life once, and I promised you that it would be yours from that point on. I'll stand by my word. I'll leave now. I know you hate me, and I deserve it. I still love you endlessly, and more than anything I want you to be happy. Just remember this when I'm gone, please."

Marcel refused to give him a parting handshake. Only when Tommy's steps had disappeared behind the door did he fall into a heap on the floor and burst into tears; over his sister, over the man who had become her unwilling executioner, and over himself, because he loved that cursed-to-all-hells executioner too.

Dijon

The heavy metal door unlocked, and Giselle shut her eyes tightly after being nearly blinded by the bright light that burst into her cell. She had lain in absolute darkness for God knew how long. She had lost track of time long ago. She couldn't even tell if it was day or night, and how many hours exactly she had spent in the interrogation cell, barely conscious, battered and naked.

She was slipping in and out distorted reality - or a nightmare from which it was impossible to wake from. She tried to concentrate her mind on one thing only: to be quiet. They repeated two questions with vicious obstinacy; to which she would scream *"I don't know"* until her throat gave in and only hoarse whimpers would come out instead of the words. *Where are the suitcases and where is the diversion going to take place?* And another, to which the usual denial didn't apply: *What is your name?* She nearly said, *'Giselle Legrand'* when, after losing consciousness due to the shock of having her head immersed under water, they shook her awake. *'Laure Vignon',* she finally whispered after remembering the correct answer. *Laure Vignon.*

Steady steps on the concrete floor near where she lay made her curl herself into a ball, her bloodied knees pulled towards her chest, expecting a kick in her ribs that were most likely broken.

"I know you're awake. Open your eyes."

His voice was strangely familiar. He stood against the blinding light, but all Giselle could make out was his dark silhouette when she finally forced herself to squint at him, shielding her eyes with her bruised hand.

He slowly lowered down, crouching next to her, and Giselle pulled back at the sight of the face that took shape in front of her eyes; somber and twisted, with a shadow of infinite evil glowing eerily in the charcoal of his eyes.

"Go away," she whispered and waved her hand in front of her, intending for it to go right through the apparition and make it dissolve into thin air. Her hand hit a knee that felt far too real to belong to a ghost. "You can't be here. I killed you. You're dead."

The man in the uniform tilted his hand to one side, studying her face quizzically.

"I'm here to help you," he spoke, at last, his black eyes gleaming in the dark. Giselle shuddered and inched further away from him.

"You're not real, Karl. Go away."

She heard his steady breathing, even felt it on her cheek when he leaned closer, leaning over her. "I'll help you get out of here. You just have to tell me your name."

Giselle's brows moved into a frown as she tried to process his request.

"You know my name well enough."

"I want you to say it to me. Just say it." He smelled of aftershave and slightly of cigarettes. Too human for a ghost who had returned from the underworld to torment her. Giselle shifted her weight onto one elbow, trying to make out his features.

"Tell me your name," he implored softly.

Giselle held his gaze and finally stretched her mouth into a grin. "I don't know how you survived, but I'll kill you again."

"Fair enough. But I deserve to know the name of the woman who will take my life, no?"

Giselle chuckled and cringed as a sharp pain pierced her side. "Laure Vignon. Now, go back to the hell from which you crawled from, and leave me alone."

He rose and disappeared behind the door, leaving Giselle in darkness once again.

Jürgen Sievers looked up from his morning newspaper as one of his uniformed orderlies appeared in the doors of his office.

"Well?" he demanded impatiently, without bothering to reply to the man's usual salute.

"Nothing, Herr Standartenführer. She repeated the same alias, Laure Vignon. Only…" He stopped mid-sentence as if contemplating if the information he was about to give was useful enough to report to his superior.

"Only what?"

"She called me 'Karl' and told me to go away because I wasn't real. Because, apparently, she had killed me."

Sievers rose from his seat and circled his desk, stopping in front of the young agent.

"Is that so? Interesting. Very interesting."

"I thought that maybe it was from a concussion or she had lost it after the shock. It happens to them sometimes…"

"No, it's not a concussion. I gave strict orders not to touch her face or head, so that can't be it." Sievers rubbed his chin pensively. "Karl, you said?"

"The man must have been a German."

"Do you recall any cases of any *Karls* disappearing lately in our area?"

"No, Herr Standartenführer. That's why I decided at first that she was not in her right mind and was imagining things."

"Check all the police reports for the past year, just in case. If she indeed killed some Karl, that can point us to who she really is. Most likely she took this new identity after the murder. If it actually happened, of course."

"*Jawohl*, Herr Standartenführer."

"Report to me at once when you find something."

"*Jawohl.*"

The agent gave him a crisp salute and clicked his heels before taking his leave.

Sievers leaned onto his desk, squinting his eyes into mere slits in an attempt to recall something that kept escaping his memory. He remained in the same position until his adjutant announced the arrival of his second-in-command; a former, entirely nondescript-looking colleague from the German police, who now went by the very becoming nickname of '*The Shadow*'.

"What's the news?" Sievers asked, after exchanging a firm handshake with the man.

"I've spent the whole evening and night on the tracks, in the exact spot which the husband pointed out to me."

"And?"

"Nothing. No one appeared. The good news is that we raked the entire length of the tracks from there to the next station with the dogs, and we found no traces of explosives."

Sievers sighed, looking somewhat disappointed but concerned at the same time.

"Do you think they smelled a rat and decided to cancel their plans?" he asked the man reluctantly.

"Highly unlikely."

"My thoughts exactly."

"Any progress with the woman?"

"No. I was hoping that Laure would be an easier case, to be honest with you. But she's keeping stubbornly quiet."

Both went silent for a few moments.

"Where do you think they will strike then?"

"I wish I knew, Jürgen. I wish I knew."

"Any suggestions then?"

"Tell your men to double, triple, their efforts in interrogating her. The second day is when they usually break. Beat the confession out of her before it's too late."

Sievers sighed again and had already placed a hand on the black telephone on his desk when his adjutant appeared in the door, his eyes shining with excitement.

"I'm sorry for the interruption, Herr Standartenführer. A man is here, claiming he knows where the diversion is to take place. He just turned himself in. He's a British MI6 agent, he says. He declines to talk to anyone else besides you."

"Well, what are you waiting for?" Sievers slammed the phone down. "Bring him in!"

Tommy sat in a padded chair, calmly observing the contents of the office and the two overpoweringly bright swastika banners framing the window on the opposite wall. The German in front of him, together with his plain-clothed friend, seemed impatient to receive the information he claimed he had.

"I would like a personal guarantee that you will release Madame Vignon at once, as soon as I tell you everything about the diversion."

"You're in no position to trade—" The plain-clothed man started, but the man in the uniform interrupted him with his raised hand.

"You have my guarantee that she will be granted life. I cannot, however, promise you her freedom."

Tommy nodded and stole a glance at his watch once again. The time was tight, but they didn't know it yet. If he calculated everything correctly, they would never make it in time to the place that would be blown up to pieces in a mere ten minutes.

They had agreed on the time with Arthur when Tommy had handed him the suitcases before his fellow countryman had left for Dijon.

"She isn't an active member of the Resistance; we only used her as a distraction tactic. She hasn't told you anything yet because she doesn't know anything." One thing Tommy knew how to do well was to lie convincingly. He had learned how to act and pretend ever since high school. "My friend and I organized the whole thing, just like the first diversion. We report directly to MI6 headquarters in London. We are the ones who you need, not these poor Frenchies. They've suffered enough at your hands; let them be. Especially her. She's a lady, after all. It really is a shame what you're doing."

The plain-clothed man began to argue with him, but his superior raised his hand once again, stopping him.

"Just name the place."

Tommy leaned over the map spread out on the desk in front of him, and indicated a tiny spot, watching both men become pale as realization dawned on their faces.

"But it's… It's…" The plain-clothed agent looked at his superior helplessly.

"Why are you still here?! Call all the brigades to go there at once!"

Tommy concealed a grin at the commotion he had just caused. *Yes, call the brigades. Maybe they will get their share of shrapnel as well.* And then, maybe Marcel would forgive him and shed a tear for him on the day of his execution. Tommy would leave this life just like he had lived it: fearlessly and without regret. *Yes, call the brigades, call all of them, sir.*

———————————

Arthur stopped in front of the *Soldaten Café*, reserved specifically for German officers and the rare Frenchmen who could afford to dine there. He checked his watch and fixed his hat, generously lent to him by *the Chief* himself, together with a suit and a heavy woolen coat he was also wearing. Now he was a British demolitions expert, dressed as the finest French bourgeois. The suitcase that he carried was made of the finest patent leather, its buckle shining in the sun. Inside, the timing mechanism was already counting down the minutes, previously set up by Arthur in the train station bathroom. A second suitcase had been left in the same station, inconspicuously placed near a pile of luggage, set to blow up later than the first one, just as the train started gaining speed. No one would be hurt, but the damage would definitely stop the wood shipment that the Germans in the Eastern front expected.

Arthur walked inside the café, tipped his hat gallantly to the officers enjoying their lunch and beer, thanked the waiter who offered him a table in the corner, and slid the suitcase under his seat. He ordered coffee, smoked a cigarette, bought "the gentlemen" at the bar a round of drinks, raised his glass and even said *"Prost"* to their victory, kindly asked the waiter to bring another coffee, and inquired as to where he could make an important call to Paris.

"Outside, Monsieur. There's a phone booth across the street. We have a city line here only, I'm afraid." The waiter spread out his hands in a helpless gesture, much to Arthur's relief.

"Splendid. If I order soup, I suppose it'll be ready by the time I return?" Arthur got up from his seat, leaving his hat and his coat hanging near his table.

"Most definitely, Monsieur."

"I'll be back in five minutes."

Arthur threw the waiter a glance, inwardly regretting that the Frenchman would become an unwitting casualty, but then regained his composure, reminded himself that the waiter was a collaborator and was eating from the Nazis' hands, and walked out of place with a resolute step.

He stopped near the phone booth across the street, glanced at the clock on the building in front of him and stepped inside the booth, preparing himself for the deafening blast.

Chapter 25

The orderly stepped away after unlocking the heavy metal door and assumed his position behind the two visitors. Jürgen Sievers faltered in the entrance of the dark cell, observing the lifeless figure on the floor with a pensive look on his face. Blanche craned her neck from behind his shoulder, scrutinizing the body on the floor with an unhealthy gleam in her eyes. She felt a surge of disappointment shoot through her as the figure moved her arm to cover her eyes from the bright light. Blanche had been hoping to find the prisoner dead.

Sievers cleared his throat and turned to the soldier behind his back, irritation written on his face. "You just left her on the bare floor like that? Give her a blanket or something, for Christ's sake!"

The orderly clicked his heels and ran along the corridor in search of the needed item.

"Why such mercy?" Blanche voiced her thoughts with unmasked hostility. "You're going to kill her anyway, aren't you?"

The look that Sievers shot her made Blanche's cheeks flare up. She lowered her eyes, unable to hold his gaze which was full of contempt.

"She deserves to face her fate with dignity, after all she's been through," he replied curtly and refused to speak another word with Blanche until the orderly appeared again, holding a thin woolen blanket in his hands.

"Cover her!" Sievers barked out.

The orderly dutifully obeyed, shaking the prisoner's shoulder slightly in the hope of waking her up.

A small smile touched the corners of Sievers' mouth as he searched the prisoner's face thoroughly, not discovering any damage. The rest of her body would heal; but having a weakness for art and everything refined, most of all Sievers loathed destroying what was pleasing to his eye, and she was indeed a remarkable woman, this Laure Vignon. Even now, barely alive and unable to stand up, she was looking at him with such scorn and defiance, that Sievers couldn't help but admire such stoicism. Yes, a remarkable opponent indeed.

"I came to congratulate you, Madame Vignon." He stepped inside the cell but kept a respectful distance, even though she had managed to wrap herself in the blanket; more to keep herself warm than minding her modesty, he thought. Closer up, he noted that her forehead was covered in a thin film of sweat. She had likely caught a fever spending the night naked on the bare concrete on a freezing October night. "You won after all."

She rubbed her eyes as if trying to remember who he was and what she was doing there.

"I did?" Her voice came in a raspy whisper, and she cleared her throat.

"Yes. Your people not only caused damage to the tracks for which we were fearing, but blew up our *Soldaten Café* as well. Twelve of our officers died."

A crooked grin appeared on her face. Sievers forced himself not to smile in response.

"I must say, I never expected you to hold on for so long."

"Trust me, I didn't expect it from myself either," she replied, her eyes closing against her will. "Is it over now? I'm really tired."

"Yes, it is, Madame Vignon," he said in a mild voice.

Blanche regarded the woman in the cell with a triumphant sneer. *He'll kill her after all, and it will be her and him again, just the two of them.*

"I also owe you an apology," he continued. "You probably know how we're all taught in the Reich how blood is above all, and how the German race is superior. I'll admit, that's exactly what I said to this young lady, fraulein Blanche, whose father happens to be German, in order to persuade her that we're much closer kin to her than the French, and that she deserves better than how her fellow countrymen treated her, and that she's much better than her fellow French folk simply because of the blood that runs through her veins. You see, it's rather easy to persuade someone to your side when you ceaselessly repeat that they are superior. Once you separate former allies, you can easily beat them one by one. Everyone wants to belong to the group that holds power. Everyone wants to be superior. However, a desire to be superior and the ability to act superior are two very different things. You read Nietzsche, so you must know what I'm referring to. I don't want to bore you with my musings as I know that you wish for this to be over with, and I assure you, you'll have plenty of time to rest soon. I only wanted to apologize for thinking less of you than I thought of fraulein Blanche, simply because she's part German. She turned out to be a disappointment. But you... You, Madame, have gained my utmost respect, even though I'm not supposed to say it to you. I had to tell you this though so that you'd know how much I respected you and that I would give anything to have you on my side. But I already know what your answer will be, and I won't insult you by insisting on it. I would only like to shake your hand, as a farewell."

He held out his hand. She looked at it for some time and then slowly slid her palm into his.

"Help me up, will you?" she asked, without releasing his hand.

Sievers carefully held her by the elbows as she rose to her feet, still swaying slightly from her injuries and high fever.

"If you respect me as much as you say you do, I would like to die with dignity." She still held his hand firmly in hers as she spoke with determination, her palm sweaty and burning. "I want to get shot, not hanged, like a common thief. Will you do that for me?"

Sievers grinned, an impish light appearing in his eyes. "I will if you tell me your real name. It would be a shame if you die as Laure Vignon, a factory girl."

She pondered for a moment, but then nodded and whispered so quietly that Blanche only just heard her as she watched them from the threshold of the room. "Giselle Legrand. My real name is Giselle Legrand."

Sievers closed his eyes for a moment, shaking his head as the recognition shone in his face.

"Karl Wünsche," he said, at last, chuckling. "That's the Karl that I was searching my memory for. You killed one of my kin, Mademoiselle Legrand. In cold blood."

"Not as cold as you think," she muttered, a dark shadow crossing her features.

"Well... Congratulations, Mademoiselle Legrand. You truly are one of the strongest individuals I have ever met." Sievers pressed her hand once again and turned to the door, his expression changing. "Orderly!"

The guard appeared in the door, awaiting orders.

"Take her to the backyard and hang her. I don't need her anymore."

As soon as the sentry stepped inside the cell to get the prisoner, Sievers tilted his head to one side, a devious grin playing on his face.

"No, not her. That *fraulein* over there." He motioned his head towards Blanche.

Blanche pressed her hand to her chest, stepping away as she gasped.

"No, Jürgen, please!" she cried in horror, watching the guard approaching her with a blank expression. Apparently, he didn't care much as to who was going to die that day. "I will work better, I promise! I will help you with everything I can—"

"The cell is gone, Blanche," Sievers stated, his voice cold and sarcastic as he watched the sentry cuff her hands behind her back and her feeble attempts to resist him. "They all scattered. You've failed me countless times, and I don't forgive failures. I have no need of you anymore. There's no chance that you can infiltrate another cell as those *résistants* will warn everyone else against you. I'm doing you a favor, really. If they caught you, your death wouldn't be as easy."

"Jürgen, please, I'm begging you!"

She continued screaming as the guard led her away, out another door that was locked behind them.

When they were left alone, Sievers turned back to his prisoner, smiling. "Now that is out of the way, we can talk discretely. My offer still stands, Mademoiselle Legrand. Work with me. I'll release you today; I'll even secure new papers for you."

She regarded him for some time, grinning. "I just told you that I killed a man who occupied virtually the same position as you, and you still want me near you?"

"I'm willing to take the risk, Mademoiselle."

"Execute me and save your life, Herr Sievers. Because you'll end up just like Karl if you don't."

Sievers seemed to think over her words for a few moments but shook his head eventually. "I'm afraid I can't do that, Mademoiselle. The world will become too boring without you."

"You can't release me either."

"No, I can't."

"What are you going to do with me then?"

He was quiet for a few seconds, and then replied in an odd, hollow voice, "Something you will hate me for, I'm afraid."

When Giselle recollected herself, the train had stopped. She couldn't force herself to open her eyes, so she lay motionless and resigned to her fate. When a rough hand picked up her wrist and let it drop lifelessly, she allowed her entire body to go limp.

"This one too." The voice came out of the void, with a strong German accent; he was saying these words on every stop, freeing the space around her as the train made its way east. "Take her out."

"Dead?" The voice was that of a Frenchman, soft and soothing to her exhausted soul.

"Nearly."

"But what am I supposed to do with the ones who aren't dead yet?"

"What do you mean what are you supposed to do? Bury them together with the corpses. You can shoot them first if you're feeling charitable. But, personally, I wouldn't waste my ammunition on them. They deserve what they get. Communist rats."

The German spat somewhere on the floor, or maybe on someone's "nearly dead" body; Giselle couldn't see which one it was.

"No, Herr Officer," the Frenchman muttered in a rushed and appalled manner. "That I can't do. No, I didn't sign up for that! Communists or not, they're people, and they're still—"

"You volunteered for the *Waffen-SS, scheiße!* Which means you are to follow your new German commanders' orders! And your new German commander orders you to take these people out and bury them, and so you will do, or you will join them for insubordination, you hear me?!"

"Allow me to handle the matter, Herr Officer," another voice said, deep and painfully familiar. "I'll do it gladly."

"By all means." The German snorted with laughter. "Enjoy yourself."

"I certainly will."

Giselle winced as strong hands picked her sore body up from the rough floor and forced herself to look at the man who carried her. All she could make out was a German uniform with SS markings. After spending – hours? days? weeks? – in darkness she couldn't possibly tell who it was. In her worsening state, barely dressed in some thin dress and a blanket that Sievers was kind enough to leave her, having slept on the concrete floor in her cell and then on the hard, wooden floor of the train, that was, of course, unheated, Giselle struggled to regain her normal senses. A feeling of relief washed over her that it would all be over soon.

He carefully laid her out on the ground, right on the snow, and started making his way back to the train to bring more people out. Giselle forced her eyes open to watch his tall frame disappear from view, and turned her head to her left, to see a line of fellow Frenchmen right next to her; unlucky ones who weren't strong enough to make it to Germany. Or, maybe it was the contrary, and she was the lucky one, for she would be laid in peace on her French soil, in a grave with her fellow countrymen, together with those who had also fought for its freedom.

Her fever-induced shivering had turned into violent convulsions and then back into subsiding trembles a few days ago, but her body was still fighting for its existence. Now, she barely felt anything at all, not even the snow under her bare skin.

"Shall we leave you to it?" It was the first German again.

A shovel hit the ground near her head.

"Of course! Why waste time waiting for me to bury them all? The ground is frozen, so it will take hours... I'll finish just in time for the following train to pick me up."

"Well, tell them who your commanding officer is, and they'll tell you where to go once you cross the territory of the Reich."

"*Jawohl.*"

"*Danke, Kamerad!*"

The train started moving just as the shovel sliced into the ground next to her. Giselle began slipping back into unconscious bliss when she swore she heard his voice calling her name.

———————————

"Giselle!" The familiar voice fell faintly on her ear. He was shaking her again, her tormentor who refused to leave her alone to meet her death. "Wake up, Giselle! Look at me!"

She didn't want to look at him. She wanted him to let her die in peace, but she guessed she didn't deserve an easy death for he wouldn't leave her be for even one second. The worst part was that she couldn't even fight him as he rubbed her skin with a rough rag, over and over, flipping her from side to side like a broken doll; he did seem to carefully avoid touching her broken ribs, though.

"Giselle. You owe me, Giselle. I can't allow you to die, and you know it. Now, open your eyes and look at me!"

She fluttered her eyelids and tried to focus on the dark features of the man leaning over her. His coal black eyes lit up as a smile transformed his usually somber face. *Karl.*

Giselle allowed a cynical smirk to appear on her grayish face as, thinking with distant curiosity that maybe the Bible that she used to mock didn't lie after all: maybe she was dead already, and this was her personal hell, and he was the demon who would torment her for eternity.

"Do me a favor and swallow at least a spoonful of soup, will you?" Karl shifted her to a seated position, propping her against a haystack, judging by several painful jabs from pieces of straw that pricked her back. He held a spoon near her mouth. "Giselle, please. We need to get some food into you."

Why, if she was already dead?

He touched her lips, cracked and broken from when she had bitten them, trying to lessen her pain, the tantalizing aroma of the broth awakening her senses. Giselle opened her mouth and allowed him to carefully slip some broth between her lips. She smiled, savoring the taste; she couldn't recall when she had last tasted any kind of food. Karl was smiling as well.

"That's my girl. Now, one more, for me."

He kept feeding her spoon after spoon, gently wiping the corners of her mouth with his handkerchief and muttering something encouraging about how they were both safe now, and how they would disappear as soon as she was strong enough, and how great their life would be. *Together, just you and me. They think you're dead, you know. No one will look for you anymore. You're safe with me. I'll look after you, just like I promised I would…*

Giselle kept scrutinizing his familiar features, trying to make sense of it all. Karl was dead. She killed him. Yet, he had appeared in her cell earlier, to offer salvation; he had taken her off the train heading to Germany; and now, he was feeding her very real broth in a barn and talking about their future together.

"Just one more," he cooed, navigating the spoon into her mouth. "Good girl. Now, rest. I'll hold you tight to keep you warm."

She peered into his eyes as he lay next to her, covering them both with a woolen army-issued overcoat with SS markings on it, his body far too real and warm.

"Why?" Giselle finally managed to whisper, summoning all her strength. She hasn't spoken in days, and her voice was weak and raspy, even after the warm broth had soothed her aching throat a little.

"Why what, *chérie?*"

Giselle frowned. Karl never called her *chérie. Schatz* or *herz,* but never *chérie.* He despised everything French, well, except for her.

"Why nurse me back to life, after what I've done to you?"

A frown crossed his handsome features, and another subtle smile replaced it as he brushed her hair off her forehead softly.

"Well, you do happen to have the most terrible temper I've ever encountered in a woman, and you tend to climb on your high horse far too often, but…" He sighed and planted a gentle kiss on her forehead. "I guess, I love you, Giselle."

Karl had never told her he loved her. He didn't, and she knew it well enough, just like she had never loved him. The two were a pair, a new breed of people as he called it, far too intelligent for any lowly, human feelings; utter nihilists purposely denying everything moralistic simply because they belonged to a generation that had grown up on Nietzsche and despised everyone who thought otherwise. The will to power was the idea that allowed his people to take lives without any regard to humanistic qualms; ironically enough the same will to power allowed her to take his, for she had turned out to be stronger than his breed, exactly because of those moralistic feelings that she had so carefully denied in herself. A perfect paradox.

"You don't love me," she argued, willing for her eyes to stay open for another few moments until she could make sense of everything. "You can't love me. You can't even be here. I killed you."

His gentle smile dropped, his expression turning confused and sad for some reason.

"Giselle, who do you think you're talking to?" he asked her quietly, after a pause.

"Karl," she stated the obvious, a little irritated with his unusually compliant state.

He scowled, shook his head slightly and kissed her once again, feeling her burning forehead with his lips. "I'm not Karl, Giselle. Karl is dead. You killed him. He's in your head only. I'm Philippe, your no-good husband-communist, remember?"

With her last reserve of power, Giselle lifted her hand to his face and touched it with mistrust. Her vision started blurring again, and Karl's features slowly morphed into a different face, one that belonged to a man she didn't mind falling asleep next to. *Yes, Philippe. Her no-good, husband-communist.*

"Where did you get the uniform then, *comrade?*"

"I secured a new passport and volunteered for the French Legion of the *Waffen-SS*; it was my only chance to get near you. Besides, I thought you'd like the look, you *Boche-lover!*"

"It's better than your workers' overalls."

He chuckled, with relief as it seemed. Giselle grinned serenely and allowed her eyes to close at last.

Epilogue

Lyon, November 1941

Marcel wept, clinging to Etienne's overcoat until his legs gave out and he fell to the floor, burying his head in his hands. Augustine dropped to her knees right next to him, soothing him with her words and gentle hands on top of his head.

"Pauvre garcon, mon pauvre garcon…"

There was nothing that could be said to console him now, and they all knew it. Only three people were left of their cell, and they all stood in a tight circle around him.

"Tommy died a hero, Marcel." Etienne lowered his hand on Marcel's shoulder, shaking with sobs. "Just like Giselle did."

"I killed him." Marcel's words came out in ragged breaths. "It was me, my fault… I told him to go; I said such terrible things to him!"

"He did what he felt was right," Etienne's tone was level, masking the subdued emotion he was trying to conceal. "He tried to save your sister."

"And now, they're both dead! All because of me!" He burst into tears again.

"No, all because of Lucienne," Yves remarked with ice in his voice, also lowering to the floor next to the crying man. "At least, she's dead as well. The

Gestapo hanged her; Tommy faced a firing squad, like a soldier. It's a noble death, befitting a hero."

"What are you saying?" Augustine shot him a reproachful look, still cradling Marcel's head on her chest. "Noble death! They killed the poor boy, for nothing, the beasts! Just like they did—"

She stopped herself before finishing the sentence, but Yves understood everything well enough and bit his tongue inside his mouth. *Just like they killed her husband.*

"We'll avenge them both, I swear to you," he whispered, catching her wrist, and then let his arms drop over Marcel's shoulders to enclose him in a tight embrace.

It had been so long since he allowed anyone to get so close to him, refusing himself the right to any kind of human companionship, separating himself from the rest with his black robe and a guarded look. But now, these people, united with nothing else but a common goal – a country free of its gray-clad invaders – had become closer to him than any family kin could possibly be, and Yves swore to himself that he would gladly give his life for any of them.

"What happened to Philippe?" Marcel lifted his wet face to Etienne, who had just returned from the Occupied Zone.

"I only know that he wasn't arrested. He's disappeared it seems. We lost contact. I don't know what happened to him."

"Where did they bury Giselle?"

Etienne lowered his eyes and shifted from one foot to another. "I don't know, Marcel. I tried to ask as subtly as I could, and I found out from one of the Germans connected to the SD in Dijon that Giselle Legrand was put on one of the transports heading to Germany, and she died from fever during the transportation. That's all that I could find out. I'm sorry."

"I won't even have their graves to visit." Marcel shook his head, tears streaming down his face. "Both of them, gone…"

"They're not gone." Augustine stroked his hair again, knowing his pain better than anyone there. Her husband disappeared the same way, buried somewhere with other Jewish prisoners of war, in an unmarked grave with no one to lay flowers on it. "They will live forever, in our memory, and in the memory of the people who they helped. One day, people will write books about them, and build memorials in their honor. No, they didn't die; on the contrary, they will outlive all of us, as heroes of France."

Marcel sat without moving for some time, sniffling quietly and pondering something. Finally, he turned to Yves, his eyes much clearer and determined.

"Could you say a prayer for them, please?" he asked quietly. "Tommy was an atheist; well, he wasn't too fond of the church because… well…"

Yves smiled and nodded. "Of course, we'll say a prayer for them both. It doesn't matter who Tommy was; to all of us, he will always be a hero and a dearly loved brother, first and foremost."

Marcel's grin came out pained, but he still breathed out with relief. "Thank you, Father."

"It's Yves. Just Yves." He kneeled and clasped his hands together; his head lowered in a solemn bow to his chest.

Etienne, Marcel, and Augustine joined him, repeating the words of the prayer together with the priest.

"Today we bury our dead," Yves concluded, opening his eyes and looking each one of them in the eye. "Tomorrow, we kill our enemies. They might be stronger just now, but the righteous cause is on our side. And we won't stop until every last one of them is gone, or dead. Whatever it will be, is up to them to choose."

Day was breaking over the orphanage, as children slept in their beds upstairs, undisturbed and blessed in their peaceful slumber. From the cellar, the four *résistants* made their way upstairs, coming out of the darkness, ready to face what the new day brought, more determined than ever.

Paris, December 1941

Michel Demarche, the owner and editor-in-chief of the Demarche Publishing House, cleaned his hands thoroughly after spending another night in the cellar of his building, printing copies of *La Libération* – the Resistance newspaper which had survived against all odds and even travelled as far as the Free Zone thanks to his late friend's son, Etienne Delattre. He hadn't heard from the young man for a long time, accepting the news of his appointment as a Sub-Prefect of Lyon with a dose of concern and skepticism.

Having no children of his own, Michel always thought of his writers as his children, and Etienne even more so, as he still remembered rocking the boy on one knee when Etienne's father visited his publishing house in Paris. Hopefully, the boy had grown into being a fine young man with the sharp mind and diplomatic abilities of his father, and wouldn't get dragged into anything that would end up badly for him. Michel chuckled, observing the new copies of the underground newspaper, still smelling of fresh ink and ready to be picked up tomorrow by one of the *résistants* working in Paris.

Being used to moving around the dark building at night without the help of a flashlight, Michel made his way upstairs into his office where he would once again spend the night on his sofa. His back would hurt the next day, but that was a rather low price to pay to keep his fellow countrymen's spirits high, especially before Christmas. The news from the Eastern front was that the *Boches* were regretting their blitz against the Soviets more and more every day, freezing by the dozens in the severe Russian temperatures. He was busy all day, composing articles so they were ready for the late-night print, allowing fresh copies of the newspaper to travel around Paris the following day.

Grinning, Michel pushed the door open and walked over to his table in absolute darkness, feeling for the cognac bottle that he had left there before heading downstairs. A shot of the finest French brandy was his reward for his day's work – the only indulgence he allowed himself.

"*Salut,* Michel."

The voice, coming from the other side of the room, startled him so much he dropped the glass on the floor, spilling the cognac on his patent leather shoes. Michel spun on his heels, facing the figure sitting on his sofa. Two figures, mere shadows against the subtle light coming in from the blackout curtains.

"Did you miss me?"

Michel faltered before stepping forward, refusing to believe the music that her voice was to his old ears.

"Giselle?" he whispered, holding his breath while waiting for a response. "Is that you?"

"*Bien sûr, c'est moi, mon ami.*" She burst into laughter, something he had missed so much, and jumped to her feet to enclose him in the tightest of embraces. "Remember Philippe?"

Laughing through his tears, Michel held out his hand to the other figure that had also stood up and found his palm in the darkness.

"Philippe, my friend! Giselle! What are you both doing here? I thought you were dead, *ma petite!* The German papers said…"

276

"The German papers lied, like they always do, Michel. As for what we're doing here, I came to tell you such a story which, once it's published, will become a best seller like you won't believe."

Michel could swear he saw her give him a coy wink before taking a serious air once again. "But before that, Michel, my friend, we have some *Boches* to get rid of."

Also by the author:

"The Girl From Berlin" series:

"The Girl From Berlin: Standartenführer's Wife" (book 1)

"The Girl From Berlin: Gruppenführer's Mistress" (book 2)

"The Girl From Berlin: War Criminal's Widow" (book 3)

"The Austrian" series:

"The Austrian" (book 1)

"The Austrian: Book Two" (book 2)

"Emilia: the Darkest Days in History of Nazi Germany through a Woman's Eyes"

Connect with the author here:

http://elliemidwood.com

http://www.goodreads.com/EllieMidwood

https://www.facebook.com/Ellie-Midwood-651390641631204/

83802769R00156

Made in the USA
Lexington, KY
15 March 2018